Enjoy!

Fatal Refuge
A mystery/thriller

Sharon Sterling

D1617504

Fatal Refuge
A mystery/thriller

Sharon Sterling

Changing Lines Press
Green Valley, Arizona
USA

Published by
Changing Lines Press
P.O. Box 546
Green Valley, AZ 85622

To contact the author or order additional copies of this book
http://SharonSterling.net

This edition was prepared for publication by
Ghost River Images
5350 East Fourth Street
Tucson, Arizona 85711
www.ghostriverimages.com

ISBN 978-0-9969408-0-1

Printed in the United States of America
November 2015

Preview

The Old West town of Yuma, Arizona is once again the site of murder and mayhem in *Fatal Refuge*. Here, just miles from the Mexico border, Kim Altaha, a beautiful but troubled Apache woman and her search-and-rescue dog Zayd team with social worker Allie Davis to solve the first of a set of grisly killings.

A severed head, the headless body and top-secret, drone-mounted laser weapons from nearby Yuma Proving Ground complicate the horror, while a mentally ill woman dubbed the "Peace Poet" and a clinically sane but morally deranged killer clash in mortal conflict. Between pages and among lines of suspense, a romance blooms and a friendship deepens between characters who are real enough to lead full emotional lives.

Nearby Kofa National Wildlife Refuge, the Colorado River, a famous casino and the Old Town Yuma barrio are unique, historic settings for encounters between the players in this intense drama. They keep the action churning and psychological motives emerging until the end, when readers will know *why* as well as "*who* done it."

Acknowledgements

My heartfelt thanks to my friend and fellow author, Sue Peterson, the first reader of my story. Your help in critiquing, suggesting, encouraging and supporting me while I wrote *Fatal Refuge* was tremendously valuable to my writing and my spirit.

Much gratitude and many thankyous to Priscilla Barton, my editor, for your professional discernment, insight into the art of story-telling, for all your suggestions and corrections and for your patience and kindness.

Thanks also to Thomas R. Schenek, Jr., former U.S. Marine Corps Corporal and currently with the South Tucson, Arizona, Police Department. The information you provided about police and military procedures kept me on track and accountable to reality as I structured the novel.

Not to be forgotten is Matt Schenek, a Cleveland, Ohio firefighter and EMT who took time out from his work as first-responder to supply me with vital details about EMT workers and their vehicles. Thank you, Matt!

Last, I want to express my appreciation to the members of the Tucson Chapter of Sisters in Crime for your continuing support, education, encouragement and comradery.

Chapter One

KIM ALTAHA

Kim left Yuma in the stillness before dawn and reached the turnoff to Kofa National Wildlife Refuge before the sun mounted the eastern peaks for its daily assault on the land. Her jeep bumped along the dirt access road headed due-east when the first shafts of daylight struck her high-boned cheeks like a challenge.

She parked the red Jeep Cherokee in the tiny dirt lot at the trail head and with confident, long-legged strides began her hike into the Refuge. The trail soon faded to nothing. Undeterred, she bush-wacked over the rocky soil, skirting boulders, brittle bush shrubs, bear grass, and desert agaves.

After an hour she slowed her pace and quieted her steps, wary she might startle the endangered pronghorn antelope she sought. Three months before, she had teamed with volunteer Marines from the base in Yuma and with local Fish and Wildlife agents to trap, transport and release three dozen of the endangered species here. She had actually touched the delicate young animals, stroked their tan and cream coats and felt the warm breath from their nostrils on her hands before watching them rise on wobbly, tranquillized legs and escape into the hills of their new home in the Kofa. It had given her a certain sense of ownership. But where were they? She smiled to herself and answered her own question. *Living up to their reputation as the ghosts of the desert.*

So far she had seen scant signs of life – a few turkey vultures soaring, distant against the thin blue sky, the surreptitious chip-chip of awakening cactus wrens, the scuttle of a lizard.

She felt the sun's rays stab the burnished-copper skin of her forearms and press a skull-cap of heat on her blue-black hair while she walked. The shards of sunlight were so intense they had pierced the atmosphere, drained from it the last drops of moisture and stilled the feeble breeze of early morning. Reluctantly, she pulled a cloth hat from under her belt and put it on.

With an Indian's acceptance of the natural world, she neither welcomed the heat nor resented it. After all, in late spring, at only ninety-seven degrees, this part of the Sonoran Desert was not yet threatening spontaneous combustion.

Suddenly, she saw the bighorn. She swept off her hat and sunglasses, raised her new Minox binoculars, narrowed her eyes against the glare and adjusted the focus until she had the ram. He stood in profile atop the rise a quarter mile away, head raised and horns in dark contrast against the sky, a defiant pose that asserted his right to be here and questioned hers. He stood more than four feet tall at the shoulders and must weigh two hundred pounds. His horns were massive. They appeared too big for his head to support. They had grown back, down and forward in a wide curve, the bottoms level with his shoulders. The grooves of the ridged horns showed a tinge of green, suggesting the growth of lichen, a badge of age. She guessed he was about fifteen years old, a patriarch of the herds, which numbered eight hundred bighorns in this preserve of over six-hundred-thousand acres. The ram remained stock-still under her inspection, as if looking straight ahead, but he inspected her, too, with his acute peripheral vision.

Kim ended the staring match by releasing her binoculars to let them dangle from the strap around her neck. She picked up her sunglasses and blew off the fine, dry dirt before replacing them, then took the cloth field hat from between her knees and pulled it onto her head. With a last glance at the bighorn and a deep breath, she turned to take in the high desert landscape, to listen to the silence.

Half-way up the ten mile climb that formed the base of the rugged Castle Dome Mountains, she turned back toward the west where she had entered the trail head. The parking spot appeared no bigger than a postage stamp and her red vehicle a pencil dot.

Resigned that she would not find the antelope today but happy about the unexpected gift of the ram, she started back down. She remembered the advice of a Hopi Indian friend, "Never retrace your steps," and chose a slightly different route than the one she had climbed.

Memory of the Hopi friend brought to mind thoughts of her own Apache ancestry, one remnant among many native tribes. The presence of White settlers had started as a trickle – pilgrims debarking the Mayflower – and had grown exponentially with each decade and escalated the decline of native humans, animals and vegetation. The settlers' and pioneers' progressive and relentless conquest of the wilderness drove antelope and other wildlife to the brink of extinction and drove Native humans to reservations.

It was ironic, but just, Kim thought, that now the Whites called the antelope and other animal survivors "endangered" and studied, tended and nurtured them; thus the descendants of men who had once almost destroyed the species now sought to preserve it, lavishing the survivors with the balm of remorse.

Her thoughts soon yielded to the wordless enjoyment of her senses: the smell of sage and creosote, the skitter of a zebra-tailed lizard, the sudden scarlet of penstemon blooms brushing against her legs, the sun's heat on her shoulders, the sound of her own steady breathing and solid footsteps. Soon the ache in both thighs reminded her of old wounds, and that descending from a height was often harder than the climb, a simple metaphor for life itself.

When she remembered the Kofa's strangely diverse history Kim began to keep an eye out for dangers other than rattlers, scorpions and mountain lions. The name Kofa began as "K of A", an abbreviation for the name of a gold mine called "King of Arizona," an ostentatious name from the floridly ostentatious and optimistic Victorian era. The miners' avid search for gold, silver, manganese and lead ended after only a few decades when the ore petered out. The miners left behind open pits, drift tunnels, deep vertical shafts and slopes of scree that could send the most sure-footed hiker sprawling.

Along with those relics, huge holes in the ground, called tanks, dotted the land. Some were natural, a few man-made and they were often filled with water. The tanks were the main source of water for Kofa's larger wildlife. Rabbits and other small wild life quenched their thirst at *tinajas*, shallow, natural scour holes in bedrock.

Open mine pits, tanks and other hazards, along with detritus from military trainings during World War Two were rare within the perspective of hundreds of thousands of acres until an unwary hiker stepped into or onto one. What nature had created pristine over millennia, three generations of mankind had made inroads to destroy.

Aware of the danger as well as the beauty around her, Kim became more vigilant. Soon she spotted a metallic object on the ground ahead. She dug her heels in to stop on a downward slope, skidded and almost sat down hard before she saw what it was. Not an unexploded artillery shell, just an empty beer can. She removed the water bottle from her day pack and hooked it to her belt to make room for the piece of junk. The metal felt warm on her finger tips as she shook off ants and loose dirt and put the can in her pack to discard later.

Three miles from the entrance to Palm Canyon and five miles from her parked vehicle, the odor of decaying flesh fouled the hot air. She stopped. *Oh, no. One of the antelope didn't make it.* Her next steps produced a whirr of vulture's wings rising from fifteen feet downhill. Her eyes followed the flight of the vulture to where others soared high above, waiting their turn. The area was partly shadowed by a large boulder. She couldn't see what lay on the ground there.

Dread slowed her steps. When she saw the carcass she felt a flash of relief followed in a split second by disbelief. Not a graceful antelope body with long slender legs and split hoofs. This body was smaller. This was a human being. The arms and legs were shriveled and discolored by decay, clothing stiff with dried body fluids, feet hidden inside tan hiking boots. It was a woman's body lying face down in the dirt.

• • •

Chapter Two

WINSTON VERBALE AND CINDY CAMERON –
Two weeks earlier

"Winston, will you please stop looking out the window. Nothing's going on out there."

"This damned rain! We came here to bird watch, not hang out in this dismal hotel. It's barely stopped the whole three days we've been here. We could have seen more birds if we'd stayed in Yuma."

"Kofa gets some wonderful migrating species in the spring but I've seen them all. We're in Costa Rico to see the tropicals."

"Well, how many have we been able to see through this damned rain? And don't call me Winston." His mouth tilted in irony. Now that we are what you call 'lovers,' get used to calling me 'Win'."

Cindy put down the magazine, a Spanish-language version of *People*, and slid further down under the bed covers. "Better to be 'lovers' than 'friends with benefits.' That expression is so crude."

"And 'lovers' is sentimental tripe."

An angry denial flashed into her mind but she didn't voice it. She refused to be led into a dispute. "Win – I can't decide if the name reminds me of a pack of cigarettes or New England, old-money, living-off-the-interest snobbery."

He flung the curtain back into place and turned with a look of annoyance. "You know I'm not in their league."

"Not if money is a league. Anyway, Winston does have a classy ring to it."

"I guess my mother figured with the last name Verbale, she'd better come up with a more American-sounding first name. I like it. 'Win' for winner."

"You haven't told me much about that – winning at the casinos and card games back in Chicago."

She saw his face brighten and imagined his mind fixed on distant memories until he snapped, "I wish I hadn't mentioned it to you at all. It's behind me. I'm cut out for better things."

"Okay. . ."

"There's more to me than someone who can win games!"

"Don't growl at me like that, Win. It isn't like you." Cindy was more puzzled than offended by his recent silence, then this ill-mannered funk. In the two months she had known him he had given her more attention, more compliments and more flowers than any man she had ever known. She didn't like it but now she needed to placate him. "You're a natural born competitor, alright. Bet you were the first kid on your block."

"As a matter of fact, I was the up-and-comer. And if I was first at something I wanted people to know it. I got my picture in the local paper more than once."

"Were you a prodigy of some kind? It reminds me of how little you've told me about yourself."

"Not a prodigy, exactly. I worked on my badges to reach Eagle Scout. When I made it the newspaper printed a half-page spread about me. And I played trumpet in the school band. I ran for senior class president. People noticed me. At least in high school they noticed me." His lips tightened.

"I notice you, Win, and this isn't high school – thank the Lord."

Ignoring her, he sat down in the upholstered chair, took off his shoes and socks, then pushed back the drapery with one hand and again stared outside at jungle-green foliage shined glossy by the steady downpour. The only sounds in their small hotel *casita* were the monotonous white-noise of steady rain fall, the whir-whir of the ceiling fan and the background whispers of Win's dejection.

Cindy was attuned enough to hear his unhappiness, spoken or unspoken. From the bed she could see only his profile but every nuance of Win's face was already familiar to her: broad, clear forehead, short nose, wide mouth, thin lips and a rather small chin. She could imagine him when he was a boy, a sprinkle of freckles across his cheeks, hair a sun-streaked yellow instead of a sandy color. His body, too, held a suggestion of whip-thin youth that was denied by a gestating little pot-belly. Sure, she had been charmed by her image of him as a fresh-faced, wholesome young boy. What she was beginning to realize was that boy could not have grown into this man. She needed to reconcile image with reality. She asked, "So how did someone who likes the spotlight end up in Yuma? It's such a low-profile, no-happenin' place."

He replied without turning. "You've got to start someplace if you want to go into politics. I guess you could call me the big fish in the small pond. People in Yuma government are beginning to know me." As if stimulated by the thought, he stood abruptly and began to pace the tile floor of their room.

Finally she voiced her impatience. "Will you stop, please? You're harshing my mellow."

"Harshing your. . ? That's one thing I've never been accused of doing to a woman, whatever it is."

"Mellow, Win. You're just too intense. You're harshing my mellow. Why can't you relax?"

"Is that surfer or stoner slang?"

"Never was a surfer and I'm not a stoner – well, not anymore. I admit I did a little toking in high school and that first month in massage school." She stretched her bare arms up and behind to touch the headboard. "After my handsome Marine deployed it was either go back home to a thoroughly whacky mom, or find some way to make it on my own. I had to work and pay my way through so there were a few luxuries, like the weed, that I had to give up."

"A massage therapist who gawks at birds. You might just be a little peculiar, you know?" The tone of his voice seemed to bring in the sodden humidity from outside.

"Well, aren't you playing judge today? Remember, marijuana is legal in some states. And I can tell you how I got interested in birdwatching. It's not peculiar at all."

"Sure," he mumbled. He stopped pacing and went back to the chair to stare out at the rain, making her wonder if he was really interested and if he would really listen.

"It started when I finished school and was trying to build my massage clientele. That's when I got sick."

Win leaned back and propped one ankle on the other knee. "What does being sick have to do with being a bird-watcher?"

"It was when my fibro was at its worst. I was in pain all day, every day. And I think I had a lot more going on than just fibromyalgia. I had a lot of what's politely called intestinal distress. But the doctors couldn't diagnose it and they couldn't help me. Even the right kind of weed didn't do it. I couldn't eat and when I did, I'd throw it up or shit it all out again in less than an hour."

"I'm glad I didn't know you then."

"Yeah, it was gross. I fainted onto the bathroom floor more than once."

"You're not the fainting type."

"I was then. I felt like I could have died there, hugging the porcelain, but no such luck. After two or three months I got so skinny my clothes hung on me. Then I developed agoraphobia. I couldn't go out of the house, not even to get the mail or pick up some milk."

"That doesn't sound like you at all."

"It was me back then. My stomach just couldn't digest real food. I used to watch cooking shows on TV – all that beautiful food – and just weep."

"Well, you don't look undernourished now and you did fine at dinner last night. You still haven't explained the bird-watching."

She smiled and propped her head on one hand, letting the sheet fall away from her bare breast. She knew that she was attractive to Win, with or without clothing and without a touch of makeup. She continued. "Back then I was so sick I'd lie in bed by the screen door, the big sliding door to the patio, and listen to the doves outside. Such a sweet, cooing sound. They woke me so gently in the morning. During the day they reminded me there was a world out there and they soothed me to sleep when I had to nap."

"You love the little feathered dinosaurs, don't you?"

"Of course. They were company, then. They were comfort. They were my only connection to the real world – the healthy, functioning world. Then, when I got a little better, I'd sit on the patio and notice other birds, and I'd want to know what they were, so I got a bird book. And then I got binoculars. And that was that."

Win crossed his arms. "Yeah. You've made quite a name for yourself at the local Audubon Society. And with those articles in the birding mags."

She said nothing, wondering if he expected an apology for her success or assurance he would someday surpass her in the narrow, competitive world of serious bird-watching.

Suddenly he pounded the arm of the chair with his fist. "Damn! I hate doing nothing. With the weather like this it's too crappy to go out, and with no wifi in this excuse for a hotel I can't even go on line to make plans for another trip."

"Win, don't you like bird-watching just for the fun of it?"

He stared at her.

"The excitement of the hunt, the glory of the birds! Well, aren't some of them gorgeous? When I look through the binoculars they take my breath away."

She couldn't read his expression. Then he said, "Very smug and self-satisfied about your little hobby, aren't you?"

"It sounds nasty when you say it that way. But as a matter of fact I'm very satisfied with my life right now, not just the birding. I love my work and my clients, and I love the birds. I'm the 'Life is good!' girl." He didn't answer. A rush of disappointment filled her solar plexus with heaviness and her mind with remorse. She had taken this trip with Win hoping it would be the beginning of a long and loving relationship. Now she couldn't get her mind around it enough to create a pleasant fantasy.

"I know you're not enjoying yourself, Win. Maybe it's not just the rain. You and I come from such different backgrounds."

"What is that supposed to mean?"

"It means maybe we aren't good for each other."

"That's crap. I don't have to be like you. You don't even understand who I am, and you're starting to think about ending us?"

"Then tell me who you are."

He sat forward in the easy chair with both feet on the floor and his forehead in his hands. Finally he said, "When I sit around like this, not accomplishing anything, not earning any recognition at all,

I feel useless. It's like I don't even exist."

"Don't even exist? How can you say that? You get a lot of recognition when we're home. You do a good job as H.R. director, you belong to those two civic groups, you even got into the "most eligible bachelor" section of *Yuma Now*."

"You're right. I'm being a complete pig. I adore you, Red, and I know you love me too much to think of leaving. It will be okay when we get home tomorrow."

Cindy fell silent, mute with uncertainty and indecision. The full emotional connection and satisfying sex life she had almost tasted with Win might still be in reach. Words failing, she slowly lifted the sheet and bedspread from her naked body and pushed it all the way down with her feet. She watched his boredom give way to interest, his eyes focus and grow avid.

"Come here, Win," she said. "We'll find out how many parts of you exist."

"When all else fails, let's f. . ."

"Win! You know I don't like the F-word."

"Whatever. At least for this I won't need my freaking binoculars." He stood and began to unbuckle his belt.

She fell back on the pillow and laughed. "No, you don't need binoculars for sex, Win, not even spiritual sex."

She saw his eyes on her diaphragm and stomach and knew he was mesmerized by their rise and fall. His eyes lingered on her pubic patch. The rich, red color never failed to arouse him.

"Damn," he muttered, looking down at his groin. "You always hit me like a jolt of electricity." He quickly lifted his shirt off and carefully unzipped his pants over the obstructing erection.

When he reached the bed, he stopped, as if her words had just registered. He looked down at her. "*Spiritual* sex? Spiritual *sex?*"

"Haven't you ever. . .? No, I guess not." She closed her eyes and said softly, "Sometimes when the emotion is there and it's slow and lovely, the world disappears and you're just floating in space – both of you in one body, but without a body. It's. . .it's heaven. It's pure."

She knew he hadn't heard. The urgency of his arousal had rendered him deaf. Naked, he climbed onto the bed. She rose to her knees and pushed him onto his back. Moving her hands down his body, she spread his legs far apart, leaned her head to the side and with exquisite slowness trailed her long, silky, red hair from between his thighs up and over his quivering genitals.

• • •

Chapter Three

Kim realized she was holding her breath, whether from shock or to block the odor of the decaying body, she didn't know. She closed her eyes for a second, forced herself to open them again and took a deep breath, resigned to take in all that demanded to be witnessed. On the thin rocky soil in front of her the terrible stillness of the woman's body contrasted with a perceptible stir of activity. Ants, beetles, flies, lizards, things pale and squirming, were active around, on and inside the dead flesh.

The woman's less fleshy parts, the wrists, fingers and lower legs appeared partially mummified. The smell of decay emanated from the woman's mid-section and open chest. Kim stared, thinking it must have been a mountain lion or coyotes that consumed her internal organs, because powerful jaws had twisted the rib cage upward. The positioning was a bizarre pose never seen in life, upper and lower body face-down, with midsection tilted upward so the ends of the lower ribs on one side were visible. The arms and hands were out-spread with fingers claw-like, death-blackened nails still digging into the dirt, as if the woman had made a last, desperate attempt to claim the earth, claim life.

Kim coaxed her mind toward analysis and reason. The woman was probably a hiker or bird-watcher who became lost and died of heat stroke. Her shorts and shirt, stiff and darkened by the process of decay, were just what a hiker would wear, although now they appeared too big for the shriveled and decimated body.

Kim had seen worse death scenes, both in her job as a Yuma City emergency medical technician and as a dog handler with the Yuma County Canine Search and Rescue team. This wasn't so bad. There was nothing vital, flesh colored or contoured about this body. It wasn't bleeding and there was no question of saving it.

She stood stock still, staring, almost as immobile as the body in front of her. She was relieved the woman lay prone, face hidden. At the thought, a prickle down her back gave way to a shudder. She realized her eyes were focused on the ruined color and pattern of the woman's shirt, but her mind refused to retrieve a memory associated with it. Her focus moved to the woman's head. The long red hair had fallen into a part down the back and spread around the skull in a mat, the color dulled by dust and dirt but still striking in this landscape of tans and muted greens. Above the nape of the woman's neck, the hair appeared caked with a round crust of dark gore Kim recognized – dried blood and brain matter.

Suddenly, something she had been holding back clicked in. Her eyes widened and her head jerked back. *Damn! That hair and the shirt. I know her! She was wearing the same green and yellow shirt.* The living person her mind pictured, Cindy Cameron, was the only person Kim had ever known who had such a long, thick mane of gloriously red hair.

No longer a professional observer, Kim was flooded with the overwhelming wrongness of this: a young and vital human being bereft of life, ravaged by animals and abandoned like so much garbage on long-suffering ground.

• • •

Chapter Four

SARA

The 1999 Chevrolet long-bed pickup truck is parked on the gravel driveway of a rest stop on the outskirts of Yuma, Arizona. This rest stop is unlike those on the interstate, which accommodate fifty cars and trucks with all their passengers and resemble a busy shopping mall; this rest stop serves a two-lane side-road. Its shallow pull-off is lined by dry native shrubs and provides space for two vehicles. There are no buildings here, but a concrete table and bench suffice for both dining and repose. Behind it a few thirsty trees hold back the desert.

The truck, a faded blue in color, appears to need its rest under the shade of a Cottonwood tree. It is fitted with a green camper shell scavenged from a salvage yard. The once-vivid colors of truck and shell have mellowed with age so they no longer clash, but blend into an abstract-painting of blues, greens and rusty primer hues, with dents of varying shapes and sizes to add depth and detail. The windshield is embellished by several dime and quarter-size wounds. The heavy truck rests on tires that appear too worn and mushy to support it.

Near it, lying on her back on the bench, a small woman in her late fifties or early sixties is dozing in the afternoon heat, with knees drawn up, feet flat, an open notebook across her face. Her drugstore reading glasses are clutched in her hand. Even under the Arizona sun her short hair reflects no highlights from its mix of grey and brown. She wears khaki shorts and a sleeveless polyester shirt that reveal arms and legs thin, straight and deeply tanned.

She comes awake with a start. Someone is approaching. She sits up in one swift movement, tossing the notebook onto the table. The two vertical lines between her eyes draw deeper, sharpening her face. She looks but doesn't spot another person or another car. The interloper strolls into sight. She raises her hand in casual greeting, then leans back against the hard edge of the table, body language telegraphing unconcern. After all, it's a public place.

The man approaches, close enough to touch her with his outstretched hand. She sits bolt upright again and glares at him, warning, "Don't touch me! And don't think for a minute I'm afraid of you. I don't shake hands."

His response calms her. She listens, replies indifferently, then to another question says, "My name? What do you want with it? Yeah, I might be suspicious, but then maybe you're nosy. If you need a label, Sara's as good as any. And Sara doesn't like questions. I'll tell you just what you need to know about me, not another blessed thing."

She grabs the thick, spiral bound notebook from the table and places it on her lap before replying to his next question. "No, I never saw you before, either. I'm new here, same as you. I'm looking for someone. Who? None of your business who."

At his next comment she smiles a little, not at him, but at an inward reflection, and then speaks, "That song says it, says, 'Everyone's lookin' for someone.' They wrote that song about me."

The man has now seated himself on the bench on the other side of the table. Sara is fingering her thick notebook, fanning the one hundred lined pages darkened by penciled handwriting. Something in the manner of the newcomer challenges Sara. "You keep looking at me! What, my grey hair?" she asks. "Yeah, I'm an older woman, but no fool. No fool like an old fool? Got you fooled, then!" She hugs the notebook to her almost-flat chest with both arms.

"Yeah, I got here the same way you did, heading west on Interstate Eight. Or maybe I drove south, down Highway Ninety-five. For you to figure out. Sure didn't head north from Taco-Land, or east from Californication, that pit of sin and foolishness. But I'll tell you one thing – if you drive down Highway Ninety-five from Quartzsite in summer you'll think you're on the road to hell. You'll know it when you pass the entrance to Yuma Proving Ground off to the west. That huge war jet and that death-machine sitting there with no shame at all. Why, I'm talking about that cannon with a barrel as long as a country mile. They designed that abomination to fire an atomic bomb right from the battle field. It's out there on display tilted up and up like it wants to blast the angels out of heaven."

She pauses and shakes her head. "Yep, coming down Ninety-five in summer, not even a glimpse of fire in sight, the heat will roast your skin dry and sear your soul to desolation. If you got one."

She doesn't notice his reaction or pause for a comment. She places the notebook back on the table. Her voice is louder, her speech more animated by the importance of what she is revealing. "Then if you keep coming south, when you pass that range of jagged, rust-colored hills off to the east where the signs say 'Kofa National Wildlife Refuge' you'll know they're back in there, and I'm not talkin' about wildlife. It's a refuge all right, for what the government's hiding. You can't see it but you can feel it, smell it on the air even goin' sixty miles an hour, the stink of corruption. "What? Don't look at me like that. I know what I'm talking about and I don't need to prove it to people like you – ostrich!

"Well, okay, then. Like I was saying, miles past the Kofa, you know you're almost here when the land lowers out to flat and you see the green springing up all around, cool and fresh. Then you know Yuma isn't all bare dirt and cactus."

She pauses and he remains silent. She asks, "You haven't seen much in the valley yet, have you? There are fields here with lettuce and cantaloupes and such – and the palm trees make it look like one of those oasis kind of spots, like in the Sahara. Pretty nice down there by the river, too, under the trees. The Cottonwoods are best, but even the Mesquite shade and hide real good.

"I went down the dirt road over there and found a spot where I can park my truck near the river, but away from those homeless camps. No, got nothing against them, but got no business with them, either, 'though some say men with that much hair can't be trusted."

She looks around her briefly then realizes she is still holding her glasses. She puts them on and inspects her companion more closely. "*You're* not all fuzzy like you've not seen a barber in a month of Sundays." She draws a deep breath, more comfortable now, and continues, "Sometimes when I bed down for the night in my truck with all the doors locked tight, sometimes I feel – I feel almost safe.

"What's that look you're givin' me? Yeah, 'safe,' none of us will be safe from those death-loving ghouls in the government and what they're planning. They chose this place. I didn't. Not where I predicted Armageddon, but I've been wrong before, and I know this poor valley will see the apocalypse, birthed from the ass-hole of the devil himself – unless I can stop it. Yeah, me. I came here just lookin' for someone. Haven't found her yet, but this Yuma valley found me. It needs me, even if she doesn't. These Yumans don't know it yet, but *they* need me. They *all* need me."

• • •

Sara has found a new place to live, quiet and secluded. The place is known locally as Betty's Kitchen, but there is not a commercial kitchen within miles. This recreation and picnic area was named after the owner of a restaurant built in the early nineteen-hundreds, when the Laguna Dam was constructed nearby. Neither the dam nor the restaurant remain now in this isolated refuge surrounded by agricultural fields, where stacks of hay the size of houses separate the tilled and irrigated farm land from the hardpan-dry soil of the refuge.

Here, a good twenty minutes northeast of Yuma, the chained-off parking spots are never filled, four or five widely-spaced picnic tables provide some privacy from rare visitors, and a large, outhouse-type restroom made of concrete block, generally unused by anyone but Sara, and is clean and odor-free.

She often walks the paths of this all-but-abandoned picnic spot that meanders along the banks of the meandering Colorado. In this place the river is transformed into a shallow lagoon easing over a thirty-foot wide spillway before it continues its way down to Yuma. Oasis that it is, not a blade of grass flourishes in the alkaline soil.

Today, Sara is alone at the concrete picnic table, writing in her notebook, her glasses perched low on her nose. A worn Bible rests on the bench beside her. An unaccustomed noise finally penetrates her concentration and she turns to see someone approaching. "You just love appearin' out of nowhere, don't you?" she says. Then she chuckles, "Yeah, I know, your job is keeping an eye on me." It is the man she met two months ago at the highway rest stop, who is now her frequent companion.

"But don't bother me today," she says, pushing up her glasses with an index finger. "I'm working here. I'm reading and writing, and figuring. Trying to make a plan."

His questioning voice is a baritone, thick and demanding.

"You know 'for what'," Sara says. "Somebody's got to stop them. What Ebola and AIDS and ISIS can't do, those Marines and their government masters are gonna do. They're getting ready to launch the Third World War out there. Out there in the Kofa. They don't keep their evils bound in the Proving Grounds any more. They loosed it in the Kofa.

"I know because I saw them out there just after I got here in January, about a dozen of them with some civilians, in big trucks. And then I camped, and after dark I saw lights flashing over, not high up, but real low to the ground and I heard strange noises, like 'whoosh.' It was evil, sure as God is good. It's startin'. I can feel it."

She furrows her brow. "But not all of 'em are military. Some are civilians living on the banks of the irrigation canals, some by Smucker Park, in the Old Town barrio and nearby the orange groves.

"I know, I know," she says, impatiently. "Every place takes on the sins people do there. It's got a bad history, this town. Settlers and Indians, Quechan and Cocopah all fighting and killing each other over the land and over the poor Colorado River. Now-days, it's little more than a trickle by the time it gets to Arizona. They've dammed it and drunk it almost dry from up-river, to down here, to the Yuma farmers and Marines. Those L.A. gangs and Hollywood pretenders don't deserve it. Let them have the trickle."

She pauses, biting the end of her pencil, listening to her companion. Her face is troubled, her voice thin with stress. "God destroyed Sodom just to kill one thousand evil souls. The only hope for Yuma is its righteous ones. It's the numbers will seal their fate, one way or the other. I'm working with the numbers."

She puts down her pencil and runs her fingers through her short hair as if summoning her thoughts. Silence broken only by the listless chirping of a few birds, the rustling of dead leaves as a lizard works its way under them and the urgent scrape of her pencil on paper.

Suddenly she stops writing, drops the pencil, and looks up. "I worked out the ratio!" she exclaims, pounding her fist into the other palm. "Nine hundred people! It's the solution of Sodom. It's Abraham's righteousness ratio. Ten people could have saved Sodom when it held a thousand. This sorry town holds ninety thousand, not counting the ones that come in winter." She hesitates briefly. "No, we can't count them. Those Canadians bolt north like rabbits when the thermometer hits eighty. So one in ten is nine hundred for Yuma." Another furrow appears in her forehead. "Are there nine hundred righteous souls in Yuma?"

"It's the greed eating away at righteousness. I'm takin' aim at it first. War puts another dollar in the pocket of some heartless millionaire every time an innocent soldier dies. Listen to this…" She lifts the notebook and reads, *"I've named them now, dubbed all vile ghouls; now crime's outdated and war's the crime of fools."*

She shakes her head and rubs the side of her nose. "I know if Ruth was here, she'd be one of the nine hundred righteous. She was never a bad girl. It was that Marine that led her down the wrong path, lured her away when she was only seventeen, didn't know any better." She pauses, a shadow of grief darkening her face, her thoughts darker still. *Even if there aren't nine hundred righteous here, some can be redeemed to fill the tally. They can be educated, persuaded! But not all will learn and respond. Some will be sacrificed."*

• • •

Chapter Five

Kim was motivated by the need to report and recover the woman's body. She made the hike down the slopes of the Kofa in less than half an hour. When she reached her SUV she used the tail of her shirt to protect her hand from the hot door handle then went around and opened the other door to let the hot desert air replace the superheated air in the cab. She grabbed an old towel from behind the seat and looked around for a cool place to sit.

The only remnant of shade in sight was the vehicle's shadow, so she spread the towel on the ground by the tail gate. She checked to confirm reception on her smart phone, then paused to drink most of the water in her second quart bottle. The first call would be 911, the second to the team leader of her canine search and rescue group and the third to Allie Davis, her former counselor and current friend.

The 911 operator transferred her to a Yuma County Sheriff's Deputy Wagner. He listened to her story about the body, and said he was inclined to mosey on out with the body recovery team until she told him about what appeared to be a bullet hole in the back of the woman's skull.

A desiccated corpse was not a very surprising thing to find in the Kofa. There were many methods of meeting one's end in the desert, both natural and man-caused. A body with a bullet hole in the head usually said "suicide," less frequently "accident." The placement of this particular body's bullet hole might say "murder victim," depending on whether it was an entrance or exit wound. The deputy told her he would bring Lieutenant Raney. She knew who he was, that he wore the hats of both crime scene tech and lead homicide detective.

"I'll be waiting," Kim said to the deputy, and pressed the end-call button before he could press for more details.

She sat with her elbows on her knees and the phone in her left hand for a few minutes before she called her friend in Search and Rescue. He owned an important member of the canine team, the cadaver dog.

"Hey, Angelo, we've got another job."

"Oh, goodie. Cuddles is getting bored. He would love a new dead body. When and where?"

"Tomorrow, in the Kofa. Just body parts search and evidence search. A woman."

"Every *body* needs Cuddles," Angelo said, a corny play on the dog's name.

"Yeah, we need Cuddles, but consider burying the joke, Angelo."

"Well, don't get testy, Kim. Tell me more."

"She's only been…the body is less than a week old, I'd say. The animals have been at it."

"So Cuddles and I will search for body pieces to complete the jigsaw puzzle. You and Zayd doing the evidence search?"

"Of course. I'll call Terri for backer. She'll do Nav/Comm, take care of the GPS and the radio. But who can we get to fill in if Zayd and I wear down before we've covered the grid?"

Angelo snorted. "Not much chance of that. When have you and your pup ever needed a second string? And why can't we do it now? Cuds and I could use a good run today."

"Because the crime scene tech hasn't done his work and the body is still there. After they remove it, you'll get the official request from the Sheriff."

"So where exactly in the Refuge do we begin our latest doggie dance?"

"Meet at Saguaro trail head tomorrow at first light."

"*Her*It's a date, Tall and Gorgeous. Don't you be late."

"Of course not, since I made the date. Even if I was late you wouldn't think of doing it without me, would you? I've got a stake in this one."

"You did say 'her' instead of 'it.' What's that about?"

"Later, Angelo. Got to go. Bye."

Kim let the hand with the phone drop to the towel. She wiped perspiration from her face with one fore-arm then the other. She closed her eyes, propped her elbow on one knee and rested her forehead in her right hand for a few seconds. Resisting the urge to drink more water, she keyed in Allie's number at the mental health clinic.

At the welcome sound of the older woman's voice, she said, "Hi, Allie. I'm glad it's you and not the voice mail."

"Only because my appointment had to cancel at the last minute. But why are you calling me in the middle of your day off? Are you okay?"

"Yeah, I'm okay, but I've got bad news."

"Oh, damn. I get enough of it here." A second's pause. "Sorry, Kim. It's not about you, is it? And it's not *really* bad?"

"Not about me, but yes, it's really bad. I'm hiking in the Kofa and. . ."

"Isn't it too hot to be out there in the middle of the day?"

"I started early and I expected to be gone by now." Kim shifted her legs sideways. The sun's inexorable movement had extinguished part of her shady patch and the fierce rays were now scorching them.

"Allie, I have to ask you something. Your friend Cindy. I know you've been worried about her. Didn't you say she should have been home two days ago and you haven't been able to reach her?"

A questioning "Yes?"

"When did she leave Yuma?"

"A week ago yesterday. Why?"

"Yeah, what I thought." Kim drew a deep breath, and dug her heels into the loose dirt at the edge of the towel.

"Allie, I found a body out there today – a human body." She remained silent, waiting for her friend to ask the question.

"You. . .you're not saying it's Cindy?"

"Yes. I think so. No, I'm sure it's Cindy. She's the only person I know with that color hair, and I recognized her shirt. It was the one she wore to your cookout last month."

Silence. Then Allie's slow, deep inhale and sighing exhale. Kim could almost hear Allie's mantra, which she often expressed aloud: *It is what it is. Accept it.*

"Allie, I know you were going to start calling around to her friends to ask if they've seen her. I think you should call the police instead, report her missing."

"Missing? For heaven's sake, why? You found her. She's not missing."

"Because I don't want to tell the Sheriff who she is. They would pull me from the search job, and I want to be in on it."

"For heaven's sake, why?"

"Because it was wrong. That's not what I mean, of course it was wrong that she was murdered. But for some reason, this is personal to me. Maybe it's because she was a friend of yours, or maybe something else. I don't know. I just know I want the killer to pay for it, and I'm going to try to see that it happens."

"Are you sure you can't just let them know her name?"

"They wouldn't take my word for it, anyway. They have to have a positive ID. They'll work it out. And – you told me she had dated a guy you work with. What's his name? Yeah, Win. Don't say anything to him and don't mention my name to anyone."

She paused while Allie processed what to her must have sounded like very strange requests. Finally Allie said, "Okay, Kim. But only because I know you and I trust you. Crap! How are you doing? It must have been horrible…"

"I'm fine, Allie. I hardly knew her, just through you. You're the one who's got the loss. Sorry. I have to go now, but you can call me later this afternoon if you want to."

Kim keyed off the phone to save the battery and tossed it on the towel beside her. She breathed deeply and when she exhaled she felt her shoulders drop and chest sink with relief. The most difficult conversation was over.

• • •

Law enforcement arrived like the cavalry of old, in a cloud of dust caused not by a posse on horseback, but a patrol car carrying Deputy Amos Wagner and Lieutenant Lon Raney followed by a

Hummer carrying the body retrieval team of four Search and Rescue volunteers. The team often arrived with a trailer and ATV to cover ground faster for body extraction but today they would have to hike it. The governmental agency charged with overseeing Kofa, Arizona Fish and Game, didn't endorse the use of off-road vehicles driven by the public and tolerated it from law enforcement and search and rescue if time or distance demanded it. This job didn't meet those criteria and if it did, the terrain was steep and rocky enough to challenge even an ATV. The extraction team would hike up with Kim and the deputies, then back with the body to the Hummer. The medical examiner's van would meet the Hummer at the highway to transport the body to the morgue.

Kim waved the dust away from her face with her cloth hat while she watched the men dismount their vehicles. The recovery team busied themselves with their equipment and hung back to follow the lead of law enforcement.

The deputy wore a uniform of brown pants and tan shirt, while Lieutenant Raney was clad in light-weight grey slacks and a white polo shirt with the Yuma County Sheriff's logo on the front. Both wore hiking boots.

"Kim Altaha, isn't it?" the lieutenant asked as he approached. "We met last month at the volunteer recognition lunch, didn't we?"

Kim remembered Lon Raney as slow, serious and silent, while today he appeared still serious but revved up to work. He handed Kim a plastic bag filled with a bottle of water, sticks of beef jerky and a protein bar. He said, "You've been out here a while today, haven't you? You should always carry at least an extra gallon of water in your Jeep, along with a few protein bars."

Kim nodded with an "I already know that," expression but was silently grateful, especially for the water. She took in the lieutenant's appearance, starting with intelligent blue/green eyes, the color commonly called hazel. She thought the word didn't describe the striking effect of combined shades of blue, green and brown. His body, as well, appeared anything but ordinary. His constitutionally slender physique reminded her of a racing greyhound.

She waited while the men shrugged into backpacks loaded with their own supply of water. Lieutenant Raney carried an additional bag, a hand-held case like an old-fashioned doctor's house-call bag. As they started up the mountain, true to her characterization, he followed close on her heels with seemingly effortless strides. The deputy followed, and at a distance back, the recovery team. All were silent as they climbed the slopes.

The smell of the body hit them before the sight of it. The sun had passed its zenith but still radiated such heat that the land was now at full sizzle. The odor of decay weighed down the atmosphere even more.

Deputy Wagner stopped to let the others precede him. He puffed and blew air, his face red from sun and exertion, shirt dark with sweat stains on his sternum and around his arm pits. Kim thought it wasn't so much excess weight that caused his distress but poor conditioning from too many days spent at a desk or in the seat of a patrol car.

In his previous contacts with her, Wagner had been blatantly admiring and made comments about her body that were a little too descriptive. She knew he expected a verbal response which, even if negative, would have given him an opening to connect with her. But she had experienced that kind of crude approach before and simply ignored him. She suspected Wagner hated being ignored worse than he hated being rebuffed, and now his carnal interest in her had turned to resentment.

• • •

Chapter Six

Kim knew Wagner was watching her as she and Lieutenant Raney approached the body together. The detective/crime scene technician opened his bag and removed several items. He slipped blue fabric covers over his shoes and donned blue nitrile gloves. He motioned Kim to stay back, and went to squat beside the body. He inspected the back of the head without touching it. Finally she had to ask. "What do you think?"

"I don't think it was an accidental death." He glanced up at her quickly. "Or a suicide. This is a bullet hole and if it was a suicide, the entrance wound would most likely be in the temple or under the chin, so the exit wound would not be in the back of the head. And if this was an exit wound, it would be bigger. There would be more brain matter and bone fragments, more blood spatter. Besides, if she shot herself, where is the gun?"

"Maybe under her?"

"Could be. Where do you think the bullet is?"

"I don't know."

"If it was small caliber, it could still be in her head. When I finish photographing I'll look. The M.E. will give the official cause of death after he gets her on the table, but I think she was murdered."

"When I found her it looked to me like she was just a birdwatcher. Who would want to murder a harmless bird-watcher?"

"There are lots of questions here. Like 'who is she'? Once I'm finished with photos, I'll look for ID, a gun, the bullet that killed her. I'll be lucky if I find any of them."

He unfolded his lean frame and walked a few steps toward Kim. At six-foot-three, he looked down into Kim's face, something expectant in his manner. She waited for a question, but he voiced none, and she began to feel vaguely uncomfortable. What was he waiting for? She had told herself she would not feel guilty about keeping information from him but now the word "murder" whirled in her mind and threatened to override the promise.

She said, "I saw the binoculars there by her arm but I didn't touch them or walk around looking for anything else she might have carried with her. I didn't want to disturb things."

"Yes, very nice," he said, "I appreciate that."

"But I wondered how she got here. There was no car down at the parking area."

"He brought her here and then drove away after he killed her. I checked with Fish and Game. They told me at least six vehicles came and went in the last week. No sense in searching for tire tracks to cast." He turned back to survey the body. "No obvious signs of a struggle or sexual assault. The clothes look relatively undisturbed. In order for him to get close enough for a shot like that, she must have known him."

"Why 'he.' If it wasn't a sex crime, maybe a woman did it."

He flashed a hint of a smile. "Could be, but the stats say nine chances in ten it was a man. Big risk factor for being a murderer – being male. But – a woman perpetrator – I'll keep it in mind."

He turned to Deputy Wagner. In a soft and almost casual voice he said, "I won't be done here until almost dark. The body team can bring her down then. Why don't you tell them to find some shade and relax for now? Then look around for any belongings, anything else significant. If you see any footprints that don't look like hers, call me."

From his bag he took a set of small, orange plastic evidence markers, open triangle in shape, with numbers in white on both sides. Next came a dozen paper bags of various sizes, a few plastic baggies, a felt-tip pen to mark them with, and last, a digital camera.

Kim's eyes couldn't leave his hands and arms as he worked. His hands and fingers were long, lean, and somehow expressive. His forearms were heavily muscled, tanned and covered with sun-bleached blond hair. Evidently unaware of her observation, he turned, and watching where he stepped, he walked to the pair of binoculars and placed one of the evidence markers by it. Then he began to take photos, quickly moving back to photograph the body from every perspective. The sun had moved far to the west and the boulder no longer shaded the body. The photos would reveal every gruesome detail.

Finally he stopped taking pictures, placed the camera back in the bag, and approached the body. When he knelt beside it, Kim turned away. She heard his movements as he began to move the body. She steeled herself to turn back and watch while he lifted one side of the body to look under it then went around and lifted the other side, moved the head to look beneath it, then gently let it back down to rest in the dirt. When he stood he saw her watching and shook his head. "Nothing."

He removed his gloves, placed them in a plastic bag and sealed it, then put on a clean pair. He stood looking down at the terrain in all directions. "She might have come from this direction," he said. Focused on the ground before he placed his feet, he took a few careful steps. Abruptly he stopped and squatted to look at something.

"Kim, bring me my case, will you?"

The answer on the tip of her tongue was "get it yourself," but he had obviously found something important and she was curious to know what.

He stood to take the case from her. "I found a sneaker print large enough to be a man's. There's a partial print there, and a heel mark there, but then the ground gets so rocky there isn't a real trail. But sometimes one good print is enough."

"Couldn't it be just anybody's print?"

"I don't think so. The body is fully visible from here. If a hiker made the track after she was killed he would have seen her and reported it."

"So, maybe it was left before that."

"I checked the weather with Fish and Game. There was a high wind and even a sprinkling of rain in this area eight or nine days ago that would have obliterated a print as shallow as this one. From the condition of the body I'm guessing she was killed about a week ago so that narrows the window of time when the print could have been made. Logic *and* instinct says it's the killer's print."

Satisfied with the explanation, Kim nodded and watched silently. From the case, he pulled a metal frame about fourteen inches long and six inches wide and pressed it into the dirt around the print, working it into the hard soil until it anchored firmly. "First we take pictures with the frame," he said. "The marks on the edges of it will tell us what size the shoe is." He snapped four photos from four different angles, then put the camera away and took out an aerosol can of artist's spray fixative.

He turned to say, "Some techs use hair spray, but this has higher viscosity and works better." He shook it carefully and holding it a foot above the print, sprayed a fine mist onto the print. "This stabilizes the dirt and sand so it holds together for the casting material." He waited ten seconds, then moved the can an inch closer and sprayed again. After the third time he looked satisfied. He carefully measured a cup of dry dental cement into a plastic bowl. Next he poured water from his drinking bottle into a measuring cup, poured it into the bowl and began to stir.

Kim watched, fascinated, as bright yellow flakes in the grey material slowly disappeared, absorbed. When all the yellow was gone he said, "Now it's ready to pour." He began at the middle of the heel, moved to the toe, and back again, reversing directions and moving toward the sides until the print was covered by the mixture an inch deep. "It will take about thirty minutes to set," he said, and began meticulously to clean and replace his equipment.

Kim had lost track of time watching his thoughtful, precise actions. When he finished, the ache in her thighs intruded, along with the thought that she had hiked more than ten miles today and wasn't done yet. She needed to leave.

"You don't need me here, so…"

Lieutenant Raney interrupted. "How did you happen to find her?"

"Oh, I came to look for the pronghorns."

"Were you alone?"

"Yes."

"Do you often hike alone?"

"Actually, I do."

"Had you been here before?"

"No." With that, she realized Lieutenant Lon Raney was interrogating her. A flash of resentment hardened her jaw. Hadn't he just said the killer was probably a man with a size ten and a half shoe? She saw his eyes widen and the shadow of a smile tighten his lips. He was reading her own expression.

"I guess that does it for now," he said. "Thanks for your help."

She turned away before it occurred that he had wondered if she knew more than she was saying, which was right on the mark. If he considered no one above suspicion, it was a sign of the detective's professionalism.

With a thirty minute hike to the vehicle yet to go and almost an hour drive home, she felt eager to be done with this day and its surprises. She turned back to say goodbye to Detective Raney and started down the slope. Immediately, Deputy Wagner fell in step with her. She turned to give him a quizzical look but said nothing. She was disinterested in the deputy and preoccupied with thoughts of tomorrow. She knew he wouldn't follow her all the way down because that would leave the Lieutenant without his second in command.

After twenty or so paces, out of earshot of the others, Wagner stopped. Kim turned, shocked to see a sneer pulling down his flaccid lips and an angry flush stamped on his round face.

"This must be quite a treat for you," he said.

She stopped short. "A treat? What the hell are you talking about?"

The sneer melted into a mocking grin as he gestured back toward the victim. You work as an EMT. You get paid for grocking the gore, but this was just dessert, wasn't it?"

"Grock? What is that, a Star Trek reference? You haven't outgrown the Trekkie phase yet? And no, I get paid for helping people who are hurt and what we just saw was a damned abomination."

He appeared not to have heard her. "But then again, she wasn't scalped. Quite a head of hair on that one, huh?" He hooked his thumbs in his belt in a studied gesture of confident superiority and stared at her.

The reference struck her in the pit of the stomach. She wanted to punch him. "You jerk!"

He continued, "After all, you and your *tribe* have a reputation for torture and atrocities, don't you?"

The knot in her stomach rose into her chest. "Yeah, and you and *your* tribe have a reputation for lies, greed, and stupidity, don't you?" She moved closer to him, glad she was an inch taller, her eyes dominant as she glared at him. "So you've heard I'm Tonto Apache. You know what *Apache* means? It means "enemy." Know what *Tonto* means? It means "wild and unruly." Leave me alone, Shit-For-Brains, or I will be *your* wild enemy!"

• • •

Chapter Seven

Kim turned and strode down the rough hillside. When she was sure Wagner could no longer see her she slowed a little. His racial slur had taken her by surprise, and now in response she heard the internal voices of an antithetical message, "Be proud of your Native heritage." It had been the habitual refrain of her tribal elders, her parents, and teachers. Even most Whites had forsaken prejudice these days, although largely ignorant of any but a stereotyped understanding of Native culture and psychology.

Pride in her heritage felt as elusive now, as then. She couldn't conjure it because it wasn't pride in being Native that was the issue. It was whether or not she felt proud to be an Apache that had haunted her since the age of reason.

Her automatic footsteps slowed by degrees until she realized she could go no farther with her mind in turmoil. She sat down in the dirt, willfully inattentive to the danger of scorpions and rattlers.

In grammar school she had heard, "knowledge is power," but learning the history of her ancestors taught her that knowledge is sometimes guilt, instead. The story of the Apaches splashed a lurid and bloody pattern on the history of the Old West. Apaches were renowned for strength, tenacity, intelligence, cunning and endurance, especially Cochise and Geronimo, their bands of warriors and tough-as-nails women and children. She could feel proud of those qualities, but her pride warred with her shame at their reported capacity for cruelty and savagery.

Histories of the tribe told of Apache children given small birds and animals to torture in preparation for an adulthood of torturing human victims. Geronimo himself confessed he had tossed settlers' babies into the air to hear them giggle then caught them on his knife.

Kim pushed the grotesque image from her mind and stood to continue her hike to the trail head. But she couldn't stop the scenes of her tribe's history from playing through her mind, reel after disturbing reel, as they had in her childhood.

In the late eighteen-hundreds, when the braves among her ancestors were avidly pursuing or being pursued by soldiers they were unable to dispatch their captured enemies at leisure. They then gave the prisoners to their women to torture. The women were considered even more diabolical, more capable of inventing horrific ways to torture their victims to death.

Soon the monsters of her childhood nightmares were Kim's own tribal ancestors. She never spoke of it, but she wondered, and she learned to argue against her growing self-doubt. Wasn't pain a part of everyday life, especially the lives of nomadic people in harsh, unforgiving environments? And didn't the Apaches include themselves in their ideas about pain and suffering? They placed bravery and stoicism above all virtues; they were renowned for their apparent immunity to the most severe physical pain.

And then the doubts wormed their way back into her child's soul. Was her ancestors' apparent cruelty dormant within her? Did some remnant of their blood course through her veins? Did she harbor the gene for brutality in her own DNA?

With fierce vigor, she joined the other boys and girls of the Yavapai-Apache tribe, learning about their heritage, including the atrocities and massacres committed against them by settlers and the United States Army. She learned and spoke bits of the ancient Athabascan-root language, and danced the traditional dances in elaborate costumes. It still wasn't enough to solidify her amorphous self-image or imbue it with positive self-regard. She read books depicting the culture and customs of other remnants of the scattered Apache blood line, who exist not just throughout Arizona, but into the mid-western states. She longed to be one of those adolescent girls. She had seen pictures of them covered with corn pollen in an elaborate puberty ceremony that was meant to ensure long life.

Finally, Kim firmly told herself to stop ruminating and watch where she was going. She reached her vehicle for the second time that day and began the drive home, wishing for just a minute she could go the other way, back home to the Verde Valley and her family.

When she finally pulled into the driveway of her little home on the outskirts of Yuma she sighed as she switched off the ignition. She looked at the brick and stone of the house, and remembered what Allie had said about her determination to live in such a house. Allie called it Kim's "three-little-pigs-complex."

It reminded her that Allie hadn't called to talk more about her dead friend. Maybe she would call Allie. With that decision, her thoughts reverted to a point-counterpoint debate about guilt. Allie knew all about what had happened at Montezuma Well three years ago and Allie was still her friend. Allie knew her and wouldn't be her friend if she was bad, deep down.

At the door, Kim's Rottweiler/Black Lab mix, Zayd, greeted her with his usual tongue-lolling grin and tail wags. She wondered why his tail swung in a wider arc than usual, wriggling his body like a worm's, until she realized that somehow he sensed the possibility there would soon be a search.

She removed her hiking shoes and dropped them in the coat closet, hung her binoculars on a hook, then tore off the band holding her hair in a tight pony-tail. She bent to cup Zayd's muzzle in her hand and kiss him on the head. Her hair cascaded over his neck, matching his ebony coat in color and sheen. She gave the dog a pat on his hindquarters then hurried to the bathroom, acutely aware she hadn't relieved her bladder since early morning.

She was not yet finished when the day pack she had tossed by the bathroom sink began to vibrate and buzz. *Whoever it is, they can damn well wait,* she thought. Before answering the phone she flushed, lowered the toilet lid and sat down on it.

Lieutenant Raney's voice, slow and undemanding, "Hi. Just wanted to ask if you'll be back tomorrow with the canine team."

"Yes, Angelo and his dog, and Terri and her dog. What do you have for Zayd to scent from?"

"The binoculars. I dusted them for prints before I bagged them.

They have no value as evidence but Zayd could turn up something by scenting from them."

"You know there's not much chance of that, don't you? I mean, scent loves moisture, and there's precious little moisture out there. And it's been days."

"I know. We have to try."

"So how did the footprint cast come out?" She absent-mindedly stroked Zayd's back. The dog always followed her into the bathroom, intent on being petted any time his owner was not in motion.

"The cast came out nicely. I don't need the computer to tell me it's from mass-produced Nikes, common as dirt, and this one has only two distinguishing marks on the sole. They must have been brand new. Average size, too."

"Did you find her ID? Or a gun?"

"No, nothing in her pockets and we didn't find a pack, just a plastic water bottle. No gun, and no bullet so far. I hope Jane Doe is local and not from Lower Slobovia, or the coroner will have her in the freezer at the morgue for a very long time. I'm hoping you and your canine team can find something."

Kim thought quickly. "Can't you identify her by her finger prints?"

"The fingers look too shriveled for prints. Maybe if we soak them in water, they'll plump up enough. If so, we'll run them through AFIS. That will only help us if she's in the data base, and I mean all ten fingers. If she got printed in Arizona, it could be an issue. Arizona's on their shit list – uh, excuse me – on their list for failing, in so many cases, to get all ten or all ten readable."

"Speaking of a list, it appears I'm on Wagner's black list and right now he tops mine. Whatever's eating him doesn't matter to me, but if I have to work with him it could get ugly."

There was a pause. "I wondered why he followed you when you left. You had words?"

"Yes."

"Something about the case, about your work, or something personal?"

"Personal, if you call racism personal. But that's all I want to say about it. So, about our Jane Doe – if you get prints from her fingers why would they be in a data base? I don't think she's a criminal, do you?"

"Maybe not. But people who aren't criminals get printed, too – insurance agents, the military, teachers, day-care workers. We might have to source some non-traditional avenues for an I.D. We'll check the missing persons reports. If she's not there and finger prints don't work out, we'll get the media to ask the public. If that doesn't produce results, at least we have the teeth."

"What?"

"When I turned her over I found them intact. The bullet exited between her eyes. She had good teeth, but not perfect. I'm sure there are x-rays on file in some dentist's office somewhere. In Yuma, if we're lucky."

When he paused, Kim found herself wondering why Lon Raney had chosen to share all this information with her. She thought about the search tomorrow and turned the conversation.

"The cadaver dog won't have a problem tracking down body parts if there are any left out there, and if there's anything that belonged to her, Zayd will find it."

"Right. About five a.m., then."

"Sure. *Carpe manana.*"

• • •

Chapter Eight

It was the next day but not yet morning when the alarm rang, forcing a yawning, groaning Kim out of bed. She had laid out her clothes the night before, so she didn't find it difficult, even with eyes closed, to pull on her cotton underwear and then the gray pants and matching gray polo shirt with "Search & Rescue" across the back in large capitals and on the front, the Sheriff's Department logo.

Zayd danced around her like a dervish, sure now of the day's events. "Stop, you're making me dizzy," she said, and tried not to step on his feet as they went to the kitchen for breakfast.

Kim was sure most Rescue dogs, like Zayd, loved their work. The team called on him so often it sometimes conflicted with Kim's EMT work schedule. Zayd had been cross-trained in both air scenting and trailing/tracking searches. Unlike search dogs at disaster sites, he had been trained to be scent discriminating, able to find one individual among many others when given a scent article for targeting.

In most searches in an urban environment he worked on lead, but today he would be off lead, deployed from the site where the body was found. Kim would follow as closely as her own speed and stamina allowed while he zigzagged within the bounds of the grid established by defining the search area with the GPS navigator. Angelo's cadaver dog, Cuddles, would wait until Zayd did his thing. Lon Raney had made it clear that finding a personal article could help identify Jane Doe, which took priority.

Kim arrived at the trail head first with Zayd. She released him from his crate and the second she opened the door he scrambled out of the Jeep and paused to scent the air, then began to bounce with excitement. "I wish I could be as enthusiastic as you," she said to the dog, and made him stop prancing long enough to put on his snappy vest with the "Search & Rescue K-9" logo. She would swear he looked proud of himself whenever he wore it.

Angelo pulled in next and unloaded Cuddles from the crate in the back of the black SUV. The huge Belgian Malinois bounded over, Angelo following him at a slow and somewhat bowlegged swagger. Angelo wore a stud in his lower lip, skull earrings and tattoos on his exposed biceps. His Search and Rescue uniform struggled to counteract the Biker persona but did not succeed. Sheriff's deputies and other law enforcement staff were not fond of Angelo but he and his dog were too valuable to ostracize. To Kim, Angelo presented a study in contradictions that only deepened when he spoke. Without preamble, he asked, "Now about that secret connection you have to this case. Do tell, Sister."

She said, "When you tell me who the hell you really are, I'll share a few secrets with you."

"Let's just say I'm someone who likes to keep people guessing," he replied, placing a hand on his hip.

Kim glanced at the back of his SUV. "I see you took off the bumper sticker."

"Which one, Sweet-Pea?"

"The one that said, '*Support Search and Rescue. Get lost*.'"

"Yes, but I'm replacing it with a new one. '*I just look illegal*.'"

Kim had to smile. "You can say that again."

Cindy and her dog arrived minutes later. After the dogs' usual ritual of butt sniffing and tail wagging, they were put on leash to wait for Detective Raney. Kim turned toward the highway, and knew he was on his way by the thin plume of dust rising from the dirt access road. On his approach he must have seen that three vehicles already filled the small parking area, and swung his 2010 Crown-Vic around to park on the side of the access road.

Kim watched him climb out. Something in his deliberate but unself-conscious movements took her breath away. She turned away, aware she had been staring.

After exchanged greetings and a few pleasantries they began the hike up the mountain side. They might have been friends out for a walk together in the coolness of the dawn, except for the excitement of the dogs and the silent tension of the searchers.

Kim's mind swam with the knowledge she was withholding a secret from her team members and Raney, that she knew the victim. At the same time she felt glad Cindy was just another Jane Doe to the others. Members of the canine posse didn't want to know the identities of victims in body recovery cases, didn't want to know a name or any other detail that might change "victim" into "real person." A person with a name could be grieved for and team members who grieved, who allowed themselves to feel sad, angry, or outraged didn't last long on the team.

Finally they neared the place the body had lain. Chaos threatened to ensue. Cuddles had scented and alerted soon after being removed from his crate at the trail head, and now he repeated his "down" as if his owner just didn't get it. Terri's dog barked and strained at the leash, eager to run. In his first year after being certified he hadn't yet learned the finer points of canine search etiquette. Terri, as the Nav/Com, the backer, wouldn't need to use her dog but he didn't know that yet.

Raney retrieved the double-bagged binoculars and handed them to Kim. She untied the orange plastic bag, carefully opened the ziplocked evidence bag and gave Zayd the target scent.

Afterward, the morning was a blur for Kim from the moment she let Zayd off leash. She remembered mostly the glare of the rising sun, the sight of Zayd's jet black hind-quarters, and the feeling of her chest heaving as she followed him at a dead run. She knew Terri, who backed by keeping dog and handler within the set grid with her GPS monitor, struggled and sometimes lagged far enough behind so she had to yell her instructions to change direction. During the search Zayd alerted only once, but it was a false alarm. She lost sight of him briefly when they had been at it almost an hour.

"Done," the backer yelled, finally. They had searched the area around the body's location to a distance of two miles in each direction. It had been a marathon, with no triumphant cross of the finish line. Instead, exhaustion for women and dog. They returned to the deployment site at a wind-recovering walk, the no-find outcome contributing to mutual silence. Kim shrugged inwardly, confident no target item lay out there within the perimeter. Zayd had done his job.

When Angelo and Cuddles began what would prove to be their own slower but equally unrewarded search, Lon Raney asked her to sit and talk while they waited. They found a boulder flat enough to sit on, shaded by a gnarled mesquite tree. Zayd lay on the ground next to the rock, close to his collapsible water bowl.

Lon started and led the conversation, which made Kim comfortable. She always warned prospective friends she was not a chit-chatterer, but she enjoyed Lon's knowledge of his work, his calmness and matter-of-fact manner. They talked about the victim and the investigation, and then about what had brought them to their jobs.

Finally, Lon asked about her family. She told him about her father, mother and older brother who lived on the tiny Middle Verde reservation in north-central Arizona, one of the five separated parcels of the six-hundred thirty-six acre reservation. Middle Verde, in the town of Camp Verde, was the headquarters of the tribe. It held a small administrative building at the entrance to a neighborhood of two winding streets, mundane and quiet, and totally unlike most Whites' notion of what a reservation would look like.

Lon fixed her with an unreadable expression. "Thank you for telling me about it. I don't like being ignorant about the people I work with."

Kim looked at her bare legs and arms, acutely aware of her own body and its condition. "Can't wait to get home and shower," she said to him. "Hell, I might shower and then take a bath. It's not just the dirt and sweat. I feel like the odor of decay is in my nose, inside my lungs, on my skin. I've dealt with plenty of decaying corpses after two years as an EMT, but for some reason this is different."

She noticed that Lon's mildly inquiring look invited her to share more personal information, but when she didn't respond, he said, "I used to feel like that sometimes when I first started on the job, but it isn't really the odor. It's the mental images you have to wash away, not the smell."

"How?"

He took her hand and bend his face to the inside of her elbow. He inhaled slowly, then with hands on her shoulders he leaned in to smell the skin of her neck. She was immobilized by the deliberateness of his actions, and by the heat of her body's response.

She saw his eyes shift from her sweat-soaked shirt to the curve of her thighs against the rock, then into her face. He said, "You smell like life to me."

"Life?" It was all she could say. Her mind felt numbed, confused.

"Our jobs attract two kinds of people: those who love life and those who love death."

Kim blinked, mentally transfixed by self-questioning. *Which am I?*

Lon rested his hand on her knee. "I'd like to come home with you. We could shower together. I'd wash your back and . . . there are other things I'd do to help you forget."

For a long moment she didn't answer. She lifted her chin to look at him, feeling the fire of defiance that she hoped was in her glare. "Yes, I think you could," she said quietly. She hesitated. "And I think someday you will. Until then, if you ever touch me again without a clear invitation, I'll break your arm."

He jerked his hand back from her knee. His face revealed a split second of shock, then softened. "Yes, I get it. And I apologize. Sexual harassment of colleagues has never been my style."

• • •

Kim went to bed that night knowing she would have to rise at five a.m. Her current shift with the fire department ambulance squad started at six. She had followed her usual ready-for-bed routine, but sleep would not wash away the events of the day. Thoughts of Lon Raney and the possibilities of their relationship, of Allie's dead friend Cindy, who by now lay safe in the county morgue, kept her mind active and her muscles tense.

Most of the trouble came from what Wagner had said, from doubts and dread spilling out of the wound his words had opened. Fear she would dream about Apache atrocities hadn't fueled her insomnia since her early teens, but now, minute by sleepless minute, the fear grew into a palpable presence in the darkened room.

At the age of twelve Kim had read about Apache women's custom of giving birth under a tree. After the birth they placed the placenta onto a limb of the tree; the tree then became the infant's double. Throughout their lives, when brave or squaw felt debilitated or bereft, he or she went back to the tree to renew their life force. They customarily returned in the spring in a kind of pilgrimage at Nature's universal time of renewal.

When the Chiricahua Apache were finally subdued by the Army in 1886, Geronimo and his people were removed from their homeland and imprisoned on a reservation. The fiercest warrior of them all hurled bitter accusations at the government for the sufferings of his people. He said they weakened and died because they could no longer return to their soul-twin trees to be restored by a sacred ceremony.

When Kim heard the story, it brought hope to restore her own childhood zest for life. She asked her mother, "Where is my tree?"

"Your tree?"

"My twin tree, my soul tree."

Her mother laughed. "Daughter, the Verde Valley Regional Medical Center knows where your tree is, and it's probably at the town dump, or where-ever they put their medical waste."

And so it continued. The innocent delights of her childhood were overshadowed by the knowledge her ancestors delighted in the agonies of others. Then, should she doubt even her occasional joy, for what it might foreshadow about her? She didn't question her parents or her teachers any further, and no one questioned her. Her self-doubts and confusion went unnoticed by the adults, who didn't understand her love of fairness and her capacity for deep feelings.

Eventually she found that inner struggle leads to a search for peace through understanding. As a young adult, she read about religions and philosophies until she felt she had found her own beliefs, and along with them, her role in life. She would be a defender of the weak, a champion of justice and an instrument of karma. She believed it and lived it – until the incident with the man at Montezuma Well. Her ancestors would have approved of the very inventive manner she had chosen to kill him.

The stillness of memory gave way to a muted sound from the floor. Zayd. She rolled out of bed, dragging her pillow with her, and lay down on the throw rug beside the bed, where Zayd snored his soft doggy snore. He woke and turned to give her face one sleepy, approving lick. She pressed her cheek against the back of his neck and her knees against his warm hind quarters. She sighed with relief. This was better. Then she wondered, *Would Allie call this self-soothing, or self-punishment?* It was her last waking thought.

• • •

Chapter Nine

The 1999 pickup truck could be an apparition from the recent past, an anachronism rolling down Yuma's 8th Street at midnight, its faded colors blending with the night shadows. The vehicle's near-antique status and mechanical longevity are far from Sara's thoughts this night or any night. It has never occurred to her the truck might someday reach the end of its life cycle and stop running, and so it hasn't.

She can see over the steering wheel only because she sits on a lawn-chair's thick cushion she re-purposed years ago. She eases her spine against the back of the seat. It wears a bright yellow t-shirt, size x-large, recently purchased at the local Goodwill store for a dollar. In a newer car the shirt might have been a jaunty decoration. In the Chevy, it hides the decomposing upholstery's look and feel of un-tanned alligator hide. The shirt may be one more thing holding the vehicle together.

She turns to her companion in the passenger seat. His name is Michael, and after these many months she trusts him – completely. "Wouldn't do this on a Friday or Saturday night," she says. "Nope. Too many people wanderin' the streets, drinkin' and carousin' on the weekends. And wouldn't do it on a full moon, either." She glances up at the lunar crescent emitting an anemic glow.

She brings the truck to a stealthy halt at a corner and dismounts. Taking a large canvas tote bag from the cab, she says, "I must'a been guided when I made fifty copies of these at that office store up in Utah. Paid dear at eight cents a copy. Now comes the work.

Important work."

The sidewalks are empty. The lackluster moon and yellow street lights play foil to reality, casting pale purple shadows on the pavement and darkening the truck's color to brown, while in this altered state of existence, Sara's tanned skin takes on the greenish hue of decay.

As one very much alive and intent she moves swiftly down the sidewalk, hugging the store fronts, away from pools of light cast by the street lamps.

Soon she stops, pulls a sheet of paper from her bag. She uses her teeth to tear a strip from a large roll of packing tape, and with it presses the paper onto the store window. She moves to the next window just feet away, and slaps another sheet on it, and one on the door, then two more on the other windows. Five yards down the sidewalk she repeats the process at another store. She turns, looks around and when she sees no one, trots back to the truck where her companion keeps look-out.

Sara drives, slow and law-abiding to the upscale mall on 16th Street. She sees the City police patrol car before the officer sees her. When they pass, he inspects her and her passenger closely. She smiles because he doesn't follow them or try to stop them. He probably thinks they are nothing more than ordinary.

She begins to hum, the sound at first a mere vibration in her throat, then louder. She sings, "Has anybody here seen my old friend Martin…" She stops humming and turns to her companion. "Martin Luther, Martin Luther…King had nothing to do with it."

At the mall she exits the truck and again tapes her written manifesto to the targeted windows and doors. In large block print, it starts:

Have no love for gems! Although
bright diamonds sparkle, so do tears
coursing down pale cheeks of saints. . .

She is especially proud of the last lines:

Gold: wasted years; long labors lost.
For glint of gold, please lust no more!

The words reverberate in her mind as she works. She regrets having to exempt the jewelry stores and banks nearer downtown from her attentions, but the police patrols there are too frequent. By three a.m. she has covered all the establishments on her hit list but hasn't yet exhausted her supply of poems. She decides to tuck a few of the pages under other doors, under the windshield wipers of a few parked cars, wherever there is a paper-width crack. She returns to her truck, saying with satisfaction, "There, Yuma's first warning that greed leads to war and war will beget the apocalypse."

Then her face goes slack, deepening the furrows from mouth to chin, and emphasizing the two vertical lines between her deep set eyes. "It's the first promise they might escape it. It's guidance for their salvation. They're only words, but we have to try. It would trouble me to have to do more. But — sometimes it takes death to warn of death, what the war-mongers have in store." A sudden smile. "There, I'm rhyming again."

• • •

Chapter Ten

Before Kim could take the first sip of her at-work coffee, a call squawked over the loudspeaker. She paused, cup against her lips, eyebrows raised at her partner across the table. Both sets of eyes asked the same question: fire truck, ambulance or both? In Yuma sixty percent of calls were injury/illness calls. For those, the truck and ambulance were dispatched together. If the EMT-trained fire-fighters decided the caller needed to go to the hospital, the ambulance would deliver them. The exception happened when police were on scene first and requested only an ambulance.

The dispatcher's voice announced, "Police call, single victim injury. Ambulance rolls."

Kim gulped her black coffee and bolted from her chair in unison with her partner Jerry, who, in this caffeine-fueled work environment, was known as "Latte" for his blond hair and pale skin.

When they reached the end of the corridor and entered the bay, they slowed a little. Before they entered the ambulance, Kim nudged her partner's shoulder with hers. "Hey, Latte, I didn't even get to ask how you are today." She was fond of her younger partner, who at twenty-two still had the slender build and bland face of vulnerable adolescence. A slight slump of his narrow shoulders revealed a basically introverted personality, unusual for an EMT. His body also displayed a biologic non-sequitur, an unruly blond Afro-kinky hair style, hinting at his hereditary diversity.

Jim smiled at her, hesitated, then jostled her in return. "*Mas o menos*, Straight Up. How did your day off go?"

She climbed behind the wheel, gave his boot a casual tap with the side of her shoe. "You're too young to know, kid. Light us up."

Out of the bay, he obediently turned on the siren and lights. The conversation would have ended in any case. Kim had told her partner during their first ride together that she didn't like to talk when she drove, unless it was about the case ahead of them. Right now they had no information except that police had summoned them.

Five minutes later she pulled the ambulance into a diagonal parking place next to the police car. On the jewelry store in front of them, sheets of paper taped to the windows and door lifted and dropped languidly in the light breeze. One window of the display case had been shattered, with much of the broken glass inside. Several larger shards littered a small section of the sidewalk, some covered by splatters of fresh blood with thin red stems. The scene provided an instant crime report and an instant patient diagnosis: attempted theft, arterial bleed.

Two uniformed officers wearing latex gloves attended the victim who lay face-up on the sidewalk, emitting high-pitched whining sounds. The scruffy-looking man had been bound at the ankles with plastic zip ties. The female officer stood on his left, one foot resting lightly on his left arm to secure it against the sidewalk, although it didn't appear to Kim that he would be able to rise if unrestrained. The male officer had one hand around the victim's right wrist, holding the arm straight up, while his other hand pressed a piece of blood-soaked cloth around the victim's upper arm. "Hurry it up," he growled. "I'm getting tired of this." His prisoner commented with a deep groan.

Kim dropped her red medic bag and turned to Jim. "More gauze, then go back for the gurney." Jack trotted back to the ambulance. She turned to the officer holding the make-shift bandage. "Looks like a smash-and-grab."

He lifted his chin toward a metal bar the length of a forearm protruding from the display case. Kim's eyes followed his to where gold and gems gleamed and sparkled in multiple hues amid bits of glass, then they went quickly back to the officer and victim. The officer gave her a sour-faced nod. He held his arms straight out from his body with his rear jutting back in an attempt to get as far away as possible from any more spurts of the victim's blood.

"You're doing a great job," she said. "Just hold on for a second more. Jerry is bringing more bandages for direct-pressure and a tourniquet."

She squatted at the victim's side. The man's face had a grey tinge and a sheen of sweat. That wasn't good. She pulled his uninjured wrist from under the officer's foot and began to take his vital signs. She saw Jerry coming back at a brisk pace, carrying gauze pads but then he slowed, distracted by the sheets of paper taped to the jewelry store windows. "What's with all the papers?" he asked. "What is that, poetry?"

"Get over here now," Kim said.

• • •

Chapter Eleven

Allie sat in her worn office chair, staring at the exquisitely detailed and well-framed drawing of a Navajo girl which decorated the office wall opposite her. Above her desk hung the diplomas and license to practice psychotherapy that validated her. She knew she was procrastinating but the knowledge didn't help. Dealing with situations involving friends was so much harder and essentially so different from counseling clients.

Of course Kim had once been her client but in the three years' time since that relationship ended they had both moved from central Arizona to Yuma. Kim had found a new occupation and their relationship had evolved and deepened into friendship. Now Kim, who knew Cindy only through her, had found her friend's body.

Allie's friendship with Cindy, Cindy's connection to Winston Verbale and her own relationship with Win had put her on the spot. She didn't relish the task of telling Verbale about Cindy's death because she didn't know what to expect. The only other time she had informed a client of a death, the relationship of victim to survivor had been clear and unambiguous, which gave her an expectation of the survivor's feelings and reactions and thus how to deal with them. With a coworker she trod on uncertain ground.

Winston Verbale and Cindy had been seeing each other for just a few months, but Cindy had not discussed Verbale with her in any detail. Certainly Win hadn't said a word about it. His position as director of Human Resources at the mental health clinic precluded talk about personal issues. Sure that Cindy and Win had been good friends or more than friends, she felt obligated to reveal the news to him rather than let him hear it from the anchorman on TV or read it in the Yuma *Sun.*

Winston Verbale entered her office with a professionally genial smile on his face but his tone of voice had an edge. "What is it you need to talk about in your office instead of mine?"

Allie came from behind her desk, closed the door and sat on the sofa, gesturing Verbale to the chair next to it. If she had remained behind her desk it might imply she had assumed the role of counselor in this situation, not a message she wanted to send. "Sorry, Win, but you have glass walls and you leave your door open. People are in and out of there without knocking. My office is more private. This is something personal."

He sat and waited, looking cool and composed in green slacks and short-sleeved dress shirt of pale green. She noticed again that his blue eyes were set in an open, strangely innocent face which often disarmed others.

"Win, I have to tell you something that will be difficult to hear. I've learned Cindy is dead."

"Cindy? Cindy Cameron?" His face appeared puzzled.

"They think she died between a week and ten days ago. I'm sorry I can't tell you much more, but evidently it's going to be aired on a TV news show this evening. You two made no secret of the fact you were dating and I just thought someone should tell you in person."

"But she told me she was taking time off to take care of her mother back East. Was it a plane crash?"

"No. It happened near Yuma. Win, I didn't know her mother lived back East, much less that her mom was sick."

"We were close. She told me things she probably wouldn't tell anyone else."

"You took a long weekend at the same time she left. I thought maybe you went with her."

"No. When she told me she was leaving I decided to take a trip myself. I went back to Costa Rico for a few days." He squinted as the afternoon sun moved through the open slits in the venetian blinds and cast stripes of light and dark across his face. Allie rose quickly and drew the blinds closed.

"I remember," she said. "When she didn't answer my calls, I went to ask you about her, but you were gone, too."

Verbale shook his head as if in denial of what he heard and looked down at his knees. He rubbed his face, pressing his knuckles into his eyes. When he looked up again tears smeared his cheeks.

Allie fell silent, feeling her own eyes sting. Then she said, "I'm sorry Win. She was my friend, too." She saw him glance at the box of tissues on the end table but reject the thought of taking one, probably because he knew they were for her counseling clients and didn't want to be cast in that role. Instead, he placed the palms of both hands on his cheeks and swiped down and back in a childlike gesture.

He said, "Did you know they were going to feature her in the next edition of *Yuma Now Magazine* – about her bird watching and those articles she wrote for the national birding magazines? And she was thinking about going into local politics?"

"She talked to me about both those things. She told me you taught her a lot about politics. She wanted to get more involved, herself."

He gave her a look filled with doubt or irony; she couldn't quite read it. She asked, "So you two enjoyed your time in Costa Rica?" When Cindy returned, she had hinted to Allie that her relationship with Win had run its course.

"It was the best. Cindy was a very affectionate girl."

The word "girl" grated in her ears. She felt her emotion shift from compassion to confusion. She changed the subject. "I hear you're going to run for the vacant seat on the city council."

Verbale sniffed but his eyes brightened. "The opening was unexpected. George Smith died last January and they've been trying to get his widow to accept the seat, but she doesn't want it. So, special election." His voice conveyed confidence. "I appreciate your letting me know about Cindy." He rose to leave but at the door he turned back to her with a raised eyebrow. "If the TV reporters didn't get onto it until today, then how did you find out?"

"Um…I can't tell you. I'm sorry."

He hesitated as if about to ask something else then turned the door knob and left without looking back.

Allie remained on the comfortable sofa instead of returning to her office chair. She wanted to sort thoughts from feelings. She expected this conversation would lead to an opportunity to grieve with Verbale about their mutual friend, but he had refused to go there. He was harder to understand than his ordinary but open appearance suggested.

• • •

Win tried to wipe the smile of anticipation from his face as he opened the wide door of the wheel-chair accessible, all-users bathroom. It contained no stalls and one toilet in full view. He closed the door without locking it and approached the toilet. *What were the chances? Win, lose or draw?* The question no longer stimulated an erection, as it had when he first began this game of bathroom roulette. It was still exciting, but after pulling the trigger of an unlocked bathroom door dozens of times, it felt less and less like the thrill it replaced. The real thrill was the prickle of fear-anxiety-hope-exultation crawling across his scalp, legs quivering at the sound of dice rattling onto the wheel, eyes following the hypnotic turn, turn, and then the agonizingly slow climax as the dice settled, then his explosive exhale.

He lifted the seat of the toilet and took his wide-footed stance. He slowly unzipped his pants, and reached into his briefs for his flaccid penis. He did miss those erections, because the additional minutes it took for the hard-on to recede increased his chances for a hit. He had gotten a dozen hits recently, but no real wins. For a second he entertained the old, familiar fantasy. The woman who opened the door wouldn't start, blush, and apologize. She would quietly step across the threshold, close the door and lock it. He would turn and she would see his prick and imagine herself holding it while it grew even larger. She would approach slowly, eye to eye, knowing he would give her the best, the very best, screwing of her entire life.

He loosed his stream of urine, ignoring the familiar tinkling, listening for a sound from behind, an opening door. He decided this was not his lucky day, shook off the last yellow drops and started to zip up when it happened. He glanced around quickly to catch the look of dumb shock on the woman's face. She uttered an embarrassed,

"Oh, I'm sorry," and slammed the door.

Score! A chuckle burst from his throat like an ejaculation. He turned, grinned into his reflection in the mirror and strolled from the bathroom without washing his hands. The woman was fat and unattractive. He was glad they hadn't made it together and he wouldn't fantasize about her. But later, when he needed it, a quick sniff of urine on his fingers would bring back the memory of the ridiculous expression on her pathetic, pudgy face and along with it his feelings of triumph and superiority.

• • •

Staccato rapping on her door – Allie looked up from her note-writing in surprise. The last client gone, the next not due for an hour; other staff members would knock, then enter. When she opened the door, she was nose to nose with the tearful face of her last client. The woman's round and lumpy form filled the doorway, then she pushed forward to enter the room, almost knocking Allie down. The woman hurried to her usual place, the easy chair. She sat, grabbed a handful of tissues from the box on the end table and lowered her face into her cupped palms.

Allie remained standing and took a deep breath. What now? When she had first accepted Debbie Smith as a client it occurred to her that this woman had the soft, under-done look of a half-baked loaf of bread. Debbie's tall puffy body was topped by a large head that sprouted short beige hair over a fleshy face so lacking in character and distinction it defied description. Allie could never picture the woman's features when Debbie wasn't in front of her. Were the eyes blue, brown, or something more indeterminate? Were the lips full or narrow, cheeks high or flat? When she actually looked into Debbie's face, Allie often felt a vague sense of puzzlement, as if in some subtle way the woman wouldn't quite come into focus. Right now, her undefined features were twisted by strong emotion. She looked up at Allie, and blurted, "He...he.., I saw him...he...!"

Allie walked to the sofa and sat down next to the client chair so she could put a comforting hand on Debbie's arm. She looked into Debbie's eyes and spoke in a soft and calm voice "Okay, Debbie, slow down and tell me what happened."

Slowly and with prompting, Debbie revealed the story. She had walked in on a man in the unisex bathroom and it brought back a traumatic memory from her childhood.

Allie felt her face soften and her shoulders relax in a rush of compassion for the child Debbie had been. A sensation of warmth in her chest often filled her as she did the work she knew so well, and this was no exception. She left her hand on Debbie's arm as she acknowledged the feelings and asked the questions that helped Debbie calm down, process the incident and understand the dynamics of past trauma.

Finally, with habit born of professional necessity, she took a surreptitious glance at the clock, and felt the pressure of her next appointment encroach on both her attention and empathy. She asked, "Do you think you're calm enough to drive home now?"

Debbie hesitated. "I'm wondering what will happen if I see him again. I think he must work here."

"Why? Who is he?"

"The nice-looking man with blondish hair who always smiles. I think I saw him in the hallway once before."

Allie knew instantly. "Yes, Winston. He works here, but he's the director of our human resources department and he's a very nice person. What do you think might happen if you see him again?"

Debbie glanced around the room, as if searching for the answer. "Nothing, I guess."

"I think you're right. He's probably forgotten about it already. Just an unpleasant little accident, wasn't it?"

Debbie shook her head. Her helmet-like hair didn't stir, but another drop of mucous oozed from her nose. She wiped. "I feel calm." A long pause. "But I don't feel safe. The way he looked at me. Like he was surprised, too, but with a different expression. And something else was really strange. When I was running down the hall I thought I heard him laughing."

• • •

Chapter Twelve

Win left the office about twenty minutes after five, unable to find any task sufficiently important to keep him, and aware it was now late enough to inform anyone who might notice that he was industrious and dedicated to his job.

While he drove, he thought about Allie's news that Cindy was dead, his red-haired Cindy. He could almost feel her wise, comforting, massage-therapist hands on his body, her long, silky hair. . .then he mentally pushed the memories away, squeezing his thighs together to discourage a fulminating erection.

He drove his clean and polished, late-model Mercedes with his left hand, the other hand alternately fiddling with the satellite radio controls, smoothing his hair or rubbing his thigh. He drove at exactly the speed limit and with an eye out for pedestrians or other drivers he might know and acknowledge with a casual wave.

He had always wanted a luxury car and to him the Mercedes was the epitome. He remembered with relish the first day he drove this car. He sat in the leather driver's seat, enjoying the smell and feel. He smiled, saying aloud, "My Mercedes, my Mercedes, my Mer-kaaaa-deez." Ah, he deserved it but then Cindy hadn't appreciated it. She liked her little Volkswagen, a woman with no taste at all.

Cindy, Cindy. It had been simple but right, at first. She had been agreeable, low-maintenance and he loved seeing the envious look in other men's eyes when he told them he had hooked up with a massage therapist. Of course she would never have been a contender for wife, not his wife, with a questionable background, uneducated, in a mundane profession. She stole into his life as a pleasant distraction and then became a competitor. With her ridiculous hobby of bird watching she had gained more name recognition than he had managed in his whole life. The fact that she might actually worm her way into Yuma government was an insult, and then she had hinted she was going to break off their relationship.

What was it about her that he hadn't recognized as a threat? Thoughts of Cindy summoned the memory of his brother, thoughts slithering into his mind without warning. Yes, she reminded him of his brother, the golden boy who did nothing and got everything, everything Mom and Dad had to give. *The ass-kisser always thought he was better than me. When I had that thing at the casino and got put in jail, he stopped speaking to me, thought he was too good for a brother who spent one damned night in jail on a misdemeanor.*

But Cindy. *I'm glad she's gone. I never wanted to be a bird watcher. I should be the one who's being watched, not the one watching. If she started in politics even on the school board or some other low-profile position, she would have risen. Like my brother, things that should come to me came to her instead. Her and her, "Don't harsh my mellow."*

Home in fifteen minutes, he opened the garage door with the remote, came to a smooth stop and opened the door of his newly-built, ranch-style house. When he stepped over the threshold he had a brief but familiar sensation that the house was trying to swallow him. Cool air greeted and enveloped him, the feeling of coolness enhanced by the interior wall color they called "cottage white." He had chosen not to paint over it with color so the whitewashed effect harmonized with the cream-color of the tile floors.

His steps echoed slightly as he walked into his office. He went to the phone, but no messages from anyone important, only a telemarketer's come-on. Something new on his desk drew his attention, a bill from the housekeeper who had been here today, straightening, vacuuming the already-clean floors and polishing the sleek and functional Danish modern furniture. He liked the floors bare of rugs, the walls naked of art work or other decorative hangings that would have been distracting, too much like the old-fashioned and over-stuffed home of his parents, who had been foolish enough to think they could beget and raise children starting at the age of forty.

He sat at his teak desk, picked up pen and paper and began to make notes for his acceptance speech to the Yuma City Council. His eyes strayed to a framed photo of his deceased parents on the wall above his desk. Too bad they were gone and wouldn't see the start of his rise to success. *No,* he thought, *they didn't deserve it, especially Mommie Dear. She never had faith in me, no matter how much I did to prove myself. It was just my brother she trusted to succeed, Momma's favorite little boy, the rotten turd.*

Finally, when I'm on the Council, this no-action funk, this losing streak will end and things will be different. Articles about me and pictures will be in newspaper. I'll give interviews, maybe get spots on local TV news and the morning talk show on KYMA.

He sat back and pictured himself rushing directly from work to council meetings which might go on until nine or ten, calling constituents or getting calls from local people who had problems and needed his help. He would listen and speak with sympathy and then just a word from him to the zoning commissioner or the health department inspector would solve the issues and turn constituents into political backers and friends.

Unexpectedly, a different thought occurred – that he might look out into the crowd of citizens at council meetings and recognize a person he had surprised in a bathroom. His own crow of laughter brought him out of the reverie.

He sat forward in the chair and began to type, inspiration streaming from memory of speeches by Kennedy, Reagan, and Bush. This was good, this would work. He revised and rewrote on the computer, reminding himself he needed to buy one of those smart-looking notebooks so he could work anywhere with people around to see him.

Feeling a surge of energy, he went to the kitchen to put a frozen dinner in the microwave and sat on the stool at the counter to eat. Back in the office, he made more changes to refine the speech, tweaked it again and again, experimenting with different type fonts for printing it although he was aware no one else would ever see it.

He stopped briefly to go the bathroom, which for some reason left him feeling strange and uncomfortable. When he took the last page from the printer and sat back in his office chair he realized he was done now; there was nothing else to do this evening. He felt the silence begin to suck at him. When he was alone like this at night the house became like a vacuum, sucking his life away. The sensation was subtle at first, then pervasive. The house was removing him, molecule by molecule, cell by cell. Nothing could be guarded, nothing held back, the tiny holes in his being were growing in number, life flowing from him like water from a breached dam.

He shook his head to clear it, to dismiss the feeling of becoming nothing, an emptiness in empty space. His heart began to pound and his skin grew clammy. He pulled his handkerchief from a back pocket and wiped his forehead. There, there was no crushing pain in his chest. He wasn't dying; he wouldn't die of a heart attack. No. The certainty came…he would simply weaken, collapse, and dissipate into nothingness.

He pushed out of the chair, grabbed the remote and turned on the TV. It was tuned to the local newscast. He saw the newscaster's face, just a talking head, heard the loud and self-important words but they were just sounds; they made no sense. Then an image of Cindy's face appeared, and suddenly he heard the words, "…local woman…body discovered…Sheriff…"

There she is again! Cindy, Cindy, my little red-haired deserter Cindy, are you haunting me? The thoughts came to nothing, pushed away as the newscaster spoke other words, and other images appeared. He found himself pretending the newscaster could see him, was talking directly to him. For a moment, it worked. Then a flash of reality coupled with self-hatred extinguished the fantasy. He clicked off the TV and tossed the remote back on the table. Fleeing down the hallway, he grabbed keys from the table and ran to the garage for his car.

He had enough composure left to drive carefully, yet without knowing his destination. Minutes later he felt a bit calmer, the emptiness at bay. He would drive another thirty minutes or so then go home. When a thirty foot tall neon sign appeared by the road side he realized with a bolt of lightning through his brain that he was at the casino. *Shit!*

He drove past, wide-eyed at the parking lot with all the tightly packed cars. He took a swift glimpse back and saw people passing through wide doors into a carousel of colored lights, movement and bursting sound. *Shit!* The bile of envy and hatred rose up in his throat. *Damn. I can't because I'm not one of them anymore!* He couldn't cruise slowly into the long, wide driveway, find the perfect spot to park and then stroll into the casino like one of them. He couldn't join them because two years ago, he had put himself on the state-wide "Do Not Admit" list, the one touted by Gamblers' Anonymous as the cure. He had done it himself, wary that the bad luck in Chicago that made him lose it and punch the dealer still shadowed him. But now if he tried to enter any casino in this state he would be stopped by the guards or be told to leave at the cashier's window. It would get out. People would gossip. Everyone would know. Then, no city council.

He drove, shuddering at the crawly feel of sweat trickling from his arm pits down his sides. He swerved the car into a U-turn. *Where can I go? Where are the people who can see me? What if I stop and get out of the car and pretend to read a road map? Or pretend to change a tire?* Yes, as they drove past some unknown person would mirror him so he would know he was alive and whole. But no, eventually some pathetic fool would stop to help him, and that would not do, would not do to appear vulnerable, needy. *Not for the future city council member. Hell, I'll soon be the mayor or even, someday, the governor.* He felt his heart again, against his shirt, trying to break through.

When an idea finally penetrated his panic he pulled the car off the dirt shoulder and onto the blacktop heading back in the other direction. His expectations and then his confidence increased exponentially with each mile. *In the end, I'll stop chasing my losses and win a big one.*

A concert was in progress tonight at the convention center. The only parking space available was twelve rows back but the distance gave him time to mentally prepare as he walked toward the building. No one at the ticket window this late in the performance and when he pointed and mouthed "bathroom," the rent-a-guard waved him through the open door. He walked down the hall hearing phrases of mariachi music from the concert that sounded thin and frantic. There was no door to the men's room. The entrance and exit were at both ends of a half-circle which provided privacy for the apex of the arch, where there were three wide, handicapped-accessible stalls. The room was typically large, tiled, and fluorescent-lighted. He entered the center stall and propped open the door. He had just unzipped his pants when an old man in a motorized scooter came around the corner. Verbale turned and pointed his penis at the man. His wrinkled face took on a pained look, as well as a shocked one. The man mumbled "excuse me" and barreled toward the exit.

Verbale looked after him for only a second before he zipped up, and allowed himself, for one anticlimactic moment, to wonder what unique and imaginative things a handicapped man might do to give sexual satisfaction to a virile, able-bodied man like himself. It was just another fantasy, and not a very exciting one. It didn't help. It just wasn't enough.

• • •

Chapter Thirteen

Kim had talked on the phone to Lon Raney twice since the day of the body recovery, but he had told her little about any progress on the case. Curious to the point of frustration, she surprised herself by asking him to come to her home for a Sunday afternoon of pretzels, beer and TV baseball. Her next thoughts were about their mutual physical attraction. Maybe they needed to keep their distance. Curiosity and determination won out. She had made a commitment to herself to help get justice for the murdered woman. She had to see it through, even if it involved a few challenging situations.

After her shower and while she dressed she pondered the indefinable elements of sexual attraction and emotional connection in relationships. Thus preoccupied she didn't bother to dress for company, but drew on cotton bikini panties and a comfortable sports bra, yellow t-shirt and shorts in a burnt-orange color. A scarf around her banded pony tail completed her outfit but not her questioning.

Her attraction to Lon did not fit the stereotype of a woman's attraction to a man similar to her father. Kim's father was short, stocky, had dark brown eyes and black hair. The only thing about Lon comparable to her father was his thoughtful, deliberate silences and the intelligence in his eyes.

When she opened the door for him she hesitated, not knowing whether to shake his hand or give him a quick friend's embrace. She sensed that he was uncomfortable with the situation too, and did neither.

It took less than five minutes to show him around the small house and the back yard where Zayd sometimes did his toilet and otherwise communed with nature. Their conversation sounded stilted in her ears and the brief silences unnatural rather than easy. When they returned to the living room she determined to relax and enjoy the day and her company as if it was nothing unusual. She kicked off her sandals and drew her legs up onto the sofa. They debated which baseball teams they would watch then began a friendly dispute about which one would win.

Kim soon decided that if Lon knew her reason for inviting him here, he wasn't making it easy for her – not a word about the investigation. She felt she had waited long enough when she said, "I'm glad you were able to I.D. our murdered woman so quickly. You must have done it just a few days after you processed the crime scene."

"Right, a lot easier than we thought it would be."

"The TV news spot aired three days after I found her. But since then I haven't seen anything or read anything about who killed her or why."

Lon appeared to be considering her statement which was a question in disguise. He was perceptive enough to know she was pumping him and with that knowledge she suddenly felt both uncomfortable and guilty.

He turned toward her, bent his right knee and shifted his leg onto the sofa, laying his forearm along the back. Now they were facing each other. He might have been about to answer when Kim turned, distracted by the dog. Zayd had scrambled to his feet, ready to defend her when Lon moved closer. She smiled and reached down to pat him reassuringly. "Cool, it Dog." She gave the hand signal "down." He sank to the floor again with a sigh, ears lowered.

Lon looked from the dog to Kim, smiled, and reached for his beer. "Yes, our Jane Doe has a name now. Cindy Cameron. Although we aren't sure if that's her birth name, a married name or one she chose for herself. We didn't find a birth certificate or a marriage license and we haven't been able to contact anyone who admitted they were family. The only official record of any kind was her social security card."

"That's a little unusual, isn't it?"

"Very. At any rate, your friend Allie. . .Allie Davis is it? . . . called to report her missing the day you found her. A follow-up the day afterward with Allie and a few other people who knew her helped us nail down the I.D. It's a good thing, too. The M.E. said the fingers were too decomposed to print and getting DNA results within six months was an iffy proposition at best."

"You made the positive ID with dental records?"

"Had to. No one would have recognized her, looking at the face. She wore no jewelry, had no tats or identifying marks except for a few tiny scars, the kind everyone gets when they're alive for more than a year. It seems Cindy Cameron flew under the radar. No contact information for next of kin, just a list of massage clients. Her computer gave us the names of people she chatted with on-line about birding, but not much else. "

He wiped the bottom of the beer glass with his palm then put it back on the coaster. His multi-hued eyes appeared calm but intense. "I've been thinking how interesting it is that Allie was a close friend of hers and you're a close friend of Allie's, but you didn't know her."

Kim hesitated. She had a choice to make. Here was a man who dealt with deception, dishonesty and more despicable forms of behavior every day. How would he react if he knew she had not been honest with him? And why did she care?

She took a deep breath, prepared for his displeasure at being deceived. "I did know her. Not very well. I recognized her body the day I found her but I wanted to be a part of fixing it, part of the search team. I hated whoever did that to her and I wanted to help get them. I still do. And I knew you'd figure out who she was."

He nodded, apparently unsurprised. She detected no hint of reproach in his tone when he said, "That explains a lot. But it's my job to get them – him – the perpetrator, not yours. Anything else about her we should know?"

"No. And I *would* tell you if there was something else." She glanced at his hand and forearm on the back of the denim-colored sofa, within inches of her shoulder. He wore a tight, short-sleeved shirt that showed bare skin, tanned and warm, muscles curved and hard, not bulging. A thrill of sexual excitement coursed through her body, a shock and a mystery. She had blocked so much from her mind and body but she was not as closed off and safe as she had thought.

She folded her arms over her chest and willed the sensations away.

"You're looking at my arm," he said. "Is it the one you're planning to break?"

She continued as if she hadn't heard. "You've questioned me and her co-workers at the massage clinic. Allie said she has no relatives – had no relatives – except her mother, who I guess is among the missing. Or maybe Cindy was among the missing. From what you've said, I don't really know. And did you question her boyfriend, Winston Verbale?"

He said, "I know she wasn't in touch with her parents." He paused, and looked into her eyes, the slightest of smiles on his lips. "You're persistent, Kim, but I know when you're changing the subject. You didn't answer my question."

"I am not going to break your arm, but my karate training is still with me and my dog would eat your leg if I gave the command, so don't provoke us."

He laughed out loud, showing even white teeth.

Her mind raced with awareness of his mouth, his body and her own. "But there's a murderer we need to catch. We have business to take care of before we think of – of ourselves."

She heard the laughter in his voice and saw the warmth in his eyes. "Business before pleasure?"

She didn't answer.

He smiled. "So back to Verbale. The first and most obvious suspect. But he turned up the proverbial airtight alibi. He says he was in Costa Rico and the flight and hotel records agree. We even checked the security cameras at the airports. The M.E. put the date of death sometime between morning of May 6 and May 7, eight days before you found her. He couldn't be more exact because of exposure to the elements and animal activity. Verbale's flight left on May 6 at 11:10 a.m."

"Well, that might be cutting it close, but he still could have done it and caught the flight. It had to be someone she knew. It wasn't just a random event or a spur of the moment thing."

"Agreed."

"Then I think you should look at Winston again. I know he looks like an ordinary, clean-cut, thirty-something business man, but you know what they say about appearances." She sipped her beer and searched his face for a response.

"If Verbale killed her he must have done it early, before he took the flight out that morning. We could take a closer look at him." Then he hesitated and looked at her sideways. "Wait a second. You know this is all speculation. And you're not a member of my team."

Kim glanced at Zayd. "You're not a member of my team either. It doesn't mean we can't share our findings."

"At this point, I have no findings and no leads — just your hunch, the hunch of . . . of a friend. You know what I'm saying. Any future conversations we have about the case need to exit your head immediately and never be spoken of to anyone."

Strangely, he was looking at her hair rather than at her face. She knew his thoughts as well as she knew hers at that moment. He longed to put his hand out, lift a lock of her hair and let his fingers slide smoothly down to its tip, caressing, teasing the ball of his thumb with the ends, then. . . For some reason, she held her breath.

"That's right," he said a little too loudly, clenching the hand on his lap into a fist. "You discuss the case with no one except me."

Kim caught her breath. "Or Zayd," she said, and smiled. The dog immediately lifted his head with a questioning look. "Got it," she said, not looking at Lon. She winked at her dog.

The next hours went quickly. They watched the baseball game and spoke little. Lon prepared to leave by collecting the two beer glasses and the empty snack bowl and taking them to the kitchen with Kim at his elbow. She put the things in the dishwasher and leaned against the kitchen counter, smiling at him. She knew he wanted to say something even though the tentative expression on his face was new to her.

"I've been reading about the history of the Apache Tribe."

She froze.

"I like the stuff about Lozen, the woman warrior."

Kim was able to smile. "Yeah. Women in the military. Not a new thing at all."

"True. The Amazons and today the Israelis. But Lozen — only one photograph exists, but they say she was beautiful."

"Why does that surprise you?"

"It doesn't. More than beautiful, I read she was an expert roper, could run faster than the men, shoot as well. She even treated and cured wounds. A remarkable woman."

"Right. You didn't read about her paranormal abilities or who she fought with?"

"No. What else did I miss?"

"Lozen was the sister of a Chihenne chief named Victorio."

"I thought she was Apache."

"The Chihenne were a separate band of Apaches, but Whites didn't get the distinction and came to lump them with the Chiricahua Apaches of Southeastern Arizona – with all Apaches, for that matter. Victorio was actually quoted in one book, saying, 'Lozen is my right hand. . .strong as a man, braver than most, and cunning in strategy'."

"High praise. You know a lot about her."

She searched his face and found satisfaction that he was truly interested. She said, "The story I like most is about her and another woman, a very pregnant woman. They were being chased down on horseback by the cavalry, along with others in their band. The pregnant woman went into labor. Lozen stopped with her. They sent their horses on with the others and hid in the bushes. The cavalry passed within feet of them. Lozen delivered the woman's baby. Then they went on alone."

"Sounds fantastic. Makes me wonder if all the things I read about her are true."

"I believe most of them are. But the one you *really* might not believe is that she had power other than physical strength. She had paranormal power. She could locate an enemy when they were still miles away."

"How? What? Like ESP?"

"You might call it that. She would chant a prayer to Ussen, the supreme being, the giver of life, and turn in a circle with her arms outstretched. From the feelings in her arms and palms she could tell which direction the enemy was approaching from, even how many there were. Other people saw her do it. They swore she did it time after time."

"If it's true, it might be the one thing that made her great and kept her from getting killed by the soldiers."

"Too bad she didn't die in battle."

"How?"

"She died of tuberculosis – on a reservation."

"Damn!"

Kim said nothing.

• • •

Chapter Fourteen

By the first of June, Yuma's weather forecasters were now admitting it was "hot" in this part of the Sonoran desert, rather than insulting the public by repeating, against human perception and all evidence, that the weather was "warm." Accordingly, sane Yumans who determined to be physically active did it in the hours between sunset and sunrise, or more sensibly, at anytime and anyplace indoors with air conditioning.

On a Tuesday in the mid-week calm and cool of the shopping mall near Allie's office, she and Kim met for lunch. They went directly to the food court then in different directions to order at their favorite fast-food vendors. They returned with their trays and sat at one of the absurdly small metal tables to eat. Between bites of salad, Allie said, "Our schedules just don't mesh, do they, Kim? If we didn't have lunch here occasionally, we'd almost never see each other. And thanks for picking me up today while my car is in the shop, damned thing."

"No problem. You'd do it for me. This pizza is delicious, by the way. You should try it some time."

"I have to make do with salad – combating the middle-aged spread."

Finished with the meal, they strolled the bottom floor of the two-story mall. It seemed to be waiting quietly for cool weather, for holidays and shop-happy snow-birds from up north. The few errant shoppers and casual walkers like themselves made little impact in the vast space, except for the sound of footsteps rising from Saltillo tile floors to echo off the vaulted ceiling.

The ambiance was calculated Southwest. Mexican tile floors of burnt-orange, rich ochre and turquoise in designs on decorative columns emphasized it, along with murals made with bits of Mexican tile that decorated the walls, and huge planters sprouting palm trees and desert succulents. Contradicting the mall's uniqueness were the common shop names – Macy's, Penney's, Sears, chain shoe stores and jewelry stores familiar to any shopper in the States.

Kim and Allie walked silently for some minutes until two elderly women wearing running shoes passed them in a power-walk, arms pumping, ear buds in place, eyes fixed ahead. Kim smiled and gave Allie a thumbs up sign of approval.

"Darn right, kudos for them," Allie said. "That'll be me in a few years, you know. I'm entering the awkward stage."

"Awkward, Allie? I don't think so."

"Yes. It's the years between when men open doors for you because you're hot and sexy and when they open doors for you because you're old and decrepit – the years between lust and decency."

Kim laughed. "Are you saying men experience a motivational gap between the age of lust and the age of decency?"

"Hum. No, I guess in those between years they open doors for a woman because she is either pregnant or carrying a baby."

Kim smiled, but something was bothering her and finally she asked, "Allie, how are you doing with Cindy's death? How are you handling it? I mean, have you talked to anyone else about it? Do therapists see other therapists if they're struggling with something?"

"Of course they do. I have in the past but I think I'm doing okay these days even after losing Cindy. When she went missing it felt worse in a way. I imagined terrible things were happening to her, but I didn't know what to do. I think the memorial service helped. A lot of her massage clients were there and some of her bird-watcher friends. To tell you the truth, I didn't know so many people besides me cared about her."

"Was her family there?"

"No, and it's got me stumped. The police let me look through the desk in her massage room at the spa, and her address book at home. No relatives I could identify. The police took her computer and phones. If they found any family contacts, like on social media, either they didn't inform them in time or they just didn't show up for the service."

"She really is a mystery, isn't she?"

"Even when she was alive, I felt like there were pieces of her she wouldn't share." She stopped and turned to Kim. "They never did find the gun or bullets, did they?"

"After the canine search they did the whole grid with a metal detector. Found a few interesting items but not what they were looking for."

"Darn. When are they going to solve it?"

Kim couldn't answer. The question lingered as they resumed walking, more slowly now.

Allie asked, "You've been seeing that Detective Raney, haven't you?"

"Seeing, yes. Dating, no. I told him I'm not ready for more than casual and if he tries anything I'll break his arm."

"Kim! Have you ever thought of taking a *non*-assertiveness class?" Slowly Allie's smile faded. "It's a good thing you found her, Kim."

Kim knew Allie was referring to Cindy, even before she continued.

"Her massage clients might never have reported her missing, and Win said he didn't expect her back any time soon. She could have been out there in the desert for... But I hate to think about it."

Kim stopped and nodded toward a bench close to the large fountain at the mall's central hub. They sat. Allie crossed one leg over the other and then tugged her skirt down over her knees. For long minutes they listened to the fountain's water splash and echo in the spaciousness. Then Kim looked directly at her older friend. "Speaking of Verbale, did he say anything to you about being questioned?"

"By the police? No, why?"

"He was a suspect, of course. They questioned him but he had an alibi. They checked to verify it, but. . ."

Allie's comment came quickly. "Win's a murder suspect? He's a little strange, maybe, but..."

"Strange how?"

"He looks like an overgrown kid. His face is so innocent, but his personality doesn't match it. He's really ambitious, a hard worker, a doer and a joiner. He's just too normal. He has his heart set on getting into local politics. I guess his job as HR director isn't important enough for him."

"I met him at your barbecue with Cindy, but I didn't like him."

"Well, we all have those reactions we might not be able to understand."

"You don't like talking about him, do you?"

"He's my co-worker and I guess he just puzzles me, so what can I say? Anyway, how are you doing with your job? I'm thinking it's probably a lot more interesting than working at that hardware store in Camp Verde."

"It is. I'm glad I left for EMT training and so happy I got the job here. It's better than I ever expected, never boring."

"I'm sure."

"I've seen some things you wouldn't believe." She glanced at Allie, thinking *I wouldn't even want to describe them to her. She couldn't handle it.* "Well, almost never boring," she added. "I don't enjoy the nursing home calls, taxi service for the dear, ancient departed. It's a yawn all the way to the morgue. But there are enough pile-ups out on I-8 to keep it interesting. Three cars in a heap with six or eight people to treat and transport is a challenge but I love it, and the physical part isn't hard for me like it is for smaller women."

"I don't know how you do it. How can you just set your emotions aside, and not panic, or… or cry?"

Kim didn't try to answer. She didn't want to tell her friend that there was little room for empathy in EMT work. Empathy got in the way. A good call for most was a murder or a four-car pile-up on the Interstate that would exercise their triage skills. A bad call was a pickup at a nursing home. There was no hurry and no challenge at all if they were dead. She held her arms out toward the fountain, enjoying the errant sprinkles of cool water, wishing she could feel it on her face. Suddenly she turned to ask, "Allie, do you think I'm weird?"

"Weird? What are you talking about?"

"Maybe it's not normal to enjoy the kind of work I do, or even the search and rescue stuff. Maybe it's morbid, or ghoulish."

"Kim, I'm not your therapist anymore. It's been more than three years."

"Yes, and I remember what you said when you were my counselor. You said, 'If people could just believe three things, they wouldn't need counseling: first, shit happens; second, it is what it is so accept it; and third, no one is perfect so how can anyone expect you to be or do the impossible?' Did I remember all that right?"

"Congratulations. But to answer your question as your friend, I can say I never thought of you as weird. Misguided, maybe, but not weird or ghoulish."

"So how am I misguided? Is it the karma stuff we talked about?"

"Not necessarily, but the lengths you went to… Do you really want to talk about it?"

Kim hesitated. "No," she said, finally, "I don't need to talk about it. But by saving that disgusting pervert I tried to kill, you saved me. If you hadn't, right now I would either be in prison or consumed with guilt and drowning my sorrows in booze – or something equally destructive."

"Do you still feel the same way about karma, that you're its instrument?"

"If you mean do I still believe I'm a delivery-woman for karmic justice, including executions of the guilty, the answer is no. Even if the worst karma someone has coming is a bouquet of dead roses, let someone else deliver it."

Allie laughed. "Yeah, karma by wire, let the god Mercury deal with it. Certainly not you in a brown shirt and shorts, tooling along in a brown karma-mobile. . ."

Kim smiled at the image. They rose to walk again. Allie's hard-soled pumps clicked on the tile while Kim's soft-soled slip-ons made no sound at all. Kim continued to mull over Allie's question. She said, "I'm concentrating on myself these days. Karma's like a balance scale that weighs behavior. Everything you do counts."

Allie shook her head in assent. "You're saving people's lives as an EMT. That's what I'd call good karma – and finding lost hikers, too."

"We haven't done that in a while, but Zayd and I are up for it anytime. Allie, how much do you know about Apaches?"

"Not much, I guess."

"As a tribe, we were known for our endurance, our ability to withstand hardship and pain. We also liked to dish out the pain."

When Allie said nothing, Kim knew she didn't understand. She stopped in front of a shoe store, but her eyes didn't focus on the thin-strapped sandals in bright summer colors. Allie stopped beside her and turned, but Kim would not meet her eyes. Finally Kim said, "Let's not mince words. We liked to torture people."

She reluctantly turned to look into her friend's face and saw Allie's lips purse in puzzlement.

"*We?*" Allie asked. "When was the last time you tortured someone, Kim?"

Kim stiffened, her face solemn. "Never. But you know what they say, the apple doesn't fall far from the tree."

"Oh, for heaven's sake, Kim! So much for stupid aphorisms. Do you think the Apache tribe invented torture?"

Kim raised her eyebrows but said nothing.

"Kim, you have what I'd call shared ancestral, karmic guilt. Really, you must know the Apache in Arizona were mortal enemies of the Mexicans and the Mexicans knew a lot about pain. They probably learned it from the Incas or from the Spanish, who perfected their techniques during the Inquisition. Who knows who started the revenge cycle of torture and mayhem between the Mexicans and Apache? And yes, it continued with the 'White Eyes,' but their hands weren't lily white either. They had been torturing people for centuries. All of Europe – hell, the whole world engaged in those atrocities."

Kim nodded.

"When you learned your tribe's history, didn't you learn that soldiers and settlers retaliated in kind, or worse? Full scale massacres of Apache men, women and children. From what I've read, it was a torture contest."

Kim felt her mouth harden when she pictured what Allie described. "Yes, I've heard that," she said.

Allie continued, "What about medieval torture chambers with all those instruments supposedly *devout* Christians created just for inflicting pain? Was the *Marquis de Sade* an Apache? And if you and your people inherited a tendency for cruelty or blood lust, or whatever you want to call it, why haven't I heard of Apache serial killers or serial rapists?" She stopped, as if at a loss for more words and drew a deep breath.

Kim felt the muscles of her stomach relax and somewhere in her gut the tension eased. Allie's words rang true, and in that moment of relief she remembered again it was no longer Allie's job to understand and counsel her. "I guess you're right. Thanks, Allie."

Unexpectedly, a divergent memory clicked into her mind. "Allie, you know the story in the newspaper about the jewelry store theft and the silly poem they found strewn all over town?"

Allie nodded again, eyebrows drawn together in apparent puzzlement by the abrupt change in subject.

"I went on that call," Kim said. "The newspaper has it wrong. Lon says the police don't believe the thief wrote the poems. The perpetrator just saw the chaos and decided whoever did it would get blamed for the theft, too. The jerk is lucky the police were around the corner when his arm went through the glass or he would have bled to death."

She put her hand on Allie's shoulder. "Lunch hour is almost over. Come on, I'm going to treat you to some ice cream before I drive you back to work."

• • •

Chapter Fifteen

At the clinic, Winston Verbale had just pulled his Mercedes into the north-side parking lot where it would be shaded when a red Jeep pulled in beside it. He felt a flash of annoyance that when its door opened it might scar his vehicle's paint job. He quickly recognized Allie but not the other woman.

Curious, he waited as they got out, and heard the tall, dark-haired woman say to Allie, "Did you hear Zayd's crate rattle against the sides every time I made a turn? It doesn't do that when he's in it. I need to secure it better." She came around to the passenger side to embrace Allie in that quick hug women do.

Allie waved good-bye to the woman as the other backed the Jeep out and left. Only then he stepped out of his car looking from Allie to the departing vehicle. "Who's your pretty friend? Is she Indian or *Indian?*"

"She's an Apache."

"Is she looking for work here?"

"No." Allie's voice sounded sharp. "Not at all. She's got a job. She's busy. She's an EMT and she does search and rescue in her spare time."

Verbale was surprised at the abruptness of Allie's answer because she was usually so mild, easy-going to the point of soupy. "Just checking. We're looking for a new weekend receptionist, and your friend would dress up the waiting room."

He opened the door and followed her in, but a question lingered. "She's with the canine team? I saw the crate in the back of her Jeep."

"She is. And from what I understand, she's working with the Sheriff's team to find the killer. If I know her, she won't stop until it's over."

Win gave her a parting nod and went to his office in the administration wing. By the time he reached it an unpleasant train of thought was stirring his defenses. He sat in his black leather office chair, leaned back, picked up a pencil from the desk and then flung it down again. Allie's friend was a search and rescue worker. Their most frequent jobs were at Kofa, and Allie had known about Cindy's death before the public did. Kim must have found Cindy's body. But so what? What could she know that might impact him?

The answer eluded him, the question eclipsed by the memory of an arrogant Sheriff's detective, a Lon Raney, interrogating him about Cindy. The cop was tall and cool-mannered, probably thought his dick was gold. The cop suspected him, in spite of his alibi. The detective's manner had been professional but his questioning persistent in spite of Win's efforts to charm him. He had to face it. He was still a suspect in Cindy's death.

The heat prickling his scalp brought him to self-awareness. His face was flushed and that might look strange to anyone walking by the office. Employees could see him clearly through the open door and glass wall panels. He sat up straight and picked up the phone, pretending to press in a number. Now anyone walking by would think he was blushing at an off-color remark or, more likely, an effusive compliment. He had always been able to manipulate the drones.

Soon he put the phone down and rubbed his palms against his eyes, tired of miming. He picked up his pencil again and began doodling on the margins of the large desk calendar. When he realized the futility of trying to deny the truth or distract himself from it he stopped, unable to suppress the rising feelings of being on uncertain ground, of being crowded, pressured.

That Raney dick, with the cool manner and soft-voiced questions – that is not the kind of attention I like. That detective, Allie, and the bitch Apache are all crowding in on me, pressuring me. I have enough to worry about with the council election coming up. My life is one big gamble with no payout since the bathroom trick stopped working for me.

He tapped the pencil on the desk. Now he needed to divert

negative attention and suspicion from himself. He needed room, space to play his own game in his own time. Maybe eliminate one of the players — but which one? It would be easy to take Allie out of the mix. More complicated but certainly possible to eliminate the Indian and her mutt. He was certain he could outsmart the detective and it would be a pleasure. But was the detective the biggest threat? Which one really had to go?

• • •

At the fire station Kim and her partner finished their four o'clock to midnight shift. Jerry showered first then stood watch for Kim since there were no separate facilities and more than one fire-fighter had "accidentally" walked in on her. Kim wasn't happy about needing her partner to spot for her but the alternative was to go home on some occasions wearing fluids or residues from other human bodies. That made her less happy.

About to finish up in the locker room, Jerry glanced at her sideways a second time with a speculative look in his eyes.

She asked, "So, what's up, Latte? Something on your mind?"

"Not really. Uh, I was just wondering what you'd do if you lost your EMT license."

"I don't know. I've never thought about it. You'd have to do something pretty stupid to get reported to the NPDB and get your credentials yanked. Why?" He didn't answer, his usually bland and cheerful face closed.

"Wait, Jerry! You're not in trouble are you?"

"Naw. Just wondering."

His manner didn't sit right with Kim. She wondered what would surface if she answered his question. She said, "Well, if I couldn't do EMT, I'd try somewhere else to qualify for fire-fighter. Maybe sign on as a hot-shot, fight forest fires. More exciting than a city fire-fighter's job."

"Ha. A big city fire fighter doesn't get excitement?"

"I imagine it would be like this job: long hours of boredom for the occasional adrenalin-rush."

"Boredom? Speak for yourself, Thrill-jockey."

"Okay, Bench-warmer." She smiled at him with real affection. Leaning down, she pulled on her shoes and fastened the tongues with a slap, preparing to leave.

"Wait."

Kim looked up, surprised at the tension in his voice.

"I'm sorry to tell you this — actually I don't want to tell you at all but I think you should know…"

"Out with it, Latte. I don't blame the bearer of bad news if he didn't instigate it."

"Amos Wagner, the Deputy at the Sheriff's North Station, has been trash-talking about you."

"That doesn't surprise me. The last time I talked to the jerk we almost came to blows."

"So now he's spreading around talk he's going to file a report with the National Practitioners Data Bank and have your license."

Kim shrugged and zipped up her tote bag. "His mouth is as foul as his brain."

"What's he got against you, Kim?"

"You mean the complaint? Nothing I can think of. He must have invented something. So how do you know this? How do you know him?"

"I don't. My friend Bill works with him. I hear he's a pain-in-the-ass jerk, alright, but I wonder if he really could get you fouled up with the EMT Bureau?"

Her mind raced with the question as she threw her tote bag over her shoulder and turned to leave but the seeds of concern were swept away by a flood of anger as she remembered the malice in Wagner's eyes and the assault of hateful words unleashed on her a month ago.

She turned back to Jerry. "It takes more than nasty words and lies," she said. "It takes a whole army and fifty years of fighting to bring down people in my tribe, Latte. No worries."

His blue eyes widened in surprise at the rarely-spoken reference to her Apache heritage. Amused, she slapped his shoulder and went out to her Jeep.

She reached her home on County Avenue C, on the outskirts of the East Cocopah Indian Reservation, just after midnight. An isolated location for a home with no street lights and no other houses nearby, it felt right for her.

She welcomed the sound of gravel on the driveway crunching under her tires when she pulled up next to the house. The home had no attached garage, a fact she didn't regret. She cherished the 1960s, cracker-box shaped house of brick and stone, happy she had found it. Her modest craftsman style home felt real and authentic. Before finding it she had rejected a score of newer homes with a two-car garage abutting the sidewalk, interior door leading directly to the kitchen. She had once told Allie, *Modern architecture echoes the modern world's obsession with food and cars.* She secretly pitied homeowners who went from car to kitchen without ever enjoying the comforting ritual of unlocking their front door and entering their living room.

Her musing created a picture of a more typical home – with herself and two children in residence and a man, obviously a husband, who she suddenly realized bore a suspicious resemblance to Lon. She dismissed the image as absurd but thoughts of Lon remained. She had never felt such a strong physical attraction to any man and at the same time no man had earned her admiration and respect as quickly as he had.

She got out, locked the jeep and walked to her front door, listening for the usual soft chuffing of her dog. Zayd always conveyed his delight at her approach with the muffled combination of whine and bark but tonight she heard a low growl and then a sharp bark as she turned the key in the lock.

When she stepped over the threshold he didn't welcome her in the usual way, a nose-guided inspection, his whole body wiggling as he sniffed her clothing, legs and feet, followed by a few wet kisses. Tonight he stood in the opened door looking past her into the dark. The hair on his shoulders and back stood on end.

• • •

Chapter Sixteen

"What's up, Zayd?" she asked, as she ruffled the thick coat on his neck. "Coyotes again? We'll scare them off when we go out." She put her bag in the coat closet. "A quick drink of water for me and off we go."

She finished her water, grabbed his leash and a flashlight from the table. She retrieved a single house key on a ring from pegs on the kitchen wall. During the day Kim never locked her door or put her dog on a leash to take a walk but at night she was more cautious. She hooked the leash onto his collar, opened the door and stepped onto the concrete apron which was dimly lit by one lamp on the brick exterior.

She turned and locked the door. Zayd growled again. Crack! Something whizzed past her face, something struck her cheek. She dropped into a crouch. The leash jerked from her right hand as Zayd bolted off the stoop into the darkness of the front yard. Crack! A second gunshot. Zayd yelped with pain. She stood. "Zayd, come!" she screamed. No response. She looked toward the road from where the shots had come. She saw the dark outline of a car. Then a flash of light on silver hubcaps, the squeal of tires and the roar of an engine as the car sped away. *No headlights, no tail lights*, registered in her mind, tightening the grip of fear in her chest.

"Zayd!" Her voice sounded in her ears like someone else's, weak and breathy with panic. She had dropped the flashlight and the house key. Now she groped for the flashlight where it had rolled off onto the ground. She found it, pushed the switch. No light. She shook it. No light. Now she had to find the key. She looked down at the cement, turned in a circle, frantic. A glint of metal near her foot. She picked up the key but her fingers trembled so it took a few seconds to fit it into the lock. Finally the key turned. She pushed the door open hard; it bounced back against the door stop. She ran to the drawer in the kitchen for another flashlight.

She raced back outside with it and swept the light over the front yard, calling Zayd's name. With each sweep her fear grew. Why didn't he come? Would the narrow ray of light find him lying dead? No, the yard was empty. *Not here! Where is he?*

She ran to the road. The sound of the retreating car was distant, unwinding. She saw nothing until lights flared, far down the road. The driver had turned on his headlights. The vehicle was still virtually invisible; it must be black or dark blue, but the headlights revealed a patch of road. Red tail lights, mere specks in the darkness, revealed nothing. And then it was gone. For an instant she heard only silence. Then the chirp of cicadas and the distant hum of traffic on Highway 19 registered, the sounds infuriatingly neutral.

Zayd must have followed the car. She began to run down the road, calling and sweeping the light back and forth. Finally it caught the gleam of his eyes half a mile away. He was coming fast. *He can run!* she thought. *He can run! He's not hurt bad!*

She stopped and blinked back tears of relief, waiting. When Zayd reached her she dropped to her knees and wrapped both arms around him, ruffled his coat and rubbed her cheek against his muzzle as he panted, tongue lolling, dripping, then wetting her face. "Why didn't you come?" she said. "You never disobey like that."

Pain in her knees from pebbles in the road finally reminded her to stand. "Let's get into the house," she said, as if he could understand every word. "I need to get a good look at you." Like an anxious mother, she wasn't sure if she felt more relieved he was alive or disappointed at his earlier disobedience. They walked back into the house, Zayd pressed so close against her his warm coat brushed her leg with every step.

She walked through the open door without fear until a flash of red in the wall mirror caught her eye. Blood! She swiped her cheek, felt a sharp pain and something hard in her flesh. A wooden splinter. It was almost as big around as a toothpick. She leaned closer to the mirror and picked it out. The wound welled up a drop of blood. She swiped it away, then caught sight of her other hand and her shirt. Smears of blood. Her breath caught and she made a sound she didn't recognize, a noise full of shock and dismay.

Zayd backed away, confused by her alarm. She looked at him, his head tilted in question, and now in the light she saw the notch in the side of one ear, a jagged wound where the bullet had grazed him. There had been only two shots, but quickly she knelt and examined his neck, his back, his legs, looking for more injuries. There were none.

Assured he wasn't seriously injured, the numbing effects of fear released its grip and she flared into anger. Her breathing quickened. Her hands became clenched fists and she cursed out loud. "Damn! Crap! The rotten, nasty, dog-killing son-of-a-bitch!"

The urge to punch the wall and kick the decorative door stop across the room was strong until she saw Zayd back away again, his ears up and eyes questioning. Of course he wondered if she was angry at him. She reached to give him a pat and stood there letting the rapid thudding of her heart slow, catching her breath and calming herself, trying to push from her mind the sound of gunshots and the glimpsed outline of a retreating car.

No, she had to deal with it. It suddenly occurred to her that the dark car driven by a would-be assassin might circle back for another try. She retrieved her smart phone from her bag and dialed 911, while she led Zayd into the bathroom. She began to clean his ear.

The 911 operator answered within three rings. Kim put the phone on speaker. The operator's voice sounded bored until Kim said "gunshots," then it took on a more urgent tone. She demanded to know who, how, when and why, the inquiries a good reporter would make. While she gave the details, Kim finished wiping down her dog then coated the raw edges of his wound with a wax-based antibiotic that stopped the slow ooze of blood. The 911 operator promised to have law enforcement there within minutes. Kim's home lay outside the city limits, so the unit would be from the Sheriff's Department, carrying the detective on duty and a deputy.

When Zayd had settled into his dog bed by the sofa Kim had time to wash her face and hands and change her blood-smeared shirt before the sound of a vehicle drew her to the front room window. Flashing lights – the patrol car. She gave Zayd the order to stay, then repeated it with her best 'I'm serious' expression, an indication of her new lack of confidence in his obedience.

The responding officers approached slowly. When she invited them in they stopped just inside the door to introduce themselves. The one who identified himself as the detective was older, near retirement age, she guessed, average height and probably Mexican in origin, although he spoke with no hint of accent. He looked lean and muscled beneath his short sleeve shirt, his face deeply creased around a thin-lipped mouth and brown eyes, which tilted down at the corners. His calm voice conveyed both reserve and confidence as he began to question her.

The other deputy was young and handsome, with dimples in his cheeks that she knew must have earned him a lot of grief from his peers. He was very deferential to the older man. She led them into the kitchen to sit at the table. The detective took notes while Kim told her story.

Finally he said, "Judging by the distance from the road to the house the shooter used a rifle. Where were you when you heard the shots?"

"Right out there on the porch."

He fixed her with a questioning look. "What's that on your cheek?"

She put her hand up to the tender spot. "Oh, I think a splinter hit me."

He rose and went back to the front door with the deputy and Kim following. He stepped onto the concrete apron and began to inspect the door frame with his flashlight. His face changed only slightly when he spotted the spent bullet imbedded in the wood.

"He really was trying to kill you," he said, looking at Kim for long, speculative seconds. "We need to get the crime scene tech out here to photograph this and pry it out. Tonight we can look for the shell casings. You're sure there were only two shots?" Kim nodded. "You can go back in the house now." With that, they pulled flashlights from of their utility belts and began to search.

She stood at the front room window and watched them methodically sweep the yard with lights larger and more powerful than the one she had used to look for Zayd. Soon she saw the detective pick up something with a gloved hand and place it in a bag, then he approached and knocked at the door.

"We're going to leave now, but we'll have patrol drive by again tonight as often as they can to make sure things are okay here. Tomorrow morning a Crime Scene tech will do his thing outside. You don't need to be here for that."

"Thank you. I'm grateful." She extended her hand to both. The detective looked at her, his face softening around eyes and mouth. "No neighbors nearby," he said. "Don't you feel lonely or unsafe out here alone?"

"No. I like my privacy and silence is the best sound in the world." He tilted his head a fraction of a degree as if unconvinced and turned to go. She watched them get into the patrol car and pull away then closed the door, locked it and wearily slumped against the wall. She let her chin fall to her chest while she reached back to rub her neck and shoulders. Wearily, she pulled off the band holding her long hair, leaned forward and shook it out, willing away the debilitating effects of fear and anger.

What now? The thought of going to bed, her usual routine at this hour, seemed ridiculous. She went to the kitchen for a glass of wine and sat down on the sofa to relax. She needed to de-stress, otherwise the events of the night might replay in her mind or worse, in her dreams. She reached over the sofa's arm to touch the top of Zayd's silky head with her finger tips, stroking him idly.

• • •

Chapter Seventeen

She might have closed her eyes for a few minutes when the sound of a car engine and then a single rap at the door made her start and drew Zayd from his comfortable bed. *What now?* But Zayd's hackles didn't raise and his tail began to wag slowly. Whoever it was, she had nothing to fear. She went to the antique oak door, wishing it had a peep hole. "Who is it?"

"It's me. I heard about it."

She felt a start of surprise and then a rush of pleasure. She opened the door and Lon Raney walked in. He wore faded jeans, a navy blue t-shirt frayed at the neck and loafers with no socks. His hair looked tousled. He must have been in bed. She glanced at the clock above the TV on the entertainment center. After two a.m. Of course he had been in bed.

Lon gave her a long, appraising look before he noticed the dog, who had gone back to his bed. "What happened to you, Dog?"

Zayd lifted his chin from the padded rim of the dog bed. One ear stood erect while the injured one drooped. He looked from Lon to Kim and, receiving no instruction or information, let his muzzle droop again.

"The guy shot him, that's what happened." Saying the words renewed her anger. She crossed her arms, gripping them so tightly her nails dug into the skin. She looked into Lon's face, hoping to see understanding in his eyes. He put his hands on her upper arms and rubbed the red indentations lightly with his palms. "They told me you were alright," he said. "Are you?" He touched the red spot on her cheek with one gentle forefinger.

Kim hesitated. She didn't understand. Why didn't she feel alarmed or angered by his touch? Because the sensation of his body so close to hers and the warmth of his hand felt comforting.

"I'm fine. But why did you come? The detective found a bullet casing and tomorrow the tech will be here to pry out the bullet. Nothing much for a crime scene man to do here tonight."

"I'm a detective too, as you remember. But I didn't come for that, I came for you. I came to see for myself you're okay."

"If there's anything more to be found out there, Zayd's nose will lead him right to it in the morning."

He took her hand in his, saying nothing. Now she appraised him and while she did an unexpected internal shift took place. Without thinking she stepped forward to press her body against his.

For a split second nothing, while she sensed his shock. Then his arms pulled her closer. He wrapped her in safety and reassurance while his hands moved over her back, her arms, her waist, then cupped her bottom and pressed her closer.

Then they were apart. She couldn't be sure if she had backed away or if he had released her. Now he held both her hands in his and immobilized her with his eyes.

"Kim, what are we doing?"

She smiled. "This might be where I question your skill as a detective."

He refused to smile. "Kim, you know how I feel about you. I made it clear enough that day at Kofa, ass that I was. But you set the boundary and the time table. I don't want to ruin things between us by chucking it all when you're upset and might just need some comfort."

She nodded. "You've got some good insights, Detective. Maybe I am feeling needy, but a relationship doesn't work on a time table, it works on feelings, doesn't it? How could it ruin things between us?"

In answer, he embraced her again. She felt her need for his strength and pressed against him, felt his erection grow against her lower belly. She rubbed her cheek against the side of his neck.

His arms tightened around her back for a second, then his hands moved down to her waist and stopped. He groaned, a breathy growl. He inched back, hands still resting above her hips and said, "Wait. Before anything else, I need to hear what happened tonight. I don't want to read it in the report. I want to hear it from you, before you forget anything." He looked into her face and then down at her breasts. Her nipples were clearly outlined against her cotton t-shirt. His voice husky, he repeated, "…before you forget anything and before I forget *everything*."

Her eyes lingered on his mouth. Then she closed her eyes, took a deep breath and let his scent of soap and clean skin envelop her. "You said you weren't here as a detective. But okay. And when we're done, you stay."

"The night? If I stay the night…"

"Yes. Come and sit down." They went to sit at opposite ends of the sofa. She began to describe what she was just now fully realizing had been an attempt to kill her, not just her dog.

It was fine until she described the sound of the gunshot. Without warning, a flashback invaded her, an intrusive memory of the first time a man tried to murder her after her own attempt to kill him. Desperate, she mentally pushed away the memory and the shame. She would not allow Lon to see her inner turmoil.

By the time she answered his last question the flashback was pushed away by her desire to feel his touch again. "Are we done now?"

He nodded. She stood, took a step toward her bedroom and glanced back at him, holding out her hand. He stood, grasped it and followed her in silence.

Her bedroom smelled of the sage and sweet-grass she burned every month in a cleansing and renewing ceremony. Tonight the room was lit by stripes of moonlight filtering through the blinds, laying across the bed in luminous streaks.

When she closed the door he embraced her from behind, his hands slipping up to her breasts, his lips on the back of her neck. His breath sent chills down her back and waves of desire up her torso.

A sound intruded. Scratching on the other side of the door then a low "woof."

"Zayd," she whispered. "He usually sleeps by my bed." Then, "No, Zayd! Go lie down." They stood paralyzed. A pause, then the click of his toenails on the hardwood floor. He was obeying.

She was committed now. She turned around and they kissed. It was a long time before their lips parted and she could open her eyes and look into his. The tenderness transforming his sharp features struck her to the core. "My knees feel weak," she said. "I think I'd better lie down."

She took a few steps back and sat down on the forest green spread covering her double bed. Gently, he put his arms under her knees and lifted her legs onto the bed, then pulled off her shoes and socks, slipped off his own shoes and climbed onto the bed to kneel beside her. He looked into her face as he pulled off her shirt and undid her bra.

"You are so incredibly beautiful," he whispered, slipping the straps off her shoulders and pulling away the bra. "More beautiful than I imagined."

She felt frozen and yet her body was aflame. He explored her breasts with his mouth and tongue. A gasp burst from her throat but she didn't move. He pulled off her jeans, leaving her cotton panties, and she held her breath. The light filtering through the blinds was only moon-glow, but he saw the round, silver-dollar size scar on her upper thigh anyway.

Now the moment in time froze. Very softly, he asked, "Is that a bullet wound?"

"Yes."

• • •

Chapter Eighteen

On his knees on the bed, breathing hard, he stared. She knew the pale pink flaw on her upper leg told a story she didn't want to remember. He traced the circle of scarred flesh with his finger tip. Lightning bolts of desire shot from his finger and pierced her pelvis but didn't penetrate the terror in her mind.

"Tell me about it." His voice was soft, intimate.

"No. I can't."

"Try."

She desperately needed something solid at her back. She pushed herself up against the headboard. "It happened a couple of years ago. It's an ugly scar, isn't it?"

"Nothing could spoil the way they look. Your legs are a work of art. An artist should paint or sculpt them. I want to know who did this to you."

"It was nothing. He was nothing. I don't want to talk about it."

The horizontal furrows in his brow disappeared and his mouth softened. "Water under the bridge then. If you want to you can tell me about it after…" His hands slid from her ankles over her knees, caressing, then moved upward to the inside of her thighs, pushing her legs apart.

Suddenly she wasn't here on her own bed. The hands she felt were the hands of someone else. The body with a bulge in its jeans was the body and the erection of that someone else. Fear and revulsion overwhelmed her. She recoiled. Her mouth opened to scream but what came out was a guttural "Uhhhhh!"

Lon reacted instantly, rising bolt upright on his knees then moving backward off the bed as quickly as if she had yelled "rape." The astonishment on his face brought her back to the present. Now he was Lon again but clearly confused and surprised. It stung her like a slap in the face.

Damn, damn, what have I done now? She pushed back, pressing herself against the wooden headboard until it hurt. Focused on the pain and on his face, she willed away the flashback and spoke through gritted teeth. "I…I'm sorry. It's just…I can't.

"You can't?"

"I…I don't know how."

Lon's face went blank, as if he hadn't heard or hadn't understood. "What do you mean, you don't know how?"

No answer.

"How to – to make love? You don't know how to have sex? Kim, what are you saying?"

Silence.

"Are you saying – you haven't done this before?" His tone grew incredulous. "Never? That you're a virgin?"

"Yes."

"How old are you?"

"Twenty-six."

"Oh. I see." But his words were a question and in his voice only confusion. He shook his head slightly. He rubbed his face with both hands then reached down to adjust himself. He sat down on the bed and reached his hand to her.

She rolled away and off the opposite side of the bed to stand facing him. Her knees began to tremble again and she pressed them against the mattress to steady herself. She would not try to cover her naked breasts because it was not her body she felt ashamed of. How could she tell this officer of the law she respected so much that she had attempted murder? Silence. Finally she said, "There are other things you don't know about me – and maybe you don't need to know."

He hesitated. "But I *want* to know everything about you."

No response.

"I guess I can understand if there are some things you don't want to talk about yet."

No response.

"This is a lot to take in for one night, even for me. But I have to ask you another question."

"What?"

"Did getting shot at tonight have anything to do with getting shot before? Are you still in danger from whatever happened back then?"

"No, not at all. Not possible."

"Good!" The questions in his eyes faded while he looked at her, at her face. A shake of his head. "Or maybe not good. How could anyone want to harm you?"

She shrugged.

"So where do we go from here, my lovely friend?"

"I'm not sure."

"Maybe this isn't the right time for us. Maybe you were right to begin with and we need to get the person who murdered Cindy Cameron first."

She sat down with one leg on the bed and one still on the floor. "Maybe so. Are you okay with that?"

"If that's what we need to do it's more than okay with me. But how is it going to be different then, from now – I mean, will we be alright together, in bed?"

"I want us to be. That's all I can tell you."

"But finding out who shot at you tonight is important now. Two mysteries to solve. In the meantime, things between us might go back to the way they were before. You think?"

"For now." She drew a deep and regretful breath that pulled her shame and fear back into the deepest part of herself, and along with it her passion for Lon, this man who belonged to a species entirely different and exquisitely superior to that of the man who had molested her when she was a child.

Lon nodded. "I still want to stay here tonight. I'll sleep on the sofa and Zayd can have his usual place on the rug by your bed."

"Thank you." Relief flooded her, but more, overwhelming gratitude. He accepted her, he was okay with her, wounds, secrets and all.

"I can tell you're just about done in. You need to sleep. But I don't want to leave you like this. Come here, will you?"

She didn't hesitate. She walked around the end of the bed and into his arms. She felt the roughness of his shirt against her naked breasts and the soft rub of worn denim against her bare legs was good. For a strange moment she wore his clothes, as if her own arms and chest and legs were inside them and she and he were one and the same person.

He didn't hold her for long before he raised his hands to her cheeks, then smoothed back long strands of black hair, grasped the whole thick handful of it at the nape of her neck and brought it over her shoulder to rest against one breast.

"My Warrior Woman," he said. "Whatever battles you're fighting, I want to be with you. Your enemies are my enemies. Your friends are my friends. And I promise you, you will never have to fight me."

She felt the truth within her. Her head dropped forward to rest against his shoulder. A chuckle bubbled from his throat and he added, "Who knows which of us would win in a fair fight, anyway?"

"Good point," she whispered, and when she looked up she was smiling, too.

He turned to leave the room then hesitated. "I have a blanket in the car, so don't bother with bedding or anything else. When I come back in I'll set the dead-bold and make sure all the windows are locked."

"Thank you. But I'm not worried. You're here, and Zayd is here."

"Get some rest, then." When he opened the door Zayd rushed past him into the room, wagging and obviously expecting his owner to greet him just as joyously.

"Lay down!" she commanded. He went to the rug and lay down, looking up at her from solemn eyes without lifting his head.

"Oh, crap, it's not your fault." She patted him, then walked to the clothes hamper and pulled off her panties. She used them to wipe the moisture from between her legs before tossing them in the hamper and padding back to fall into bed.

Some warrior woman I am. A three hundred pound man who's fallen and wedged between the toilet and the sink, I can pry out of trouble then heft him onto the gurney. I can hold down a football player in a wicked grand mal seizure but I can't do what most normal woman my age do as naturally as putting on lipstick.

Zayd woke her in the morning with a series of polite but insistent chuffs telling her she must get up and let him outside for his toilet. She pulled on a thin flannel robe that covered her to the ankles, and went out to the living room. Lon's blanket lay folded on the arm of the sofa but he wasn't there. She heard him stirring in the kitchen. She let Zayd out and went back to her bathroom to shower and dress. By the time she finished and went to the kitchen, Lon had set two mugs of steaming coffee on the worn oak table.

"I guess we're all addicted to this stuff," she said, feeling strangely shy.

"It's the least I could do," he said, "because I couldn't find enough to make breakfast. And good morning." He stepped over and gave her a quick, firm hug then sat down at the table, stretching his long legs under it and slouching just a bit in the round-backed oak chair. He held his mug in both hands and just looked at her.

She sat down. "Did I hear voices just a few minutes ago?"

"The crime scene tech. He's out there finishing up. He took some photos of the tire tracks the guy left last night when he pealed out. Most of it blurred, but a couple of patches might be identifiable."

Kim sipped her black coffee. "People in my job don't usually make enemies. The only person I can think of who obviously doesn't like me is Amos Wagner."

"My first thought too, but he was supposed to be on duty last night. I'll check it out but it doesn't seem likely to me even if you do have a personality clash. Not the kind of thing would make a man want to kill a woman. Unless there's more to it."

"No, Lon, no. We never had a relationship. I barely know the guy but he has it in for me. From what he said to me that day, I think he just doesn't like Indians, and in particular, Apaches."

Lon plunked his mug on the table, hard. "He is an ignorant, obnoxious… But never mind. He's allowed to be a juvenile prick, but if it was him last night we will nail him to the wall."

"What about the guy who killed Cindy Cameron? I'm wondering if he'll get away with it. And I'm still wondering if it was Winston Verbale."

"Before we go there, I want you to promise me something. I

want you to call me every morning when you get up, and every night before you go to bed."

Kim didn't answer, wondering why the thought was alarming, seductive and reassuring at the same time.

"I need to know you're safe, Kim. When we can't be together, I need to hear from you. But I don't want you to promise unless you're sure you'll do it. I don't want to break speed limits racing over here – or where-ever you are – just to discover you forgot."

"Of course I won't forget. Do you think I'm a ditz?" She turned her mug up to her face so he couldn't see the tears in her eyes, and quickly blinked them away.

"Okay. About Cindy Cameron. We're working on it, Kim, I promise you. The coroner did some testing with the maggots on the body but he can't come up with anything more exact than a twenty-four hour window for when she was killed. Theoretically, it would give Verbale time to kill her and drive back to hop on a plane to Costa Rico. It would be a good alibi, if the timeline excluded him completely. If he used his car his GPS would tell us he was at Kofa within the twenty-four hour window. But so far we have no evidence that would allow us to get a search warrant."

"What about Cindy's car?"

"In her garage. It told us nothing. No GPS. She certainly wasn't killed at home, no evidence of that and whether the car went to Kofa that day is anybody's guess. We're questioning the neighbors about what they might have seen. It's the usual slow-moving, methodical steps that sometimes actually pay off. We haven't found a mobile phone, but we have her computer and we're checking who she's been in contact with. We're questioning her massage clients, especially the few men. She participated in a couple of computer chat rooms for bird-watchers. I've learned more than I thought there was to learn about yellow-rumped warblers and vermillion flycatchers."

• • •

Chapter Nineteen

As she gets into the station wagon Sara realizes she is frightened or maybe just a little apprehensive. It is not a familiar feeling and she dislikes it intensely. She reminds herself that the brave aren't those who feel no fear; the brave are those who are fearful but proceed anyway. Her job tonight requires that kind of courage.

She pulls out and drives toward Yuma, tires marking her path on the dirt road. Most times when she goes into town, she stops alongside the agricultural fields where crops of lettuce, broccoli, and other vegetables grow according to the season. After the harvest she often walks the rows looking for enough remains to serve as her dinner, reminding herself of women in the bible who gleaned in the fields. She has never gone into an un-harvested field to pick vegetables. It would be stealing.

Today, from her camp at Betty's Kitchen, it takes her thirty minutes to drive down Laguna Dam Road, connect with Highway 95 west and then head south on Avenue 3-E and onto County 13th Street. The abandoned gas station she spotted on an earlier reconnaissance makes a perfect place to watch and wait for dark. She parks on the north side of the building, where she and the truck will be in shadow even before the sun sets.

It is almost cool here, with all the windows rolled down. The sheen of perspiration on her face, arms, and legs picks up each puff of breeze and helps to cool her. She listens to the silence and deeply inhales the desert perfume of sage and creosote and baked earth.

She gazes at the horizon. It has just sliced the bottom off the sun's yellow orb and is sucking it down into darkness. She is deep in thought while she waits for the fullness of night. She wonders who might be found tonight, who might be redeemed, and who might die. She is thinking she is not immortal. This could be her final attempt to rescue the world, in spite of her companion's reassurance she will survive. When she told him, "You know I've got to get my message across to the heads and parts," her companion knew she spoke metaphorically, that by "heads" she meant heads of state and politicians, and by "parts" the military and others they influence. Why had she felt she had to explain herself to him: "We have to stop them before they reach the point of no return with their schemes."

Now her self-justifying thoughts continue. *It wouldn't have come to this if they had let me on the base, those uniformed robots they call Marines. That one at the main gate looked so thin and sharp and well-pressed when he came to the truck. He reminded me of one of Ruth's dolls, that Ken-doll, too perfect to be real. He was polite, but gruff about it, too. That gun he had on his hip was real, a boy like that with a gun, a whole platoon inside that forbidden zone with guns.*

She shakes her head. *But it isn't their fault, those Ken-doll Marines. They're only protecting what their masters don't want real people to see, them preparing for the destruction.*

She grits her teeth and closes her eyes. *I'll stop them. They'll come to reason when they read my words. The first ones didn't do it, but if I keep it up, they'll learn. And this one is good.*

Sara has spent the day preparing her declaration in verse and then laboriously handwriting three copies, *one for the chief honcho of the base, one for the man they call the public information officer, and one to tape to that war jet. They display that obscene death machine right at the entrance, with no shame at all.*

She handles the four pages gingerly, careful not to smudge the pencil lead. The original page. . . she decides to leave it here, where it confirms her ownership and includes the truck in her efforts for good.

In the fading light, she re-reads the message one more time. The last lines are the most direct, *"Your callous attitudes could jeopardize: One nuclear war will all earth martyrize!"* She nods with satisfaction. This is her most direct and most eloquent plea. Surely they won't ignore her now.

Looking at the pages she realizes the light has faded so she can no longer see the words. Out on the desert floor, only outlines of cactus and shrubs are visible against the pale glow of a darkening sky and the defunct gas pumps nearby masquerade as hulking monsters crouched in a row. Now that the dark is her ally, it is time.

She starts the motor and drives away, toward the base. Soon she pulls onto a gravel road more closely paralleling its southern boundary. The pale sliver of a waning moon has just slipped surreptitiously from under the horizon.

A bumpy and dusty mile later she switches off the headlights and jerks the wheel to the right, propelling the truck off the road, jolting onto unpaved desert terrain that provides an even rougher ride. This is risky. Vicious cactus spines can pierce a tire or a jagged rock she hasn't seen can tear out the vehicle's underside.

For three minutes she and the pickup truck jolt over rock and cactus. Her muscles are tense, teeth clenched and chin jutting with determination. At one point she suddenly realizes she is holding her breath and coaches herself to breathe normally.

In five more minutes she applies the brakes, puts the truck in park and switches off the engine. It dies with a hiccup and a sigh of relief, as if in communion with its owner. The only sounds are an occasional muffled roar of a commercial air plane taking off from Yuma International Airport and her own breathing. The Marine Air Station shares the airport runways and facilities, but tonight the military jets and helicopters remain on the ground.

Sara lifts her hand to feel the pages tucked safely into the front of her shirt, and feels her heart pumping beneath them, racing with each excited breath. She reaches for the folding camp shovel on the floorboard and when she exits the truck she closes the door carefully so it makes only a faint click. There is not a single person near enough to hear but an interloper's guilt has settled around her like a shroud, with it a demand for silence.

She starts toward the perimeter of the Marine base which is guarded by a barbed wire fence. She carries nothing to light her way. In this flat terrain even the tiny glow of a flashlight can be seen from miles away, so ambient moonlight must suffice. She can't clearly make out the details of the ground at her feet so she moves in a shuffle. When she does see a patch of ground clear of obstacles, she strides forward.

The hum of a mosquito invades her ear, loud as a violin's cry, then a sting on her cheek. She doesn't bother to squash the thing. Mosquitos don't usually favor her tough skin or her blood. Here in the desert there are worse predators to fear or kill.

She reaches the wire fence. Inspecting it as best she can, she decides there is no hope of going over it. It is six feet high and at the top there are five extra rows of barbed wire leaning outward. Aided by dim lights spilling from the base itself, she searches the fence for what she fears – a fine wire running along it to electrify it or some object that could be a motion detector or a camera. Her search reveals none.

She checks right and left for the guards who patrol the perimeter in their low-profile Hum-Vees. None in sight. The only movements that catch her eyes are those of a few figures far away inside the base near the buildings.

Pausing for a few seconds, she tells herself that a person who won't risk her life for a cause she believes in doesn't belong on God's good earth. Then she unfolds her compact camp shovel and begins to dig. The soil is hard, dry, and rocky. It takes a long time to dig a furrow long and deep enough to belly-crawl through. When the digging is done she reminds herself to be thankful she is short and slender. She kneels and for a split second she feels the sanctifying significance of her position.

Then she sprawls down full length. The soil still retains the heat of the desert sun. It is hot against her bare arms and legs. She ducks under the lowest wire of the fence and squirms forward, ignoring the scraping of rocks against her knees and the bruising hardness against the heels of her hands and her fingers. Almost through, she feels a tug on the back of her shirt. Caught! No, just one of the wickedly sharp barbs catching at her. She wiggles back an inch, tugs down the tail of her shirt and manages to free herself without ripping the cloth. Another few seconds of determined crawling and she's through.

She stands quickly and brushes the dirt from the front of her black cotton t-shirt and black shorts. She feels blood trickling down to her wrist. It is a puncture wound on her inner forearm. *From a barbed wire spike*, she thinks. She wipes it with her palm then swipes her palm against her shorts.

She looks around to orient herself, and decides the heart of the base is straight ahead and the main gate far to her left. In any case, she can't remain here in the shadows. She must move into the lighted areas to locate her targets. She squares her shoulders and hopes she appears confident and normal as she begins to strides forward. Soon her foot strikes a large rock and she stumbles, catching herself before she falls. Then a tree root trips her and she goes down on her hands and knees. There are many such unseen obstacles in the un-landscaped verge. She thinks, *This ground was designed to trip me up, but I won't let it.*

She is relieved when her foot makes contact with asphalt — a road. Sure-footed now, she walks briskly toward the heart of the base, passing buildings where uniformed men and women and some in civilian clothes enter and exit, going about their private business.

There is scant traffic on the road, and little noise. Sounds of an occasional shouted greeting from people entering or leaving a building and muffled words of a friendly argument rise and fade in the distance. The quiet and order is not what she expected. *Shouldn't there be marching, or people with big guns over their shoulders?*

Never mind, she says to herself, *I have a purpose here. They think they're fighters, like superman, 'for truth, justice and the American way.' But they're only pawns destined for destruction.* She turns left onto another street she believes will take her to the fighter jet at the main gate of the base.

As she walks, strangely, her thoughts turn to Ruth, memories of Ruth as a baby, then vivid mental pictures of her daughter as a plump toddler with a cap of unruly red curls, a rowdy middle-school child with freckles, a spirited teenager, then grown-up too soon. The baritone voice of her companion cuts through the images.

"*She's gone.*"

Michael! She looks around quickly, searching for him but he's nowhere in sight. A chill erupts from the base of her spine and rushes upward, prickling her scalp. *Why can't I see him? Where is he? What is happening here?*

Less confident, she continues to walk and then she is in a

neighborhood of modest, ranch-style homes with children's Big Wheels and tricycles parked on parched lawns, and garbage cans on curbs waiting for pick up. *Why…what is this place? Families here? Could my Ruth could have been here? She could have married the one who stole her away. She could have had children by now…my grandchildren.* The thought is deeply disorienting. The voice comes again. "*You know she's gone.*" This time, the voice is different. It makes her want to drop to her knees and pray to it, although it's meaning is clear. Ruth is gone. It's as if she never existed. Ruth does not exist.

Tears roll down her cheeks, unchecked. Her mind begins to race, but she tells herself she is in control of it, repeats the word *control…I control it, gonna roll with it, get that jet, you bet…* And then she realizes she is walking away from main gate, and she turns around and walks back toward it.

The lighting along the road is stronger here. She starts to pass a woman coming from the opposite direction, a woman who might be her Ruth. She looks into the face, but the not-Ruth looks back at her with a strangeness on her not-Ruth face.

Now there are more people passing her, looking into her face… *why are they doing that? Who do they think I am? I am, wham, bam, wham, I am, I am, I can, I can.* She asks herself, *what am I doing here? What is this place?* No answer comes, but the chanting in her head won't stop, *not tell, very well, hell, hell, smell hell.* She turns to her companion, who should be here but he's not here. *Where, not there?* She is alone, alone, deserted, bereft. She doesn't know she is sobbing.

People are all around her now. Do they expect her to help them, to save them? Do they know why she is here? A young woman in a loose cotton dress and flip-flop sandals touches her arm. "Can I help you?" she asks, in a strange voice that doesn't sound like a human voice should. Fear stabs her. The hand is hot, like some wild creature's paw. Sara shakes loose and runs.

Out of breath and more confused, she can bear it no longer. She stops and holds out her arms, palms upward in a plea for understanding. Her body is shaking. She screams, "Are you blind? Are you deaf? The smell. Don't you smell it? It's the stink of corruption. Lies, lies, everyone dies!"

Then two men, then three of them, talking to her but she doesn't understand what they are saying because they are not real. They are the Ken-dolls. They pretend to talk but out of their mouths comes the roaring of lions and the growls of tigers. Then she realizes. They are gathering to destroy her! She runs.

A man grabs her arm. "Listen to me!" she screams. She reaches into her shirt to pull out her plea for peace. "Read this, read this, then you'll understand!" Before she can finish pulling out her poem, a hand grabs her wrist, forcing it open. The pages are flung to the ground. She reaches to retrieve them, and sees a booted foot step on one.

She strikes out, kicking and punching. She hears nothing but the distant sound of incoherent screams and muffled grunts when blows land on flesh. Her glasses get knocked from her face, fall to the sidewalk. A booted foot crunches them. Now everything she sees is as blurry as the thoughts in her mind. Then she sees the guns, guns on the bodies around her, more kill-weapons, earth's destruction. She reaches to grab one and throw it away, and then she isn't there anymore, anywhere anymore at all.

• • •

Chapter Twenty

Sara wakes because her bladder is pressing for relief. She is lying on her back. She hates lying on her back; she never lies on her back. *No spread-eagle, crucify me, have your way with me position – in bed or out!* She begins to rise but something jerks at her arms and legs, pulls her back down.

Her vision is blurry; she is not wearing her glasses but she can see her wrists and feet are strapped with leather restraints attached to a metal bar. She moves her arms and legs and feels the inside of the leather cuffs chafe her ankles and wrists. She's lying on a bed with white sheets. Soft, white cotton clothes her body. *A hotel?* She turns to see metal bars run the length of both sides of the bed. *Not a hotel. A hospital.*

A distant memory of another time and place of innocent white fabric and wicked leather restraints threatens her. It came soon after her Ruth ran away, a time of fear and anger, bewilderment, voices, devils screaming their accusations and hatred at her, threatening her. She doesn't remember how she got to that hospital, but she remembers the injections and the endless talks with people who told her to trust them because they knew what was real and she didn't.

Panic rises from her gut trying to constrict her throat but she disciplines her mind and defeats it. She focuses on her body, assessing her condition. She feels the sting and throb of scrapes and bruises on her arms and legs but mostly her body is telling her she needs the bathroom and she knows that is real.

"Hey," she says in a normal voice, hoping her companion is nearby. No answer. "Hey," she yells. "What happened? Let me up." No answer. Louder, she says, "I have to use the bathroom," and jerks her arms and legs against the restraints to punctuate her demand.

Two people enter the room. Only then does she crane her neck to look around and inspect her surroundings more closely. The room has only one door and beside it a large window. She can see nothing at all through the window. The walls are painted a pale, sickly green. The room contains nothing else but her and her bed, and now these two people she has never seen before, a woman wearing green nurses' scrubs and a man in uniform. The uniform. A Marine! Now she remembers. The base. She stares at the gun on his hip.

"Are you going to shoot me because I need to pee?"

The woman in scrubs answers. "Of course not. I'll bring a pan."

"Didn't you hear me? I don't need a pan. I need to pee."

"We can't get you up yet."

"Unstrap me from this bed and I'll get myself up. And bring me my glasses. I need them."

"We can't do that." She and the man stand just looking at Sara. She sees their eyes, too curious and too knowing. She thinks, *It's as if their eyes are trying to drain my soul when it's my bladder needs to be drained.*

Her head falls back against the pillow again. She looks away and tests the integrity of the straps in earnest, using all the strength in her wiry arms and legs. It hurts, chaffs the skin of her wrists and ankles but accomplishes nothing else. She inspects the restraints more closely to see if she might be able to slip out of the loops and when she is sure she is too firmly bound, she screams for her companion, "Michael! Michael!" *He always comes when I need him.* "Michael! Where are you? Michael!"

A man wearing a white cotton medic's coat comes through the door. The other two stand back. The man in white grabs her arm and jabs her with a needle. Nothing.

• • •

She is not sure when it happens, but someone is unstrapping

both her wrists and ankles and helping her get out of the bed, into a bathroom with a white toilet, so clean and cold but nice to sit on both for elimination and to let her head stop spinning. Later, a woman in scrubs brings food. She is fearful of poison but one bite reveals a flavor she can't resist. Her right wrist is unstrapped and she is given a tray with the food and a plastic fork they take back the second she is through.

People come and go, but Michael, her companion, doesn't come. Her mind feels strange. Her thoughts won't come, or they come slowly, with effort, as if she has to pry each one from her brain, where they are stuck, clogged with fear. *What am I doing here? Why are they taking care of me if they're going to kill me?*

A man comes, another uniformed man, to ask her questions. Then another day and another man who wears a business suit, an older man with deep-set eyes and a gentle manner. What does he want? It seems all he wants is to listen to her. She talks about herself and about her poems, about her mission to save them all from destruction. But the other person she talks about, Ruth, doesn't seem very real any more. Ruth is gone.

Now she isn't sure whether this is a hospital or a jail. The woman she saw earlier – a day ago, two or three days ago? The one in nurses' scrubs is gone. Now a very big man with dark skin, also in scrubs, comes to unstrap her arms so she can eat and takes her to the bathroom, standing with his back to her while she uses the toilet or while she showers. There is no mirror in the bathroom, and no cabinet or towel rack and towels. The man hands her a towel and when she's finished he takes it and leaves with it.

After these rituals have been performed in virtual silence many times she asks him, "What's your name?"

"Bruce."

"Why are you pretending to be a nurse?"

"I am a nurse."

"But I'm not sick."

"Would you like something to read? I can bring you something."

"No!" When he leaves, she mutters, "Not without my glasses, you dope!" She begins to talk to Michael again, this time in a whisper because when she yells, they come in and strap her down again or give her a shot. "Michael! We have work to do, and we can't do it in here. These are the ones! These are the ones we have to stop."

Just then the man who questioned her before, the one in a business suit, opens the door to come in. As before, he is carrying a plain wooden chair to sit on while he talks to her, and then he will take it with him when he leaves. She remembers, *This is the nice one, the one who listens to me. He's not one of them.*

The man is short and solidly built, with grey hair and deep-set brown eyes with lower lids that sag a bit. They ask and ask but tell nothing. She can't understand what lies behind them. Then she decides, *That's okay because there's nothing at all that's evil behind them.*

"Who were you talking to just now, Sara?"

"No one."

"His name is Michael."

"I don't know what you're talking about."

Suddenly she has the strangest feeling of unreality. *They think I'm crazy. I'm not crazy. People used to say I was crazy, but that was years ago, and I'm fine. I only want to help people. Don't they know that? They took my poems. If they read them they'll know.*

The man is looking at her closely. "Sara, my name is Doctor David Sirota."

"I told the other man I'm not sick so I don't need a doctor. And don't try to give me a shot. I don't need anyone trying to control me *or* my thoughts."

"I'm going to ask you again, as I'm sure the officer did – are you any relation to a woman named Cynthia Cameron?"

The name brings no memories, no hint of recognition. "No, and why are you asking me? Cameron is a very common name. How do you know my name, anyway?"

"The MPs found a car registration in your vehicle – a very old car registration from Oklahoma with that name on it. Are you Sara Cameron?"

"Of course I am. Who else would I be?"

He hesitates. "Would you like to get out of here?" he asks.

"Out of where? Where am I? You tell me – and why I'm here in the first place."

"You've been here three . . . three and a half days. This is the

Marine Corps Air Station sick bay. We have to go to a meeting now, then we'll decide," he says, but he doesn't move. Bruce comes in and he is carrying her clothes. They are folded in a bundle and wrapped in clear plastic but she recognizes them immediately. A pair of glasses tops the package. She starts to grab for them, but remembers her manners and holds out her hands. He gives them to her without comment. They aren't her old glasses, but when she puts them on she can see smaller objects clearly again when she looks through them. "Thank you."

He nods and hands her the package of clothing.

She hurries to the bathroom to change. Minutes later with her clothes on again she feels better, calmer, as if these familiar garments hold a protective power. *There, my own clothes, mine, myself.* She says her name out loud, "Sara" and feels as if a friend has just greeted her.

Doctor Sirota and Bruce are waiting for her. The doctor takes her elbow gently and escorts her out the door with Bruce close behind. Sara turns quickly to take in her surroundings but sees only the corridor and at its end part of a room and one chair. Before she can assimilate other details of her surroundings they enter a much bigger room. It contains little except a large oblong table with many chairs and a flag standing in the corner. The room is carpeted in a dark blue, flat-pile carpet like the ones in public places, the kind of carpet that wears well. The seats of the office chairs are the same color. There are pictures of men in uniform on the walls. She instantly recognizes one – President Eisenhower.

Doctor Sirota pulls out a chair for her, and then sits next to her. Bruce stands on her other side. Three men are already seated around the table, one of them leaning into the back of his office chair that gives enough for a shallow recline.

Dr. Sirota nods at the other man, then says, "Sara, this is FBI Special Agent Manning. The gentleman to his left is Major Connolly, the base commander, and on his other side is Detective Reed from the Yuma Police Department. We're here to talk about what happened three nights ago."

Sara is wary. She shakes her head and says nothing, unwilling to participate in what is evidently going to be some lying conspiracy against her.

The man they call the commander sits forward in his chair and puts one forearm and hand on the table, fingers splayed. "You do remember three nights ago when you snuck on base? When you broke in?"

"I didn't break anything!" she says, with emphasis.

Now he sits back looking angry, his hands grasping the metal arms of the chair. His voice is stern. "You entered the base illegally, at night, and created a disturbance. When the MP's tried to talk to you, you became belligerent and assaulted them."

"They assaulted me. They had guns!"

The FBI man speaks quickly, impatiently. "Mrs. Cameron, do you know you committed a Federal crime?"

She doesn't answer. She feels confused, and the words sound as if they come from a great distance away.

He leans on the table and glares at her. "This is a Federal military installation. You were trespassing. You could be tried and sentenced to years in Federal prison. The only reason we are considering releasing you to the civilian authorities is that you appear to have no weapons, no history of arrest, and thus far you have made no threats, as such, against anyone." He shakes his head as if in disgust, and adds, "The civilian authorities have valid charges against you."

"Sara," Doctor Sirota says, " Did you come here to hurt someone, or damage something on the base?"

Sara shakes her head to clear it. Finally she says, "No! I don't do those things. I just came to hand out my poems, to make you see war isn't the answer. Yuma can be saved. The world can be saved. I know the nine hundred are here. I need to. . ."

"Sara!" Doctor Sirota turns to calm her again with his eyes. His face somehow absorbs every word she is thinking and returns only understanding. "Do you have a plan to hurt someone on the base?"

"I don't hurt people."

"Do you have a plan to destroy anything on the base?"

"Destroy?" Her voice rises in volume with her frustration. "That's what I'm trying to stop. They're the ones. They specialize in destroying! Why don't you understand?"

The base commander is leaning back in his chair now, arms folded over his chest. He stares at her, then turns to the others. "Our sick-bay isolation room is no place for this woman." He stands and says, "The meeting is over, gentlemen. Thank you, Doctor Sirota, Agent Manning. She's yours, Detective Reed."

"Give me a minute with these two gentlemen, will you?" the officer says to the Commander, indicating the FBI agent and Doctor Sirota. The Commander nods and leaves the room.

Bruce takes Sara's arm and she understands he wants her to leave also. "Wait a minute," she protests, turning to each of the men in turn. "You can't talk about me behind my back. It's not right. You're treating me like a child, like a criminal! I haven't…" Bruce has her up and out the door before she can finish the sentence. Then he stops without closing the door all the way. She looks up into his smooth, chocolate brown face and he winks at her. He is going to allow her to listen to what they are saying.

Detective Reed's voice is loud enough for her to hear clearly. "I just want to know what we've got here. No hits on ACIC, none on NCIC, none on AFIS, none on the Watch Lists, none on the No-Fly Lists, she's not on a missing persons watch, and no social media presence at all. Is that right?"

Agent Manning's voice comes slowly, as if reluctant to leave his mouth, but clear enough. "No criminal history we could find. But she's a few tacos short of a combination plate, isn't she? And we all know what people like her can do."

Doctor Sirota: "I understand you searched the Social Security records using Sara Cameron and a birthplace of Oklahoma. Good work."

"It was luck."

"I went through the records and saw she went on disability about thirty years ago for unspecified mental issues. Probably for paranoid schizophrenia rather than cognitive deficits. She appears intelligent and organized in her thinking when she's not actively delusional. There are virtually no medical records, none of childbirth, so I understand you've ruled out a Cynthia Cameron connection."

The FBI man: "That wasn't our concern. What we feared was another Uni-bomber – someone deranged enough to kill people *and* think they can justify it by writing a bunch of opinionated trash. We didn't uncover any mention of the President or anyone else in

Washington in her scribblings, so we haven't alerted the Security Service, but she needs to be locked up, now. Isn't that what you concluded, Doctor Sirota?"

"No, it isn't." The doctor's voice carries both tension and irritation. "Your psychiatrist and I agree that Sara displays an unusual variation of delusional thinking for a paranoid schizophrenic. She generalizes the fear of being threatened or targeted. She extends it to include the world and the whole human race as potential victims."

"Yeah. She thinks people like Reed and myself are the enemy, not to mention the whole Marine base. Is that what you're saying?"

"It's true she sees the military and politicians in general as threats, as persecutors. But she's managed to deviate from the idea of violently retaliating against those she considers enemies. Instead, she's obsessed with the idea of saving the ones they threaten."

The sound of Manning's laugh emerges smooth and sibilant. "Saving the world by writing asinine poems?"

Dr. Sirota's voice has a tone that suggests he is losing his patience. "It's an understandable variation of the Messiah complex that fits with her delusional thought system."

Agent Manning: "We have your report, Doctor." The sound of a chair-back rebounding as its occupant rises alerts Bruce and Sara. The FBI man is coming. Bruce grabs Sara's arm and pulls her across the hall into an empty room before the FBI man emerges.

• • •

Chapter Twenty-One

Detective Reed glanced at the FBI man's back as he left the room then turned to Doctor Sirota and lifted his eyebrows. "Okay then. Our problem now. City of Yuma has her for littering and maybe theft if any of that mountain of stuff in her truck was stolen. I was with the FBI when they went through it. Sure didn't look like anything in there was worth committing a crime for."

"They told me she has a lot of books, including the complete works of Shakespeare," Dr. Sirota said, with a faint smile.

"That and a bunch of old albums and 8-track tapes of folk music – mostly 'make love not war' type lyrics, some books of poetry and just a lot of junk. The FBI will turn it over to us. If we want to inspect it again, it will take days. I think she's one of those hoarders."

"Probably not. Obsessive people collect things. Schizophrenic people accumulate things. She finds and keeps the things that support her ideas, delusional as they may be."

"Then is she crazy or not? Likely to start howling at the moon or stuffing mashed potatoes into her ears?"

Doctor Sirota didn't smile. He shook his head. "I doubt it. More people than you suspect have paranoid schizophrenia. They can appear normal and behave normally if they're on medication, which of course she should be."

"Why isn't she?"

"We gave her an anti-psychotic and tranquilizer cocktail by injection several times in the past three days, but it has a relatively short half-life. Today there's enough residual effect to keep her relatively coherent and under control. Tomorrow – no guarantee."

"I would hate it if she got violent and I had to restrain her – a skinny old woman like that. Don't even like to touch someone like her. All that negative coverage in the news media about excessive force. A few abusive cops out of tens of thousands of good ones puts us all on the defensive."

"She's not likely to become violent, but then I don't know her full history. Acute stress or a severe psychological shock could send her into another psychotic episode."

Reed shook his head. "No guarantee to keep her stress-free in the Yuma County Detention Center. The judge has to see her within twenty-four hours to get her plea. *If* she pleads innocent and *if* she's lucky, the judge will release her on her own recognizance. But if she goes off the deep end in the meantime, we'll send her to the local psych unit."

"I'm medical director there. If she shows up she'll be my patient."

"Good. The County Attorney isn't eager to keep people with a psych diagnosis locked up, unless it's for a violent offense, a felony. We might even drop the charges if it turns out she's just a nut who likes to litter."

They rose, shook hands and left the conference room together. Doctor Sirota went down the corridor in one direction, while Detective Reed walked the other way to the unmarked door where Sara had been held for three nights. He had to read her her rights.

When that was done, he handcuffed an incensed Sara, walked her outside and now she was locked in the cage-like back seat of his patrol car where she sputtered that she had never been arrested. She leaned forward, bumped her head against the plexi-glass partition and asked, "Where is my truck? Where is all my stuff?"

"It's in safe keeping. Don't worry about it."

"Where? When can I get it? And where is my notebook? I need my notebook."

Detective Reed sighed, then reminded himself to be grateful that so far this prisoner was behaving just like any newly-arrested pain-in-the-butt. He had not had to touch her except for the brief act of handcuffing. At the station he finished booking her and congratulated himself silently when he handed her over to the female guard.

The guard was middle-aged, dumpy-bodied, and coarse featured, her face red with blotches of a parasitic infection called rosacea over which she wore a mask of bored indifference. She grabbed Sara's arm to take her for processing. Sara's hands were still handcuffed behind her back but she pulled back and jerked her arm free. "Don't touch me."

"Don't touch you, Lady? You'll get touched a lot while you're in here if you act like that." The guard grabbed her prisoner's arms, and pushed her down an empty corridor.

Sara couldn't feel herself stumbling and tripping as the woman behind her pushed her down the corridor. Instead, shock sent her consciousness out of her body to hover near the ceiling. She didn't feel anything, but saw her body in the grasp of the guard as they walked clumsily down a hallway. From the worn concrete floor to the blank grey walls, their scraping footsteps echoed a raspy whisper of despair.

Then somehow she came back, back in her body again, walking. She looked into the empty cells with iron doors and imagined the one that would slide shut on her and suddenly it all became real. She imagined the confinement, the boredom, the hopelessness and the complete dependence on others for the basic needs of life. No. She had to do something. "Wait! I get a phone call, don't I? Isn't that what they say? I'm entitled to make one phone call."

"Yeah, sure." They turned and the guard led her down a different corridor. They entered a concrete square of a room totally bare except for three old-style telephones mounted six feet apart on one wall. The phones were black, the cords only a foot long when kinked at rest. The guard picked up the receiver of the nearest phone and said, "I'll dial for you."

"I don't know the number. I have to see a phone book."

The guard went to the adjacent wall and from her pocket pulled a lanyard with a set of keys on the end and inserted a key into a recessed cabinet. She produced a phone book, handed it to Sara and folded her arms across her chest to wait. She didn't move but looked away, a gesture that implied she was giving her prisoner some privacy.

• • •

Yuma Sun crime reporter Jane Myers kicked off her retro-style wedge heel shoes with the thought that everything old should *not* become new again. She toed the shoes under her desk and took her first sip of a café Americano. She stared at the orange scone, indulging in guilt feelings that would not prevent her from devouring it, when a call from the receptionist came in. "Jane, this one's for you. Line four."

"Hey, isn't that an old beer commercial? Got a cold one for me?"

"Ha. You wish." The receptionist chuckle cut to a dial tone.

Jane took another quick sip of coffee and pressed line four. "Hello, this is Jane Myers, what can I do for you?"

"I'm being held illegally in the jail, and I…"

"Illegally? Why is it illegal?"

"Because I'm trying to save people, not hurt them. They won't listen to me."

Jane sighed and bit into her scone. Another call from the County Detention Center by a person innocent in no reality but their own deluded one. She chewed and asked, "What are the charges against you Ma'am?"

"Charges? Oh. They said littering, but that Marine knocked them from my hand and…"

"A who? A Marine? What Marine, Ma'am?"

"On the base. It was my best one yet, but they took them from me, and they have my truck and they won't give me my notebook."

Jane was tempted to toss the phone back in its base and finish her scone, but an unfortunate vulnerability to guilt guided and informed her ethics. Even a person like this deserved a professional response. "What makes you think your truck and your notebook and a charge of littering are news, Ma'am? Wait a minute, what's your name?"

"Sara. Sara Cameron."

The words of dismissal were on the tip of Jane's tongue when the last name triggered her memory. "Uh, Mrs. Cameron, tell me a little more about when and why and where you were arrested."

The narrative that followed was disjointed, sometimes vague and sometimes painfully detailed, but eventually it became clear to Jane that the caller was the poet with the anti-war message. The scattered poems had created a minor nuisance and earned only a few paragraphs in the paper. But…there might be a human interest story here, and better yet, this Sara Cameron might be related to the dead woman at Kofa.

She glanced at the clock on the wall. Visiting hours at the Detention Center would be over soon. "Okay, Mrs. Cameron, I'd like to hear more but I need to come and visit you. Now."

"Here? You'll come here?"

"Yes. I'll be there in about ten." She hung up the phone, downed her black coffee, and with a wistful grunt wrapped the partly eaten scone in a paper napkin. She decided against recording the woman's voice with her smart-phone. Instead she grabbed her tape recorder and headed out.

Yuma traffic was nothing compared to some cities where she had worked but at three o'clock in the afternoon school buses, car-pooling parents and school zones to drive through at agonizingly slow speed complicated the trip. She made it with only fifteen minutes visiting time left.

Jane had interviewed inmates at the Yuma County Detention Center before, but today she was especially annoyed by the check-in routine that ate up so much time. The uniformed officer inspected the contents of her purse, directed her through a metal detector, remotely unlocked the door to the main unit where another officer escorted her down the hall to the visiting room. There, she sat in a cold, hard metal chair in the empty room wondering again how she could establish enough rapport with someone to do a good interview while separated by a wall and a window. But this time she might actually get a story – the prisoner had seemed very eager to talk.

The guard entered with Sara, who spotted Jane immediately and came to sit on her own hard metal chair on the other side of the window. They looked at each other through the glass. Neither spoke. Jane registered a stab of mental resistance to the fact that a vulnerable and harmless-looking older woman like this could end up in the Detention Center. She was sincere when finally she said, "I want to hear more about you, Sara."

"When I came to Yuma, I didn't know I'd be doing this. I started to look for my daughter. But when I saw what they were up to in the Kofa, and realized what's going on at the Marine Base, I knew I had to try."

"I'm not sure what you mean about Kofa and the Base. Please, tell me more."

"I saw it back in January, when I camped there. Trucks with military and civilians driving right up the mountain side. Strange noises and lights at night, and the jets flying over all hours. Back in the Second World War they tested guns and tanks and such at the Proving Ground, but now their evil is something else, and it's spreading into the Kofa. It will be the end of us all if I can't stop it. We need the nine hundred, and you can help me..."

"Wait, Mrs. Cameron..."

"Call me Sara. It's a Bible name and a good one, not some made-up word nobody ever heard of. Call me Sara."

"Okay, Sara. Listen. In January, a group of civilians and some Marine volunteers from the base transported trucks full of antelope to release into the Refuge. Maybe that's what you saw. And I'm not surprised if you saw strange lights and heard noises at night near the Proving Ground. They're still doing testing there."

"Didn't you hear me? What they're doing there will kill us all!" Sara's features seem to shrink to the center of her face, giving it the drawn effect of a shriveled apple. When she spoke again her voice sounded both accusing and sad. "You're not one of the nine-hundred, I expect." She looked down at the floor.

Jane lowered her voice to the tone of a gentle inquiry rather than a question. "What nine hundred is that?"

"Never mind." Sara turned away as if about to leave.

"Wait, Sara. I want to hear more. You spoke about the poem you took to the base. I want to see it. Do you have a copy?"

"The copy is up here." She tapped her temple with an index finger.

"You memorized it?"

"Of course. I know the whole thing, but this is the important part." She recited, "'Heads: War gambles with the breath we breathe. Humanity merits a permanent war-reprieve. Parts' callous attitudes could jeopardize: One nuclear war will all earth martyrize!'"

"Very good. I've got it on tape, and I'm going to write about you and put it in my story." Jane glanced at the guard, who stood behind Sara looking at his watch suggestively. At any second the loudspeaker would blurt, *end of visiting hours*. She said, "But I have one more

question before I go. Are you related to Cindy Cameron?"

"Cindy? No. I have a daughter named Ruth. Ruth Cameron. But…but then. . ."

Jane waited through a very long pause.

"Seems like when she hit those teenaged years she did say she didn't like her name and she took to calling herself Cindy."

Jane sat straight up in her chair. "About thirty years old, right? Beautiful long red hair?"

"Guess she would be thirty-something now."

"Mrs. Cameron, I'm so sorry for your loss."

"Well, that's right good of you to say. Some people blame the mother if a youngster runs off."

Jane cocked her head at the peculiar answer but then, this woman was definitely not ordinary. She took her phone from her purse and scrolled to the newspaper's photo of Cindy at her high school graduation. She held it up to the window, hoping the woman could see it well enough through the scarred and dulled safety glass. "This is your Ruth, isn't it?"

Sara's eyes widened as she stared at the photo. "Where did you get that?"

"A friend of hers gave it to us when we interviewed him about the murder."

"Murder, what murder?"

Jane hesitated. Something wasn't right here. "Her murder, on May 7th."

"She – someone killed her? She's dead? My Ruth is dead?"

Jane was speechless. *Damn! The murder is news to this woman! Doesn't she read the paper or watch the news? Isn't she the next of kin? Why didn't they notify her?*

Sara stood very slowly, as if to walk away.

"Wait, Mrs. Cameron…"

Sara took three steps and stopped. An ear-splitting scream, "Michael!"

Jane and the guard jumped, startled. The guard reached for Sara's arm. A transformation overtook Sara's body before she could grasp it. One second Sara appeared weak and soft, as if she would melt to the ground in a faint, and then she froze, her ropy muscles rigid and still.

Jane felt a stab of remorse. What had she done now? Guilt and regret overwhelming her, she rose, tapped on the glass, but Sara didn't turn. She was as unmoving as a statue, one of the living statues in department store windows or on the plazas in Europe. The reporter thought herself immune to surprise but what happened next stunned her. The guard took Sara's arm and pulled gently to guide her away. Sara did not budge and appeared not to breathe. The guard stared at Jane, no doubt wondering what she had done to the woman. Jane could only shake her head. The guard tried again. Sara's arm lifted a little when she pulled at it but the rest of her body remained as immobile as if imbedded in the concrete floor. The guard raised her grip to both Sara's arm pits and pulled harder. Sara's body remained rigid, and began to topple forward. The guard caught her and pushed her upright again. Sara's face was as immobile as her body. Sara's body was there. Sara was somewhere else.

• • •

Chapter Twenty-Two

Winston Verbale had formed the habit of stopping in at Allie's office shortly before eight a.m. to chat while he sipped his coffee. He had almost slopped the steaming brew into his lap during one such chat a week ago, when Allie told him someone had tried to kill her friend's dog. He knew he hadn't gotten the dog because the mutt came chasing after his car but he thought he had nailed the Indian bitch, who dropped like a stone after his second shot at her. He wondered if she was stupid enough to think the dog had actually been his target. At any rate, it had been a good bet to try to take her out rather than Allie, because Allie was proving to be a valuable informant. Today she sat in one of the office easy chairs reading the morning *Sun* when he walked in.

"What's Yuma's earth-shattering news *du jour*? Are the lettuce and cantaloupe doing well?"

She looked up. He saw shock on her usually serene face. She turned the paper so he could read the headline, "Yuma's Poet-at-Large is Murder Victim's Mother."

Now he was shocked.

Allie's voice rose to just above a whisper when she said, "I'm still reading it."

He turned and went to retrieve another copy of the paper from the waiting-room. The table there always held the morning edition and a few tattered magazines. He grabbed the paper and began to read when the receptionist walked in. She stared at him, raising an eyebrow, both inquisitive and flirtatious. He returned the look with a glare. The slut wanted him, of course. He walked the corridor to his office, trying not to look rushed. He closed the door before he sat down to read.

His hands shook as he skimmed through the absurd poems about gold and heads and parts. There wasn't much else, just that a bit of detective work by the reporter had found the victim's given name was Ruth, not Cindy or Cynthia, and her mother was Sara Cameron and Sara had been arrested. Nothing about where the mother came from or when. He read it twice, let the paper fall to the floor at his feet. Cindy had never told him anything about her mother, including whether the woman was dead or alive. What a mistake he had made when he talked about her, once only, but in a crucial context. Now here she was in this one-horse town in the middle of nowhere, able to make a liar out of him.

A knock at his door. Allie entered. Without preamble, she asked, "Win, how are you taking this? Are you okay?"

He stood, picked up the newspaper and folded it, careful not to reveal his discomfort. "I'm fine. The poor woman. I'll have to visit and extend my condolences." He sniffed and turned his mouth down at the corners.

"Yes, I think I'd like to do that too. But why didn't she come forward before? It's been two months since they discovered her daughter's body. You said Cindy told you she had to go back east to take care of her mother but her mother has been here in the valley since January."

"I never knew what Cindy was up to. Not the most reliable person, kind of quirky and unpredictable with all the bird-watching stuff…"

Allie's face silenced him. Evidently she had really liked the red-haired witch. She looked down at the newspaper still in her hand and said, "I guess it's not important. But being hit twice in one day with important news can be – upsetting."

Her words and tone were expectant, but he didn't know what she wanted him to say. Then it registered. "Twice?"

"The article about the vacant seat on the city council. Didn't you read it?"

Her voice sounded faint with dismay. He was beginning to dislike the woman, useful or not. He answered, coldly, "No, I didn't. Why?"

"I guess the council seat isn't vacant any more. Debbie Smith decided to accept the mandate to finish her husband's two year term."

Allie paused, still looking at his face. He knew she could see how stricken he felt. Might have expected it from her, the bleeding-heart do-gooder. Memory flashes of Debbie Smith rose with the bile in his stomach. He pictured Debbie Smith shaking his hand once at a town hall meeting. Then he remembered her face in a different context. The fat slob he had encountered in the office bathroom a few weeks ago and failed to recognize.

He cleared his throat. "That's the way the dice roll. Now, if you'll excuse me, I've got…" Allie must have known he had dismissed her because she left without another word, sparing him more dishwater sympathy.

He sank down in his chair. His thoughts chased themselves in frantic circles. No council seat, no recognition, no reward for all the handshaking, ass kissing and image polishing. No. It wasn't right. The way Allie had looked at him wasn't right, as if she didn't like him or suspected him of some wrong-doing. He just wanted what he deserved and had never gotten. Rage came then, the blood rushing to his head and pounding in his ears until he thought his skull would split. It was all he could do to remain seated while his muscles twitched and heart pounded. Without conscious volition his head lowered and his eyes stared at the floor, seeing nothing.

Now there would be no reward for giving up the casino and all its delights. But. . .maybe he would go back to gambling. Back to the life of excitement and suspense, pitting his wits and will against the dealer or even more valiantly, against the house? Memories. . .the ecstasy of winning, the forgettable despair of loss. . .

Then another memory surfaced, the memory of killing the red-haired bitch who had tried to outshine him, threatened to challenge him in the game of politics and then hinted she would leave him. No one like that would ever leave him, refuse to speak to him, imagine themselves better than him.

The sight, sound, feel and taste of it came back to him: sun and shadow, blood and dirt. He remembered the power of fulfillment that overwhelmed him while he watched Cindy fold and sink face-first to the ground, twitching and gasping, life pulsing out of a hole in the back of her head. It was a simple matter of eliminating anyone who would eliminate him. Rid himself of competition, distractions. Now another spoiler, another stealer, Debbie Smith.

Other memories came that placated him just a little. He remembered the stupid faces of the stupid people who had walked in on him in the bathroom, and how he had laughed at them. He imagined the look on the Indian bitch's face when she thought her mutt was dead. Slowly, with the help of imagination, the devastation gave way to constructive thought and clever planning. He would do what all great men had done. He would turn a set-back, what might look like a defeat, into victory. He would use the red-haired bitch's mother and her absurd poems and he would win it all, yet.

In less than a week he had developed and rehearsed the plan and now his performance. He wiped the sweat from his upper lip with his fore-arm because his hands were covered by nitrile gloves. He flattened himself against the siding of the house. Behind the tall shrub of yellow bell flowers in bloom, neither moonlight nor street lamps could reveal his presence. He had studied her schedule and knew it would be almost ten o'clock before she returned. In the hungry silence, with only the rise and fall of his chest for distraction, he knew he had never before felt this keyed up. *"Hyped,"* the kids would call it, but not fearful or anxious, no. Waves of anticipation washed over him, strong and rhythmic, cleansing him of doubt, feeding his virility and power with the knowledge of what he would do.

The car's headlights appeared. He couldn't see her in the driver's seat against the glare, but he recognized the car by the unique pattern of smaller l.e.d. lights around the beams. His eyes locked on her approach down the quiet, residential street. The closer she came, the harder his heart thumped against his ribs.

The car pulled into the driveway slowly, giving the remote time to lift the garage door. When the door was up four or five feet he crouched low and approached the car's rear bumper. Touching it, he followed into the right bay of the two-car garage then squatted behind the passenger-side door and waited for the door to close. He wouldn't move until it was down fully, blocking the view of anyone who might be outside, and until she got out but hadn't entered the kitchen, a window of action just a few seconds long.

This close, the rattle of the metal door sounded deafening. He felt the rumble in his teeth. He held his breath. Flash. Lights flooded the dark garage. He cringed. Clunk. The bottom of the garage door touched down. Her car door opened. She stepped out. A cry of pent-up excitement burst from his throat as he rushed around to her side of the car. She heard it and turned with the same look of dumb surprise on her face he'd seen in the office bathroom.

He smashed into her doughy body, almost bumping her forehead with his. It could have been a lover's embrace until his right hand clutched her neck, and he forced her down, crashing to the concrete floor. Her head and shoulders landed on the steps into the kitchen. She cried out in pain and her arms wind-milled to grasp something. Her frantic motions knocked a mop and broom from their holders on the wall. The handles fell across Verbale's back. He threw them aside, fury deepened.

He grabbed the front of her dress and jerked her upper body onto the floor. No longer immobilized by shock, she began to struggle but all her bulk was useless against him. His right hand tight around her neck pressed deep into her flesh. *It feels just like the rubber of a squish-ball!* Now he pressed down with both hands, and felt the slickness of oil and sweat on her skin. Her mouth gaped and saliva rolled off her protruding tongue. She stared up at him, emitting only gagging sounds, but mentally he heard her silent shriek of horror and her frantic question, *why*. Her terror-stricken eyes narrowed a fraction then popped wider, the whites large desperate circles around swollen black pupils.

"Recognize me now, Bitch?" he panted. "Wish you had fucked me when you had the chance?" His thumbs worked deeper into the pasty flesh of her neck, his fingers red and knuckles white with exertion.

No sound then but his grunts of effort and the futile thumps and slaps of her limbs against the floor. In a strange moment of timelessness awareness, he saw her head was topped by a helmet of drab brown hair, so unlike Cindy's flagrant, life-affirming mane. Yet the excitement, the exultation of Cindy's death was nothing compared to this. It filled him, surged through his arms, jolted through his fingers into the woman like bolts of electricity. It was good, exciting good. His hands felt something give way in her throat, and within seconds her eyes rolled back in her head. He didn't want to let go yet. It was too soon. But then it was done, the last breath of life choked out of her. She went limp, soft, unmoving and unbreathing. Dead.

Power surged through him, uncontrolled. It shook him. He didn't move. Finally, with trembling reluctance, he allowed his fingers and thumbs to release their grip. Still kneeling on the concrete, thighs straddling her body, he straightened his torso, his arms and hands hanging numbly by his side.

He stared at the limp body underneath him for long moments, silently congratulating himself for triumph over what was now so much raw meat. Then his eyes shifted from her face to the bulge in his crotch.

This was good. It was better than good. He began to chuckle. *So much for foreplay.* He unzipped his pants and with a few jerks on his rock-hard dick, he came onto her bulging-eyed, purple face.

So much for wham-bam-thank-you-ma'am. I'm not a smoker, so what comes next? He was still smiling when he remembered. *The plan. Yes, of course, the plan.*

• • •

Chapter Twenty-Three

Traditional harvest time for the early crop of Summer Kiss variety cantaloupes was mid-June, but on Guzman Farm it took place whenever Boss Sam Guzman said it would. On June 5th, he appeared at the fifty acre plot south of County 12th Street followed by a gaggle of foremen, machine rental agents, buyers, and day labor contractors. Guzman was a sun-burned man in his sixties, bow-legged and heavy around the middle but well-muscled. His aggressive stride and the intense set of his craggy face left no doubt as to who was in charge here.

From the north side of the field, he walked by ten rows, then down the eleventh furrow for five or six yards before he stooped to inspect one of the cantaloupe. Here on the south side of the raised bed it had been free of standing water while it soaked up the most available rays of sunshine.

Close on his heels, the head foreman and the machine rental agent watched expectantly. Guzman swiftly cut the melon from the vine and lifted it to carve out a slice. With the melon in his left hand, knife and slice in his right hand, he took a bite of the juice-dripping fruit. He rolled it on his palate like a wine taster, while those who watched held their breath in suspense. Finally he swallowed and declared, "Good sugar!" The harvest was on.

The next morning two tractors and a dozen workers began the task of picking, sorting and moving thousands of cantaloupe to the cooling sheds. From there they would be packed with care in plywood crates and shipped to grocery stores all over the country.

The lead tractor pulled a metal-frame trailer twenty feet wide. On the trailer, a ten foot tall conveyor belt held the fruit placed on it by the harvesters. From the conveyor belt, the melons went down a chute onto a stainless steel sorting table at the side of the contraption. There, other workers quickly sized the melons and placed them in boxes.

Most of the workers were Mexicans with years of field experience. They were adept at selecting the ripest melons to cut from the stem and place on the conveyor belt. They worked in companionable silence as usual, focused and earnest. Until Stephen Lopez gave a hoarse shout and tossed a melon back into the dirt. He shook his hands violently, rubbed them together, wiped them on his pants. He quaked, his knees threatened to buckle. Both arms pointed stiffly down to the soil, then upward to the sky. He shouted, *Dios mio, Dios mio! Una cabeza, una cabeza!*

The nearest tractor driver stopped and dismounted to look at the object the field hand had chucked back into the dirt. He approached to within inches. The thing was the right size for a melon, round like a melon, a mottled buff color like a melon, but melons didn't have hair. He extended a booted foot to roll the object over. And melons didn't have lifeless eyes filled with dirt and a gaping mouth filled with flies.

No more melons were harvested on Guzman Farm the rest of that day.

• • •

Over the past week, Kim had kept her promise to call Lon at the start and end of every day. Sometimes their conversations were as brief as "I'm okay," and "All right." At other times, especially in the evenings, Kim sat in bed when they talked with the lights already turned off and Zayd settled on the rug beside her. Their conversations then were longer and more personal and she felt Lon's presence almost as strongly as when they were together.

"I'm still at risk, is what you're saying, Lon."

"I don't want you to worry but Wagner, unfortunately, is still among the suspects. On that night, when he was supposed to be on duty, he called in sick. Diarrhea and vomiting, he said, and of course he was alone the whole night with no one to confirm it. It was a very indirect line of questioning because we didn't want to alert him he was a suspect. In the meantime, there was no match in the computer for the shell casings and the tire tracks were too smeared to match with anything. But you never can tell when someone or something cruising under the radar will suddenly make a blip."

"My name never came up with Wagner, right?"

"Of course not."

"And before that. You didn't talk to him about his trash-talking and his obvious dislike of me? If he's just the blowhard jerk I think he is, I don't want anyone fighting that battle for me."

"I wouldn't think of it."

"Good. But I guess he is the most logical suspect because I don't know anyone else who could hate me enough to shoot me."

"Maybe someone whose grudge is against Apaches in general?"

"A hate crime against Indians?"

"Out of style now, isn't it?"

"There are better people to hate now. Terrorists, the Taliban, Isis, homosexual people who get married." Kim slid further down under the sheet, and let the arm that held the phone rest on the other pillow beside her head. "I want this investigation to be over almost as much as I want you to get Cindy's killer."

"I want the psycho who tried to kill you more, Wagner or whoever."

Kim's thoughts slowed a little as the narcotic of sleep oozed into her nervous system. Her voice softened. "You know, my friend Allie called me. She's the one who works at the office with Winston Verbale. It seems she changed her mind about him. We talked about the possibility he killed Cindy."

"We haven't ruled him out completely. But what would his motive have been? Not money. She had very few financial assets and there was no insurance policy. We didn't identify another woman – or another man – involved, so no love-triangle. The way she was killed doesn't fit with that kind of motive, anyway.

She responded, "I guess there's always a motive, even if it's just some asinine thing like 'I wanted to see what it feels like,' or 'the devil-dog told me to do it.'"

Lon said, "Cindy Cameron's death was not a copy-cat a murder, the kind committed by people too stupid to delve into their own evil imagination."

"Ummm. I'm probably too tired to think about it anymore tonight, Lon. Murder doesn't make for good bedtime conversation."

"Good night then Warrior Woman?"

"Lon, please don't call me that. I am no Lozen. Have you ever seen me carry a rifle or ride a mustang bareback?"

"Umm. Stereotyping. You're right. But I like to think of your strength and your toughness. It gives me a little more confidence that you're okay when I'm not with you."

"I understand. I appreciate that. But still, don't do it."

"Okay."

"Good night, Lon."

"Then sleep well, Kim Altaha."

• • •

Lon had heard her chuckle a little in the instant before she keyed off her phone, a low and throaty sound much like a cat's purr. She couldn't have imagined the rush of testosterone it triggered.

He got up to brush his teeth, then fell into bed thinking of Kim and her Native heritage and how it must have influenced her growing up, how it had formed her perspective about life.

Soon the focus of his musings turned from her mind and personality to her body. Vivid mental pictures of Kim flooded his mind, fueling erotic fantasies that kept him awake and restless. Damn! He was not a horny teenager. This was ridiculous. He tried the usual techniques for insomnia, getting up to get a drink, replacing his pillow and cranking the air conditioner setting down for a cooler room. His hormones and his imagination did not yield to behavioral strategies or to reason. Toward dawn he cursed the ordeal and was tempted to relieve his discomfort by masturbating. He angrily resisted the urge, only to wake at seven a.m. with the sticky evidence on his thighs that his body had overruled his mind and had its way with him, something that hadn't happened to him in years.

• • •

Chapter Twenty-Four

Later that morning Lon grabbed his car keys from the holder hanging on the kitchen wall next to the garage door, aware of feeling sleepy and irritable at the start of the day. His phone rang. Impatiently, he answered and followed the prompt for a face to face. The freckled and genial visage of his friend Dean Reed of the Yuma Police Department greeted him from the tiny screen.

"Hey, Lon, we've got something here you should see."

"What's that, your favorite chick flick, Dean?"

"I don't go for them fat and headless, Raney." Reed's face disappeared. He had turned the phone toward the floor. Lon made out the image of a dark and shadowy something on the floor. A body.

"*Headless!*" Instantly Lon was wider awake. "A homicide?"

"What else? Not your jurisdiction, but there's a poem here reads like that stuff Sara Cameron wrote. There could be a connection to the Cindy Cameron case you're working on. Just get your butt over here, pronto."

Lon took down the address and backed the unmarked Crown-Vic out of the two-car garage of his house on County 9th Street. Just then his radio went live with the request to meet the man at Guzman Farm about a woman's severed head. "Repeat," he radioed back. The dispatcher did. Now he was very wide awake. *This head goes with that body of Reed's… And the victim might be connected to the person who killed Cindy Cameron.* The satisfying feeling of closing a case, recalled from dozens of previous ones came to him, but he dismissed it as self-indulgent and seriously premature.

He pulled the car over to the curb. Smiling in anticipation, he returned Dean Reed's call. "You may have the body, Reed, but I've got the head."

"What? Like in a bowling-ball bag? Don't give me that crap. This is no grade-B movie we got here."

"No kidding, Reed. I'm on my way to it now. It's in the county – my jurisdiction after all."

"No way, you greedy fool. We've got the crime scene so that makes it ours."

"Then we have to work together if we want to take a whole body to the County Attorney."

"Crap, Raney, it's not the body, it's the perpetrator we need to take to the frickin' C.A., so she can indict him."

"I know. I'm on it."

"The hell you are. Not unless you've got the suspect in a bowling-ball bag too."

"So you just found the victim. When did she die?"

"Last night, we think. The dog, one of those little, yappy ankle-biters barked all night and all morning till the neighbor came to investigate. She had a key."

Lon had no trouble finding the Guzman Farm. In this wide valley it lay at the lowest elevation, visible from the gentle slopes and low plateaus around it. In the middle of the green field, a dark circle of humanity placed the gruesome body part at its bullseye. The field workers and other employees were silent, some crossing themselves, others exchanging excited comments in rapid-fire Spanish. He and Sam Guzman succeeded in shooing the workers away just minutes before the Medical Examiner's van arrived to take the head to the morgue. A few minutes was all the time he needed to examine the gristly, pathetic thing.

Fifteen minutes later he drove down the quiet residential street where Debbie Smith had lived, busy now with its own crowd of onlookers.

He made his way under the yellow crime scene tape and past the uniformed officer. Before entering the garage he paused long enough to don blue cloth shoe covers. Inside, he saw Detective Reed talking with one of Yuma's crime scene techs, seemingly unaffected by the evil stench clouding the enclosed space. It was a dense amalgam that might have been brewed in hell: six liters of blood pooled and filming dry on the floor where the head should have been, the victim's excrement, sweat from more than one body, an undertone of oil and steel, the stench of fear and the merest hint of semen.

Lon approached Reed and the other man cautiously, avoiding contact with thousands of blood spatters. Blood defiled the floor, the car, the walls, virtually every surface. He only glanced at the headless body as he walked past but it was enough. It told him she had died and been beheaded in the spot where she lay, and there had been no genital sexual assault.

He nodded with no intent to shake the gloved hands of Reed and the tech, who he had met before. The tech looked at Lon's shoe covers and said, "No need to pussy-foot around any longer. I already took all the pictures and samples from the spatter."

Lon nodded and said, "Haven't you figured it out yet, Reed? I'd say she's probably dead."

"Better late than never, Raney? And where's the head you promised to bring? No gift for the host?"

"I'll bring a bouquet of roses to your funeral, Reed. In the meantime, what about inside the house? The perpetrator probably went in to clean up before he took her head for a ride in the country. Could be bags full of DNA evidence in there."

"No kidding, Sherlock?" Dean looked up from his note pad. "Another team is in there sweeping the place, and we're not welcome. What about the head?"

It's in the M.E.'s wagon on the way to the morgue. Didn't take long to see it was drained dry and washed before it was dumped in the dirt."

"Washed? Why"

"DNA. The guy probably came on her face."

"Disgusting…!"

"Yeah. But he could have taken a dump on her. That's been known to happen. If we're lucky the M.E. will find traces of semen in her ears or up her nose."

"You see anything else when you examined it?"

"Not much else to learn except he choked her before he cut her. Finger indentations under the chin and in the throat."

"Could be fingerprints in the flesh."

"Not unheard of. Crime Scene labs can sometimes recover prints from flesh." He turned to the tech. "But I think he wore gloves. So, what's this about a poem, and Sara Cameron?"

"See for yourself." The crime scene tech handed him a clear plastic evidence bag with a slip of paper inside. "It was pinned to the front of her dress."

There were faint, watery pink stains on the edges of the paper. Lon looked closer but saw no trace of finger prints in the stains; whoever wrote the note had been gloved. Then he read the block printed verse aloud,

"Soldiers and sailors have no hearts
For war they plot and oft.
Their selfish wishes earn no mercy,
So with their heads let's off."

He read it again, silently, then shook his head. "This is bullshit."

"What, you don't appreciate good poetry, Raney?"

"Yes, I do, but this isn't it." He handed the evidence bag back to the tech. "This is written in block print, but the ones I saw by Sara Cameron were longhand. Hers aren't Shakespeare in quality either, but this is rhyming trash."

Reed's full, pink-skinned face sank into an uncharacteristic somberness. "True. Let's take this outside." He led the way out, leaving the crime scene tech behind. They walked to Reed's unmarked car, "...away from the lookie-loos," he said, away from those who lingered hoping to get a glimpse of the body being removed.

Reed leaned against the car, oblivious to its ever-present coating of dust, crossed his arms over his chest and began to tap the curb with the tip of one shoe. He didn't look at Lon when he said, "You're right, Raney. Whoever did the deed wrote the stupid poem and we'd be crazy to like Cameron for it." He jerked his head toward the garage. "This woman was big," he said, "a lot bigger than Cameron. Cameron isn't strong enough to do what was done to that woman."

Lon nodded. "The guy trying to pin it on her had his head up his butt."

"Just to be sure she wasn't involved somehow, I called County Psych and she's still there. Has been since we sent her out a week ago. Lucky her psychiatrist was there, a Doctor Sirota. He forgot the HIPPA crap long enough to tell me she's there, in a locked ward, otherwise I wouldn't have learned squat."

Lon's head tilted. "Why did you release her from Detention? Did the County Attorney decide not to prosecute?"

"She's still out on that decision. We released her to the hospital because she had what the shrink called a 'acute psychotic episode.' Staff at the Detention Center said she went stiff as a board, like turned to stone. Screamed for someone named Michael, then wouldn't talk, wouldn't move. Catatonic. At the hospital they've been shooting her up with some heavy-duty juice. The Doc said she's just now starting to come back from La La Land."

"Who is Michael?"

"Maybe no one. I heard from the orderly at the base that she yelled that name a lot the night she broke in and while they were holding her there, like he would appear out of nowhere and rescue her."

"Did you follow up?"

"Hard to follow up on just a first name. What I can tell you is that none of the homeless we questioned knew of a Michael and an older woman hanging out together. Not one of them knew her name or recognized her picture. She kept a low profile."

"More reason to work together. We have homeless sites in the county you haven't checked."

"Yeah. I think we can get approval for an inter-agency task force. The FBI is back in the picture already."

"Why? They turfed her to local and now they're taking her back?"

"They heard she freaked out when that brainless reporter told her Cindy Cameron was murdered. The Feds gave themselves a do-over on whether or not the two were related. Turns out they are mother and daughter."

"How did that escape them in the first place?"

"Cindy's real name was Ruth. She wasn't born in a hospital, she was delivered at home and the birth was registered by Sara a week or two later. On the birth certificate she used her own name as 'Mother' but under 'Father' she put 'Evil Smiles'."

Lon laughed. "Any relation to the daredevil?"

"We'd have to get DNA to confirm it. That's how the FBI nailed it with Cindy and Sara. Isn't it amazing that it takes months for us to get DNA results, but the Feds can finesse it in weeks?"

"National security, Reed. Have some respect for our guardians of freedom."

"Yeah, yeah. You know this just complicates our job."

"Right. Instead of a relatively harmless but wordy psychotic, we have another murder suspect on our list."

"What list?"

"A short list. Okay, a blank list. But we're working on it, Reed. Have some confidence."

"I have no confidence that the woman murdered her own daughter."

"No, it doesn't seem likely but we deal with the unlikely all the time."

"How about the M.E.'s report?"

"Yeah, it says the bullet trajectory aimed slightly downward. That means the shooter had to be someone taller than Cindy, or her mother stood on a rock to shoot her only daughter."

"I'd put a 'U' for unlikely next to Sara Cameron's name."

"Agreed, but I'd still like to see the inventory of items in her station wagon."

"It's a mile long and reads as boring as the telephone book, but I say you're welcome to it."

• • •

Chapter Twenty-Five

Allie pulled into the parking lot of the Psychiatric Hospital, which staff members humorously called The Resort. One reason she liked the two days a week she worked at the hospital was the element of surprise. She never knew who or what she would face. The private practice she was trying to establish didn't keep her busy five days a week and the hospital gave her a fascinating set of different experiences that required different skills. It was a challenge she hoped kept her alert and learning.

On the down side, many of the hospital patients were psychotic and sometimes abusive or violent. Most of the psychiatric nurses and psych techs had been kicked, punched, spit on or hit with foreign objects, including chairs. Allie had never experienced an assault, although one patient, who had to be twenty-five years her senior, referred to Allie as "that old bitch," a name so inappropriate it bounced off her back. As difficult as the hospital population could be, she liked spending professional time with people desperately in need.

When Dr. Sirota had asked her to see a new client she was shocked to discover the woman was the newspaper's "Peace Poet," Sara Cameron, the mother of her friend who had been murdered. She hesitated to take on the counseling job because ethical considerations always came into play if a therapist had some connection to a client. The issue was whether she could remain both objective and effective in counseling the client.

She had discussed her hesitation with the doctor and reflected long and hard. In the end she knew her compassion and motivation to help the woman would be no more, no less, and no different than what she experienced with other seriously mentally ill clients.

The next morning she read Dr. Sirota's psychiatric assessment of Sara, which made no attempt to downplay the severity of the woman's mental illness. The signs and symptoms that helped him reach a diagnosis for Sara were her paranoid delusions as well as delusions of reference and last, her failure of the ability to think abstractly. He tested her abstract thinking by asking her to interpret the meaning of common allegories. To the one about not crying over spilled milk, Sara said that you can always mop it up and only cry-babies cry over a little thing like that. Her thinking was consistently concrete, and would probably remain so even if other symptoms of schizophrenia were held at bay by antipsychotic medications.

Allie's office in the corridor of the north wing of the hospital always felt chilly, even in the blazing heat of July. Here, no windows allowed the golden sunlight or relieved the indifferent ambience of uncarpeted floors and smooth plaster walls. Down the corridor from Allie's were three other offices, for the head nurse, the psychiatrist and the director of the facility. On one end of the corridor was a double-door exit to the outside and at the other the door to the ward where patients were housed.

At today's appointment time Allie left her desk and looked down the hall to watch Sara approach, escorted by the psych tech. Sara wore the unit's uniform for men and women – cotton scrubs in an orange color which cast a muddy hue on her wrinkled face. Her shuffling gate was demanded by the over-sized rubber flip-flops she wore, all adding to an impression of age and fragility.

It struck Allie that Sara bore no resemblance at all to her daughter. She was short and wiry in stature while Cindy had been above average in height and full-bodied. Sara's short, salt and pepper hair indicated she was not the one who had endowed her daughter with a head of glorious red hair.

Allie stepped forward to greet her but before she could speak Sara demanded, "Who are you, and why do you want to talk to me?"

"My name is Allie and I'm a counselor. Doctor Sirota asked me to talk to you about losing your daughter – so much sadness. Please, come and sit down for a minute."

Sara entered the office slowly then sat down in the chair near the door, rigidly upright and unsmiling. "I didn't lose her, she ran away with a Marine."

So, no time for the pleasantries, Allie told herself. "Uh, yes, I understand. You hadn't been in touch with her for years, had you?"

"Just because I couldn't find her."

"And what did you learn about her recently?"

Sara looked down at her feet. Finally she looked up, her face blank, her voice emotionless. "She's gone. Three times she's gone."

"Three times? How can that be?"

"Gone when she left me, just a teenager. Gone when God's voice told me she was gone, there in the Kofa. Told me it was a sacrifice I had to accept so I could concentrate on saving this place from Armageddon. And gone the final time when the newspaper lady showed me her picture."

"Did the newspaper lady tell you why she's gone?"

"You mean that someone murdered her? Yes, that's the lady's job, the news. Now I'd like to go back and finish my poem." She shifted in her chair, but Allie didn't budge from hers. Her intuition had told her counseling Sara would not be easy. Establishing rapport would be challenging but if things went well she might eventually be able to understand the origin of Sara's desire to prevent an imagined global conflagration. She asked, "You're writing the poems to try to prevent a war?"

"Isn't that worth doing? You got any ideas for saving people?"

Allie refused to be disarmed. She said, "Sara you look like you might be cold. Would you like me to ask for a blanket to wrap around you?"

"No. No thank you."

Allie leaned back in her office chair and crossed her legs in a gesture of ease she didn't feel. "So you get ideas to save people. Where do you get those ideas?"

"Different ways, different times, different people."

"Oh, do I know any of the people you're talking about?"

"Could be."

"Let's find out. What are their names?"

"My conscience speaks to me. She doesn't have a name."

Allie smiled. "I guess not. Mine doesn't either. But if everyone heard the voice of their conscience and paid attention, we'd all be better off, wouldn't we?"

"Sure enough."

"Do you hear other voices, Sara? Do you hear voices telling you to do things, or saying bad things to you?"

"The only bad one is Borbour. I call him Borbour for short."

"Oh, Barber. What kinds of things does Barber say to you?"

"That I ate too much or ate the wrong things. Oranges and tomatoes, that acidy stuff sets my stomach to growlin' something awful. He's a nag with a grudge, that Borbour."

Allie stopped with the next question on the tip of her tongue and stared at her client. The word *borbourigmy*, a medical term for a noisy gut, came in a flash, along with the knowledge that this woman was playing with her. Sara was not willing to reveal herself. She didn't trust Allie yet. Allie tried again. "Sara, have you ever heard different voices that other people can't hear?"

"You mean like auditory hallucinations? Naw. That's for crazy people, and I'm not crazy. I might be the only sane person on this poor, doomed planet."

"Is the planet doomed? It would help if you'd tell me more."

"Wars and hatred is why it's doomed. People cutting people's heads off and those heathen countries getting nuclear bombs. I stopped reading the papers years ago, but I still hear about it, like it or not."

"There is a lot of bad news in the papers. But I think the idea of a doomed world might have come to you before. When was the first time you had those thoughts?"

Sara's eyebrows lifted, as if she was startled by the question. She remained silent for a very long time. Allie waited, hoping she hadn't triggered an abreaction, a memory of trauma that could catapult her client back into psychosis. Finally Sara began to speak and Allie knew the question had by-passed Sara's defenses and summoned a memory.

"When I was seven years old, my best friend Betsy died. I knew what that meant, from our dog that died. I asked if Betsy fell down a well or if a mountain lion got her, or a rattler. They told me no, it was a germ. I didn't understand germs. I asked my teacher. She told me germs are little beasts so tiny we can't see them, and they're everywhere. She said they kill a lot of people, even babies and kids, without people knowing they're even there."

"That must have been a very frightening thing for a seven year old to hear."

Sara gave her a faint smile. Allie waited without speaking. Finally Sara said, "You're too old to be one of the nine hundred."

"Nine hundred?"

Sara began to rock back and forth in her chair, her flip-flops scraping the floor. She recited in a sing-song voice,

"Youth sees a peace-maker as an enterprising fox
but to old destroyers, peace is so unorthodox.

With a satisfied smile that said she had just had the last word, Sara stood, opened the office door, walked down the corridor and stopped at the locked steel door to the ward. She glanced back at Allie, who had followed close on her heels. Allie keyed open the heavy door and summoned the psych tech inside with a wave of her arm. Sara walked back into the ward.

Allie returned to her office shaking her head. She was fascinated by her glimpse into what might be the origin of Sara's paranoia and was eager to learn more. Nevertheless, the woman's name calling had gotten to her. She knew not to take these things personally but when she sat at her desk she bent her head and rested her face in her cupped palms. *I'm barely pushing fifty, yet I get tagged "the old bitch" and an "old destroyer."*

• • •

Chapter Twenty-Six

Allie knew that during her three weeks at the Mental Health Clinic's inpatient unit, Sara was also seen and assessed by a second psychiatrist, who agreed with Dr. Sirota that her diagnosis was paranoid schizophrenia and she was gravely disabled. That diagnosis and that designation meant Sara would be classified as seriously mentally ill.

The process of court-ordering her to submit to both in-patient and out-patient treatment followed. The hearing took place in the Center's large conference room. A judge experienced in mental health law presided. Sara was present with her attorney, appointed for her because she was indigent. There to testify that she must be court-ordered for treatment were the two psychiatrist, two psychiatric nurses and one of the psych-techs.

Allie had been asked to testify, but she refused. She wanted to keep the marginal amount of trust that Sara had been able to place in her. She knew the hearing was a formality; no one would testify that Sara was *not* disabled by a mental illness. When they released Sara from the Unit, Allie would continue to see her on an outpatient basis once a month and Sara would report to the Clinic monthly, where Dr. Sirota would inject her with anti-psychotic medication in an extended release form called a decanoate, which lasted thirty days.

Allie's next meetings with Sara went well. She again talked about her childhood. The death of her friend at age seven had truly been a pivotal event. It filled her young mind with vague but pervasive fear, a malignancy waiting to metastasize into paranoia. Trauma triggered its dissemination into schizophrenia.

By the time she reached age twelve, Sara's reaction to the awareness of invisible organisms that kill was the desire to fight them, to become a bacteriologist or even a doctor. But she was one in a family of seven children born to uneducated and hard-working farmers on five acres of land in Oklahoma, where hard work and stoic acceptance of hardship were the prime virtues. She and her family lived much as the early pioneers had. When Sara's younger brother broke his arm, her father set it, splinted it with sticks and it healed. When Sara came down with measles one summer, she kept on working in the fields, feverish and red with rash every scorching day for a week. Her eyesight suffered in consequence.

It wasn't surprising to Allie when Sara spoke about her parents' belief that cities were proverbial "dins of iniquity" and education was an indoctrination that contradicted God's laws. They refused to send her to school after the eighth grade.

Allie needed to talk with someone more knowledgeable about Sara and her prognosis. She stopped by Dr. Sirota's office a week before Sara's release date. The room appeared comfortably furnished and comfortably cluttered with stacks of books, papers and professional magazines. The psychiatrist's tie hung over the back of one of the chairs and his desk held two empty coffee mugs. He had just hung up the phone when he saw her in the doorway.

"Come in, come in, Allie," he said, sitting back in his chair, a warm smile implying he welcomed the interruption. "What are you up to today?"

Allie sat in the chair across from him. "Doctor Sirota…"

"Call me David. We'll both be more comfortable."

"Oh, okay. Well, I just want to talk about Sara Cameron a bit. I think I may have stumbled on one of the factors that contributed to her psychosis. The trouble is, having the key to paranoia doesn't seem to unlock it."

"You're exactly right. Welcome to the world of hospital mental health, or behavioral health as we now like to call it. We don't treat the kind of ills that knowing the cause of produces the cure."

"But – David – she is so intelligent. It seems she should be able to see the flaws in her thinking."

"We haven't given her an IQ test but people with paranoid schizophrenia are often highly intelligent and certainly capable of higher levels of education."

"When they're psychotic it's hard to see that," Allie said.

"I know. Schizophrenia is a strange disease. When it's in remission, many people behave as normally as you and I. When it surfaces, it produces some of the most bizarre and disturbing behaviors of any mental illness."

Allie nodded. "I've seen some of that first hand. Not pretty. I heard that psychiatrists used to think it was the result of bad parenting – bad mothering, actually."

"Bad mothering or bad parenting in general probably contributes to any psychiatric diagnosis. But schizophrenia occurs at about the same percentage rate in every population in the world, so we know it's a product of nature, not nurture. It has a biological basis. It's in people's genes."

"Then why is it still such a mystery?"

"The brain is complicated, in case you haven't noticed." He smiled at her again, and stretched with his arms over his head. He leaned further back in his chair before he continued, "Studies of identical twins show that although they're both equally predisposed to the illness biologically, one will manifest it and the other won't."

"How can that be?"

"Life happens. Traumas of various kinds can bring it on. From what you've already told me, I'd say being denied the education she thought was so important was Sara's trauma. If she had become a professional whose job was to combat diseases, that might have relieved her fear and given her a focus for her intellect. She might have become a successful doctor or researcher with no trace of mental illness."

"Or she might have been a poetess."

Dr. Sirota smiled and put his hands on the arms of his chair as he leaned back a bit more. Allie thought his smile was now indulgent.

"Well, listen to this one," she said. She pulled a scrap of paper from the folder in her hand. "After we talked about how hot it's getting she recited it to me. I liked it so much I wrote it down. It's about seasons having moods.

> *'Winter is cool esprit. Spring seems, to me*
> *Impetuous glee. Summer's tranquility.*
> *Autumn, obviously is Nature eager to acquaint*
> *the world with all her stirring moods of paint.' "*

"Just keep her talking, Allie, and writing poetry if that's what she wants to do."

In their twice-weekly sessions, Sara's personality emerged more as her thinking became more logical and organized. Allie knew she was coming to like Sara and she struggled to stay professional. She believed that Sara came to like her, too. The woman always gifted her with a few lines of verse in farewell when she left the office.

Their last meeting in her office also signaled a beginning. Allie asked Sara how she adjusting to being on an antipsychotic medication.

"It has its good points and its bad points. I feel just a little more connected with people and with things around me, you know?"

Allie nodded.

"But I also feel slower, somehow, like things are more of an effort. Even my mind feels slower at times, like someone poured syrup on my brain. My poetry doesn't come to me quick and clear like it used to. And I'm gaining weight. My appetite has never been this strong."

Allie told her, "I know this is a hard adjustment for you, Sara. But now you have a place to live and a chance at a more normal life, a more comfortable lifestyle."

"I was comfortable before and I don't give a hoot about any kind of style."

Allie had no answer for that. Finally Sara said, "I know what you're talking about. Normal people don't sneak onto military bases or get arrested."

"I didn't mean it that way, Sara, I …"

"It's okay. I can still write poetry, even if it is harder. As long as I just hand the pages to folks instead of pasting them up everywhere, I can still get the word out."

Allie nodded "yes." She had not succeeded in shaking Sara's

core delusion, that it was her responsibility to save the world from destruction. And who was she, anyway, to deprive a woman of such a cherished goal? Still, she wanted to mitigate Sara's fear, if just a little.

She moved her chair a bit closer to her client's. "Sara, last night I was reading a biography of H.G. Wells. Do you know his name?"

"Oh, the War of the Worlds guy. Why?"

"Here is some of his advice." She reached back for a note pad on her desk and read from it. "He said, 'While there is a chance of the world getting through its troubles, I hold that a reasonable man has to behave as if he were sure of it.' "

Sara shook her head. "But a reasonable *woman* can still have her doubts."

Allie had to let it go. "Since this is our last session, do you have any questions for me, anything I can do for you?"

"There is one thing."

Allie felt pleased and wary at the same time. "What is that?"

"You said the County buried my Ruth when no one claimed her body."

"I'm sorry, but that's true. In the cemetery in Somerton."

"But I know her spirit isn't there. I want to go where my daughter saw the last light of day. I want to put a cross where she died, and flowers. She might have been misguided, but she was a good girl, my Ruth."

"Yes. I knew her, Sara. We were friends."

Sara sat bolt upright. "Friends? You were friends with her? Why didn't you tell me?"

"I didn't think it was important for you to know. You had enough to deal with, coming to terms with your diagnosis and being court-ordered for treatment. The fact that I knew Cindy – Ruth – made me want to help you more."

"You have." Now there was reserve in Sara's face and voice.

"Sara, I know they found her body in the Kofa, but I don't know where. It's a big place but I do know someone who knows and she might be willing to take you there."

"Will you come?"

"I don't know if I should. I don't normally ... well, I'll ask my supervisor. But some of the birdwatchers she hung out with might want to go with you. They loved her, too."

• • •

Chapter Twenty-Seven

Lon threw the three-page inventory of Sara's belongings on his desk and leaned back in his chair. His phone was on speaker. "I need to go through them, Reed, before you give them back to her. There could be something there that just might be important."

Reed's sarcasm came through clearly. "What, a Shakespeare sonnet? Get real, Raney."

"And I want to interview her. You said they released her from the psych unit?"

"Yeah. They put her up in that little bungalow complex on Avenue C, with the rest of the seriously weird. I imagine she'll agree to meet with you. A month ago, all you'd hear from her is vapor-speak but they tell me she actually makes sense now. And when the Assistant County Attorney dropped all the charges she made it clear to the little lady that she has to be on good behavior."

"Yeah. More when I get there."

The Yuma Police Department's evidence room reminded Lon of his grandmother's basement: dark and stuffy, an aura laden with possibilities where a breath-smothering, uncounted number of objects leaked emotion and murmured previously untold stories.

He shook off the desire to browse and pulled twelve boxes marked "Cameron" off the shelves, sneezing only twice in the process. He found a folding chair and sat in one of the wider aisles, surrounded by cardboard cartons marked with her name and date of arrest. He quickly examined and then pushed away four heavy boxes filled with books and went through the others. He shook his head at plastic evidence bags filled with pencils and pencil shavings, hair clips, underwear, lawn ornaments, an old toaster, half-burned candles, and framed pictures with religious themes. Soon, he ceased to be surprised at anything he found. He placed each item on the floor and when he reached the bottom of the box he put all of them back.

At the bottom of the eleventh box he pulled out a bagged pair of sneakers. He held his breath. A look at the soles released an explosive exhale. They were the same brand and size as the one he had cast at the scene of Cindy Cameron's murder. Two distinctive markings on one sole matched the cast markings.

• • •

"Reed, you've got to sign these out to me." Lon held the evidence bag with the shoes in one hand and wiped his forehead and then his nose on his handkerchief with the other.

Detective Reed cocked his head. "Your own Nikes not doing it for you, Raney?"

"Very funny, Reed. These could be the shoes worn by the person who killed Cindy Cameron. I need to double check them against my cast of the print, and I need to keep them safe."

"They're safe here."

"Let's not get into this turf thing, Reed. We're a task force, remember? Just get your evidence clerk to sign them out to me, and you might get some of the credit when we arrest the suspect."

"You're a demanding cuss aren't you?"

• • •

What used to be a 1970's motel was now a residence provided by the housing department of the County Mental Health Clinic. It provided basic shelter for a few seriously mentally ill clients who had been court ordered for treatment. Most of them had been homeless before entering the system, and this housing arrangement was preferable to the other alternatives – a group home or a board and care facility. Residents here were required to be compliant with medications and willing to accept supervision by case management staff.

Nine separate bungalows of salmon-colored stucco, room-with-a-bath size, formed an open square around a courtyard of compacted dirt. In the blinding heat and glare of a late July afternoon, nine window-mounted air conditioners hummed a promise of relief. Next to front doors, patched and faded walls held white plastic letters of the alphabet. Lon knocked on the door of unit D, Sara Cameron's new home. Silence from within, while the window curtains in other units parted and curious eyes inspected him. He knocked again.

The door opened a crack, and Sara Cameron's face looked up into his. "Who are you and what do you want?"

"Lon Raney of the Yuma County Sheriff's Department, Mrs. Cameron."

"Don't call me Mrs. I never married the man. The Good Lord punished me by taking away my love child, my Ruth. The innocent often pay for the sins of the wicked."

"Uh, that's what I'd like to talk to you about, Sara. I'm looking for the person who – who harmed her. Can I come in?"

"A godly woman never entertains a man in her room. But you look genuine. If my counselor can be here, then it'll be okay. I'll call her. Give me your number."

Lon scribbled the number of his personal phone on the back of his card and handed it to her. She took it and slammed the door. Lon walked away, wondering at the steel in this small woman's spine and at what must be a scrambled maze of mutated neurotransmitters in her divergent brain.

An hour later he received a call from Allie Davis, who he remembered from the murder investigation. He returned to Sara's housing unit. Allie opened the door. They shook hands. When he entered Sara remained seated on the twin bed. It was covered with a bright blue crocheted spread and someone had added other touches of color in an attempt to enliven the institutional ambiance of the room.

Sara inspected Lon, then turned to Allie. "You two know each other."

"Detective Raney talked to me about your daughter soon after – after they found her. I told you that Cindy and I were friends, so it was natural that the Sheriff's Deputies thought I might know something that would help them." She motioned Lon toward the only chair in the room and went to sit on the bed beside Sara.

Lon resisted the need to mop his forehead again. The window air conditioner made valiant noises but provided negligible relief against an outside temperature well above one hundred. He looked at Sara's feet again; he'd taken a quick glance an hour before when she stood in the doorway. Getting the information he needed required the direct approach. "Sara, I'd like to know about the Nike sneakers we found in your truck."

"My truck? You went through my things? When do I get them back? When do I get my truck back? They said I wasn't under arrest anymore, so you've got no right to them."

"Yes, you're right. Detective Reed has filled out the paperwork to release the truck and all your belongings to you, except the sneakers. They might be connected to your daughter's murder."

"I don't understand. How could that be?"

"We don't understand either, Sara. The sneakers are too large for you by at least three sizes. Who do they belong to?"

"They belong to me since they were in my truck. But I see what you're getting at. I can't rightly say who they belonged to before I got them."

"Where did you get them?"

"Most likely at the Goodwill. I shop there sometimes."

Lon had anticipated this kind of dead end to his inquiry, but he wasn't finished. "I understand you have a friend named Michael. Could it be the sneakers belonged to him?"

Allie started to shake her head at him, but his look silenced her. His attention returned to Sara. As experienced as he was with interrogation, her face told him nothing. It held the blank expression called a 'flat affect.'

Then her eyes and mouth softened, melting into both wistfulness and embarrassment. "Michael, Michael, my friend. I miss him."

• • •

Chapter Twenty-Eight

On Yuma's Main Street, the fenced patio at Lute's Casino felt shaded and almost cool, thanks to the misters that lined the eaves of the roof. Their fine spray of water cooled the dry air and coaxed the patio temperature down to the low 90's. Tourists bent on gambling often discovered to their consternation that Lute's was not actually a casino, but a pool hall, domino parlor, pin-ball arcade and restaurant with patio seating. Built in 1901, it underwent several incarnations of use before landing in the hands of the Lute family.

Lute's drew locals as well as tourists. It appealed to bikers, pool players, domino grandmothers, business men out for lunch, and gaggles of kids lined up at noisy game machines. The kitschy decor featured walls lined with posters, celebrity photos, Western memorabilia and artifacts, all capped by a mannequin's foot protruding through the ceiling in the main salon.

Lon and Kim had a rare same day off and decided to meet there to talk, drawn by the home-spun but inventive menu. The din inside the main room challenged normal conversation and few patrons braved heat of the patio so it was a place they could talk in some privacy.

Lon arrived first and requested only a glass of water while he waited for Kim. He downed it in one long gulp, remembering the days before the western droughts and global weather weirding, when tall glasses of ice water greeted each diner whether they wanted it or not.

Through the open doorway into the restaurant he saw men in jeans chalking their pool cues and ladies at a round table intent on their domino tiles. In the corner, a senior citizen with grey hair and paunch pounded away at an old upright piano. He wore jeans held up by suspenders over a faded plaid shirt, cowboy boots and a sweat-stained straw cowboy hat. The plinking notes of his piano drifted out as backbeat to the racket made by diners and players.

Kim arrived a few minutes late, leaving behind in the main room a trail of male gawkers. One youth with no character but abundant acne marking his face had followed her out to the patio. Lon rose, smiled at Kim and glared away the would-be Casanova.

Kim wore white today, a soft cotton shirt with a collar, khaki shorts and white running shoes. She had threaded her long pony tail through the back of a white baseball cap. She looked back at him and smiled. Since the night someone had attempted to murder Kim they had mutually chosen to meet in public places like this, which were not conducive to carnal thoughts much less carnal actions.

The waitress interrupted his introspection, took their order and soon they were dining on Lute's best cuisine. When their conversation turned to the Cameron investigation Lon looked around to be sure no one would overhear.

"You're saying this Michael person might not be imaginary after all?" Kim bit into her Lute's signature special, a hot dog burger, while her eyes remained fixed on Lon's face.

"It's a possibility he might be real. Remote, but we can't afford to dismiss it until we investigate."

"How can you investigate someone who might not exist?"

Lon wiped a string of cheese from his chin and finished chewing before he answered. "We'll do DNA on the sneakers. If we get a male ID, we'll run it through NCIC for someone named Michael in this area who has a criminal record. Then we might link him to Sara Cameron. The other possibility, of course, is that the shoes belonged to someone not named Michael who was Cameron's killer."

"Sounds promising."

"Not really. Chances are we won't get a single readable DNA or we'll get too many to sort and classify. They found the shoe in her truck jammed under the mountain of junk she kept in there. How many DNA traces do you think it could hold?"

"Not my area of expertise."

"If she got the shoes at Goodwill like she said, they would have collected DNA as people touched them or tried them on. It may be a dead-end, even if there is a real Michael." He pushed away his plate with remains of a grilled cheese sandwich with green chilies and drank his beer while he looked at her over the rim of the mug.

Today it was impossible to ignore the vital physicality of his platonic friend. He would never get enough of looking at Kim's tawny skin, jet-black hair and strong-boned face that somehow conveyed integrity as well as pride. He admired her beauty, her direct personality, her energy. He wondered about the pain and horror he had seen in her that night in her bedroom. It had to be the result of some sort of sexual trauma, a rape or molestation. And if she had been raped, would she have told him she was a virgin? So, molested as a child? What a devastating effect it had made on her sexuality. But other women were able to recover from that kind of atrocity, and he trusted that she would, too.

Pain leaking from horrible memories was not the only vampire-like emotion bleeding Kim's spirit. He could sense unexpressed feelings of anger, maybe guilt, and maybe even shame. Where did they come from? He couldn't untangle it all. And if he didn't understand her, didn't really know her, why had she captured him like this?

She munched a French-fry, smiling at him at the same time. His breath caught in his throat. He wondered if the secrets she guarded from him would remain a barrier between them, even after Cameron's murder was solved. If it ever was solved. How could he concentrate on Cameron, much less on the back-logged cases? Thoughts of Kim and her safety crowded out anything else when he wasn't with her. The thought that her life might still be in danger gnawed at him. Would she even survive to be in the relationship with him that he wanted and imagined every day?

She must have seen the questions in his eyes. She said, "Nothing suspicious at my place since we talked last night. No dark colored cars driving down my street at night, no one stalking me. The Sheriff's patrol cars still drive by a couple times every night, keeping an eye on me."

"The lead detective and I are working the case, but still no progress. We canvassed Wagner's neighborhood to see if anyone noticed him leaving the house that night, checked the only security camera he would have passed on the way to your place. Nothing."

Kim shrugged. "You know, it doesn't fit that someone who would do something as petty as file a complaint against me with the EMT Board would then try to kill me. He's looking less and less like a real suspect, isn't he?"

"Afraid so. So what about the Board – your EMT license?"

"Well…"

"What?"

"I did get a letter from the Board asking me to meet with them in Phoenix to give. . .what they called a preliminary, verbal explanation of a situation that led to a complaint against me. They didn't identify the complainant."

"We both know who it was, that son-of-a-bitch." It took a few minutes for Lon to stow his anger to be dealt with at a different time. "So. . ." He hesitated. "About Cindy Cameron. I don't want you to hang all your hopes on this, but you may be right about Winston Verbale. We're liking him more as suspect number one."

Kim leaned forward in her chair. "Why?"

"One of Cindy Cameron's bird-watcher friends came forward with the information that the morning Cameron was murdered she called saying she was going to Kofa with Verbale to spot a rare species of woodpecker – a 'Lewis' Woodpecker' is what she said."

"Are you going to arrest him now?"

"No. It's not even enough to get a search warrant for his home or his car. But we've got a photo of his black Mercedes and a picture of him from the newspaper – the political article from a few months ago. We're canvassing the area around her house and around his, showing them to the neighbors."

"That makes sense. Whether they went in her car or in his, someone must have seen them leaving or him coming back."

"The timing would have to fit, though. We know he went to the airport for his flight to Costa Rica. Unless someone saw her leaving in the car with him and then saw him coming back alone, it wouldn't be worth testimony in court."

Kim's chin came up, and she spread her hands in a gesture of mild exasperation. "Wouldn't it be worth knowing for sure that he did it?"

"It would. I want it solved too, Kim, but I've learned not to close my mind to any possibility until all the evidence is in." He shook his head to dismiss his own frustration and leaned back in his chair, stretching his legs under the table. His sneaker bumped hers, then their bare legs touched. He saw her eyes widen. He jerked his leg back. Did she think he was still pressing for a physical relationship? He smiled at her in a way he hoped was reassuring. She trusted him and he would not betray that by trying to seduce her. The idea of someday being her first lover was daunting enough without adding the psychological poison of guilt.

In the silence that followed their touch he considered telling her what he had been thinking about her safety and the Cameron case, but decided against it. His growing suspicion of Winston Verbale extended to what had happened to Kim.

If Verbale was guilty of Cindy Cameron's murder, maybe he knew that Kim had found the body, and feared she knew something that might incriminate him. Maybe he had a rifle as well as a hand gun and had been the one who tried to kill her.

The bullets and shell casings from the night of the attempted murder had produced no trail that might lead to Wagner, Verbale or any other shooter. Could there be something he hadn't done to help the detective in charge, even something not legally sanctioned? In his ten-plus years in law enforcement he had never before tried to bend the rules or circumvent procedures, but knowing who had tried to harm Kim would be worth it. Anything that kept Kim safe was worth it.

During his silence, Kim looked across the table at Lon and pondered the why and how of their attraction. He was too tall, too slender and not handsome enough to inhabit most women's erotic dreams. But then, she wasn't like most women. Maybe it was his intelligence and the way he looked at her as if there was something about her he wanted to know very much…but was patiently waiting for her to reveal.

During their lunch she had been mulling over her own plans and wondering if she should share them with Lon. Sara Cameron wanted to see the place her daughter had lost her life and had asked Allie to take her there. Allie passed the request to Kim, and she had agreed.

Her instinct was to tell Lon but for some reason she pushed it away, reasoning that he worried about her too much already.

She reached out to the mist descending from a nearby spigot. Gathering it on her fingers, she smoothed the moisture over her forehead and cheeks while she searched the strip of sky visible between the top of the fence and the roof. Not a cloud in sight, uniformly, unrelentingly blue. Finally she broke the thoughtful silence. "I hope the monsoon comes soon. It seems a little more humid lately, at least in the evenings."

"The rain will cool things off. Then, so much for the license plates and bumper stickers that say 'It's a dry heat'."

She nodded. "I know – the ones with pictures of a skull and cross-bones. In July and August they could picture a drowned rat."

Lon paid the bill with a generous tip in cash and they walked back through the restaurant to the exit. Their eyes were unaccustomed to the dimness indoors. They didn't see a well-dressed but rather ordinary-looking man standing at one of the game machines watching the action but Winston Verbale saw them. It shocked him as nothing lately had. *Kim the Indian squaw with the detective.* He froze, mind instantly racing to make sense of it. *They're together. Very together. What kind of game is this turning into?*

• • •

Chapter Twenty-Nine

Kim left her house in the grey light of dawn, determined to hike into the Kofa and back before that part of the Sonoran Desert came to a boil. She decided to leave her dog at home, knowing he would have loved the hike; but she reasoned that four people and a large dog in a small car was more like a circus act than a day trip.

Zayd's good-bye was very different from his tail-wagging, tongue-lolling greeting. He stood two feet back from the window, stock still, watching. He remained unmoving as long as she could see him. She wondered if he turned and went to his bed when she was out of sight, or lingered there at the window. She had tried to ease their parting by giving him a doggie treat before she walked out the door, but it went untouched until she returned. Then he would pounce on it and devour it in seconds.

It took Kim only fifteen minutes to pick up her passengers: Sara, Allie and Veronica, then just one more stop before heading north on Highway 95. She swung her Jeep Cherokee into a gas station and up to a pump. She announced in a loud voice, "Okay, everyone, law of the desert south-west: gas tank full, bladder empty!"

She got out and went around to the front passenger side, expecting to help Sara out, but Sara had already opened the door and headed for the building. Veronica followed her into the store. Veronica was in her early twenties but Kim thought she still had the lanky look of an under-active, under-fed, under-socialized teenager. Straight, muddy brown hair a shade darker than her eyes contributed nothing in the way of attractiveness.

Allie hung back to talk to Kim while she pumped gas. "Thank you for doing this, Kim. It's really important to Sara. For the last ten or twelve years she didn't know where her daughter lived or even if she was still alive. I think she needs to anchor her memories of Cindy with some geographical place. It will give her some closure, some peace of mind."

Kim leaned one hip against the vehicle. "I'm glad you were able to come along. I was a little uncomfortable with the idea of taking a hike with Sara and a bird-watcher I've never met."

"I know. Thanks again."

"I'm happy to do it, but this kind of trip sure isn't the tradition in my culture. Our ancestors – most Native American ancestors – didn't go near the place someone died. If it happened in a house, they burned it. I can't help wondering about Veronica and why she came along."

Allie said, "I don't know Veronica very well. I met her through Cindy. I have the impression the only things that really interest her are birds and eligible men. She has lots of knowledge about birds, can tell you about them all day long but I think men are a little more elusive and harder for her to get close to."

When Sara and Veronica returned, Kim and Allie took their turn in the restroom. On the road again, Kim and Allie soon paused their own conversation to listen to Veronica talk about Cindy. A group of Cindy's massage clients and bird-watcher friends had created a memorial service to honor her just a few days after her body was discovered. Veronica said she had missed the event so she was eager to pay her last respects to Cindy today.

When they reached the trail head, Kim parked the Jeep in the same spot it had occupied on the day she discovered Cindy's body. She switched off the ignition, suddenly deaf to the others' voices. A chill went through her, an unfamiliar sensation she didn't understand. Was it just the memory of Cindy's murder that was making the hair on the back of her neck stand on end? Or was it a super-sensitive awareness and warning of present danger? With effort, she managed to dismiss the eerie feeling as a remnant of Native superstition. Allie asked her a question. Grateful for the distraction, she busied herself with familiar pre-hike preparations along with the others.

Veronica took the caps off the lenses of her binoculars, hung it around her neck and pulled her field guide out of her backpack. Allie laced on her hiking boots. Sara donned a beige cloth hat with an exaggerated front brim and a back brim that flopped all the way down the back of her neck. Kim had turn away to hide her smile at how peculiar it looked. Last, before they set out, she checked the backpacks of the others and supplemented most of them with extra bottles of water.

Just minutes into the climb she pointed out that the cylinder-like Saguaro cactus, many of them fifteen feet high, had finished blooming. The cup-sized, waxy white flowers had been pollinated at night by bats and now were producing plum-sized fruit which would be harvested by some Native tribes and brewed it into an intoxicating drink.

She commented on the prickly pear cactus with clusters of succulent pads the size of small plates, bearing spines like toothpicks. In spring they had sprouted blooms along their edges which were now magenta-colored fruit covered with hundreds of stickers thinner than a hair. Some bore the bite marks of *javalina*. The pig-like *javalina* also savored the spiny green pads.

Kim's comments about the cactus didn't interest Veronica, who had been to Kofa as many times as Kim. She hung back with Sara, while Kim and Allie hiked side by side. A rattling sound stopped them. Sara, following close behind, bumped her head on Kim's backpack and stepped on her heel. Veronica stumbled while avoiding a collision with Allie and almost fell. A four-foot long Gila Monster burst from a nearby creosote bush and hurried away from them with a sinuous, almost serpentine gait caused by short legs on a wide body. It took a minute for the four women to watch it go, apologize to each other and sort themselves out.

During the last minutes of the hike Kim pictured the site the way she had last seen it and fervently hoped, for Sara's sake, that no visual trace or odor of death lingered there. She said to the others, "I think we're almost there, but let me go ahead to be sure. Just stay here and rest for a few minutes."

If evidence of the remains were discernable by any human senses at the actual site she would fudge a bit on the location. She stopped by the boulder and examined the place, a picture of the body vivid in memory. No, the blood and body fluids along with their odors had succumbed to the assimilating power of the desert. The place appeared no different than the terrain around it.

Kim walked with Sara to the spot while the others hung back a little. Sara stood looking down at the place in the dirt where Cindy's body had lain. She took off her backpack and lifted out an arm-full of jacaranda blossoms picked in Yuma that morning. They were withered now, the once-spectacular flowers, shaped like ruffled cornucopia, were a limp mass of purple color and sweet scent.

From her own backpack, Kim took the little white wooden cross Sara had brought. Together they set it up and Sara lay the bouquet at its base. They all stood in silence until Veronica said, "She was a mentor to me when I started bird-watching. She was so good. She could spot a tiny little Vireo in a mesquite from fifty feet away."

Allie put her arm around the young woman. "She was special," she said. "She loved her friends and her massage clients and she loved the birds. That was her motivation. That's why she did things – because she loved them."

Kim began to speak. "I didn't really know her, but I know she didn't deserve…" She glanced at Sara quickly, aware that Cindy's mother didn't need to hear expressions of her own outrage over the murder.

Sara said, "I think I need to talk to her alone."

The other three walked away until they were out of sight but close by, on the other side of the large boulder. They scuffed at the dirt with their hiking boots, looked for rocks big enough to serve as seats, and finally settled down. A minute later Veronica popped to her feet, reached for the binoculars hanging around her neck and sighted on something in a mesquite tree nearby, creeping toward it. Kim and Allie smiled at each other with silent amusement at her intensity.

"Cindy focused like that, too, when she had her binoculars," Allie said. She gulped and a few tears slid down her cheeks. Kim leaned to the side a bit until her shoulder touched Allie's, but said nothing. They watched as Veronica moved further away in pursuit of more birds.

When Sara began to speak Kim realized the words were clearly audible. She looked at Allie in concern and started to rise, intent on moving further away, but Allie shook her head and raised one palm. Kim settled back on the ground again, feeling guilty but unable not to listen. Allie didn't try to hide her own eavesdropping. Kim reasoned that Allie's motivation must be clinical curiosity. Allie had pushed the boundaries of a professional relationship with Sara by taking part in a personal activity like this one. Although she no longer saw Sara on a regular basis, Kim knew she liked Sara and still felt concerned about her.

"It never should have happened," Sara was saying. "No child should die before her own mother. And not this way, Ruthie." A long pause. "See here, the flowers I brought you? You always loved bright things that smell good. These came from a tree so big and such a glorious purple, like a giant bouquet set down in the dirt by the hand of God."

A long pause, with no sound at all. Kim pictured Sara arranging the wilted blossoms like a blanket on the dirt beneath the white cross. Then her voice again, "I'm sorry, Ruthie. . . we lost so many years together. I know I pushed you away. I wasn't thinking straight in those days. My fears and my stories confused you and they drove you away. I'm sorry. But why didn't you tell me?"

"Why didn't you tell me. . .?" The words went straight to Kim's gut. She pulled her knees toward her chest, wrapped her arms around her legs and rested her head on her forearms, closing her eyes. It could be her own mother's voice speaking to her. Was she herself like Sara's Ruthie? Had she run away to Yuma because of what she couldn't tell her mother? If only she had been able to tell – tell about a monster disguised as a seemingly ordinary man who had tormented her childhood for three years! If she had been able to tell, things might be different right now, different with her and different with her and Lon.

Sara's voice sounded louder and more strained. "I want you to know that I forgive you for running away. You found someone you believed loved you. We all follow love. We follow love or run from fear, Ruthie, get led by love or get pushed by fear. That was me, Ruthie, pushed by fear." A pause. "That is me."

Again, the words sounded in Kim's mind as if meant for her. She pushed them away – a cursed soliloquy in this cursed spot in the desert. She didn't want to think, didn't want to hear a truth rising from her heart to her mind.

Sara's voice again, "Ruthie, I never told you…I guess I hardly ever hugged you or even touched you. But I loved you."

Silence. Kim lowered her head on her arms again and surreptitiously wiped tears from her eyes. Sara's words had reached a part of her that she had tried to lock away, releasing an understanding that had eluded her all her life. In spite of her Apache forbearer's history of torture and violence, she acknowledge for the first time that she had been given a legacy of strength, passion, endurance and loyalty. And in spite of the secret she harbored that no mother wants to hear but every child should tell, she loved her mother deeply and she knew her mother loved her.

Silence. The warmth of the sun, the scent of baked earth and sage brush, the barely-felt passage of a light breeze carrying the soprano notes of bird song. Kim fell deep into thought. The woman she had been doubtful about and even wary of, Sara, was a person with insight and courage who had just delivered a message not meant for her, but deeply felt and personal to her.

• • •

Chapter Thirty

"I'm done." Sara's words and sudden appearance startled them.

Allie scrambled to her feet and started to hug the woman but checked the urge at the last minute. "How are you Sara? How do you feel?" she asked.

The older woman shrugged and stared into space for a moment. Then she spoke,

"Too hastily my heart and soul bow to pray,
Let all humans know much longer life.
Why should lives so soon go the dusty way
When dark still rules and wretchedness is rife?"

Her face showed no sign of tears or distress. When neither Allie nor Kim replied, Sara asked, "What's up there?" pointing to a faint trail leading up the side of a nearby canyon.

Kim answered, "The Queen Mine and Skull Rock."

"I want to see it. Let's go." She headed in that direction.

Kim and Allie looked at each other. Allie said, "It's not eight o'clock yet, and fairly cool. Do you think we have time?"

"It's not time we have to worry about, it's water." Kim reached for her backpack and checked the extra water she carried, then looked in Allie's backpack. "Yeah, I think we're okay. Veronica, how about a little side trip?"

Veronica slowly removed the binoculars from her eyes and turned. "Sure, why not?"

The trail led through more upper desert landscape decorated

by saguaro, teddy bear cholla, jojoba and creosote bushes. They climbed a saddle between hills and descended to a long, wide wash. The dry wash provided a footing that was sandy and relatively stable but steeper than anything they had climbed yet. In places the gravel was loose and deep, giving the feeling of walking on a sandy beach. After a quarter mile they entered high-walled Queen Canyon with jagged grey buttes close by and at a distance, high walls of brick red.

They hiked the wash in silence until Kim stopped and whispered, "Look!" High along the side of the mountain to their left, three prong-horn antelope walked sedately on their own path, seemingly unaware of the hikers. Kim shushed the others' exclamations of surprise. They stood quietly watching the graceful trio until they were out of sight. Kim smiled at Sara, whose mouth still formed a surprised "O." She said, "They knew we were here, but they decided we weren't a threat."

Sara looked Kim up and down as if she were seeing her for the first time that day. "Tell me about your family and your people," she said. She moved to walk beside Kim, while Allie and Veronica followed.

Kim was surprised but pleased. "I'm a Member of the Yavapai-Apache Indian Nation, if that's what you're referring to."

"Where is that, Kim?"

So many people hear "Apache" and think we're all one, but there are sub-divisions. Once our homelands covered parts of New Mexico and almost all of Arizona. Each clan had its own culture and traditions and territory."

"So which Apache are you?"

"By heritage, I belong to the Tonto Apache clan. The Yavapai-Apache Nation, the tribe I belong to, was actually two distinct tribes before they joined. We were enemies once, before the White Eyes came."

"I never understood that term, 'white eyes'."

Kim laughed. "I know. I didn't either. But after the settlers and then the army, the military relocated our band of Apaches to a reservations further south in Arizona. Now we're back in the Verde Valley, in central Arizona where we belong."

"So why did two tribes join, if you were enemies?"

"We decided that two tribes combined would fare better with

the government than two small ones separately."

Sara glanced at Kim and shook her head in understanding. "It's big and powerful, the government. It doesn't like women. All those boys, those soldiers trained to kill people. . ."

Kim was at a loss. Finally she said, "You know, our own ancestors held some very conflicting attitudes about women. When a girl had her first menstruation, they held a very elaborate puberty ceremony. It lasted four days and four nights, with the men's blessing. But when a woman committed adultery, they punished her by slitting her nostril."

Sara gave a guttural sound of disgust.

"They did it to make her so unattractive no man would want her."

And so it went, questions and answers exchanged as they hiked and took rest breaks to drink water and munch the energy bars Kim had put in her backpack "just in case."

When they resumed the hike after one rest break, Sara said, "I've seen movies about the Apaches. That Geronimo and some of the others came to a sad end, but the sins of the father…"

"What?" It sounded to Kim like a rebuke coming. "My father is not a sinner, and how can you say Geronimo was? You weren't there. You don't know."

"…are visited upon the children to the third and fourth generation."

Kim stopped, suddenly angry beyond reason. "What are you saying? That they all deserved what the military and the government did to them? That I and my Apache friends are all sinners?"

"No! Well, no more than any other tribe or race on earth. What I meant to say is that we all inherit. Some good things, some bad things. We have no control over it except what we do with it once it's ours. Seems to me you're doing a great good with yours."

Kim looked into the old woman's grey eyes for long seconds, then bent to wrap her arms around Sara's back in a hug. Allie had watched and listened to the exchange between them with alarm. She held her breath. Sara's face took on a look of discomfort, then she slowly lifted her arms and leaned into Kim's hug. Allie exhaled relief.

They hiked another half-hour. Veronica occasionally stopped to raise her binoculars at a bird, then trotted to catch up with the others. They passed a recently dug, open-cut mine, a tennis-court size gash in the rock with red tailings staining its center.

Kim stopped again, her eyes fixed on the sky.

Allie followed her gaze and saw nothing unusual. "What are you looking at?"

"That darkness in the distance. I can't tell what it is. It's too low to be a rain cloud. Anyway, monsoon storms never come this early in the day. And they come from the south-west, but that's to the north-east."

"Whatever it is, it's miles away."

"True." They continued to hike until the breeze began to stir creosote shrubs and the sky overhead took on a strange greenish cast. Again Kim stopped. The dark cloud definitely looked closer. Suddenly she said, "I know what it is. A *haboob*."

"What?"

"The word is Arabic. It means sand storm. Come on, we have to get to shelter. Fast."

Veronica laughed. "Kim, what's the big deal? It's miles away. Besides, we've had dust storms before in Yuma and survived."

"Not one like this, you haven't." She began a slow jog, and when she saw the others were keeping up with her, she increased the pace a little.

"Where are we going?" Veronica asked, her voice wavering in time with her jogging. Not waiting for an answer, she stopped. "We could just sit down here in the shelter of some bushes. The wash is deeper than ground level, so we'll be fine."

Kim shouted, "No!" and resumed the pace. Seconds later she looked back to see Allie with her hand on Sara's elbow, encouraging her to keep up. Veronica still stood on the trail, putting the caps on the lenses of her binoculars.

The wind felt stronger now, the leading edge of the storm bringing with it just a few fine grains of dirt and sand. Veronica bent over to pick up something from the ground. Her binoculars caught a gust of wind and began a metronome-like swing. The same gust blew Kim's long pony tail into a hectic dance. She motioned for Allie and Sara to keep going and went back.

"Veronica, we've got to get to better shelter. There's a cave up ahead, in Skull Rock. Just ten minutes more and we'll be there."

She turned toward the dark cloud. "It's getting closer. Come on, I'll help you."

Veronica shook off Kim's proffered hand. "Oh, all right." She fell into step again behind Kim, Allie and Sara in the lead now.

The wind picked up. Kim glanced back at the ominous, smoke-colored cloud. It wasn't just closer, it had grown. It filled the wide horizon and towered upward as far as she could see, obliterating the sky and moving toward them as if in pursuit.

Skull Rock came into view, still minutes away. "Look, that's where we're going," Kim shouted. The wind reached them, buffeting, before the wall of particles hit. Kim felt the grains of sand stinging her bare legs and face, and knew the others were feeling it too. She sprinted forward and took the lead again, up out of the wash and then west toward the Rock, the wind a tormenting enemy at their backs.

Fear gripped her, fear they would become separated when the cloud grew dense enough to obscure their destination. She reached back to grab Allie's hand and yelled, "Hold hands, make a chain. Put your heads down. Just watch the ground. Don't look up. Close your eyes if you have to." She squinted and blinked repeatedly to clear her vision. Air-borne particles invaded her ears, her nose and eyes. Her skin was being scoured raw by sand and dirt driven at sixty miles an hour and she knew the others were experiencing the same assault.

A minute later, she couldn't see her feet or anything that lay in front of her. She walked by instinct instead of by sight. Twenty more steps. They were almost on it before she saw it, the dark shape of Skull Rock, the openings up high were the eyes, the gaping mouth the entrance to the cave.

Closer. Ten more steps. The struggles of those behind telegraphed to her through the chain of linked hands, tugging on her. She imagined their fear and distress. She gripped Allie's hand tighter. Above the shriek of the wind she heard coughing. Someone yelled something unintelligible.

She stumbled into the cave, shallow but dark as a moonless night. With sand and dust in her eyes she could see almost nothing. She kept walking, trusting to memory there were no rocks or other barriers to stumble over. In twelve paces she reached the back of the cave. She pulled Allie to the rock wall beside her, and reached back to make sure Sara and Veronica followed. Yes, all here. Finally she sank to her hands and knees. The others sat around her, coughing and panting.

• • •

Chapter Thirty-One

The sound of the wind grew louder; the storm reaching its crescendo. Only a few weak down-gusts reached them at the back of the cave. Wind shrieked outside, now a background to the sound of their ragged breathing. Light filtered through the mouth opening of the cave, dim and grey as if seen through gauze.

Kim tried to blink the dirt from her eyes. Her vision cleared and adjusted to the darkness enough to reveal the others and a bit of their surroundings. "How are you, everyone? Sara, are you okay?"

Veronica yelled, "I can't see! There's sand in my eyes."

Sara coughed and cleared her throat. "Considering I've got enough sand in my nose, my eyes, my ears and my hair to fill a kid's sand-box, I feel pretty good, Kim. How about you, honey?"

Kim started to answer but instead a laugh erupted from her throat. Then they were all laughing, semi-hysterical, weak with relief. The laughter slowly died down. Kim felt cleansed of fear for the safety of the others, at least temporarily. She said, "Don't rub your eyes, Veronica. Let me help you. We'll wash them out with water. All of you. Sara, you're first." She pulled a quart of water from her back-pack. She tilted her head back and poured water in one eye, then the other. Then again, blinking as she poured.

"Why are you first?" Veronica asked.

"So I'll be able to see what I'm doing when I help you."

One by one, she irrigated their eyes. With their vision cleared a little, they used the water bottles to take long, cleansing gulps.

Allie stood to shake out her hair and clothing. The others were also beginning to take stock of themselves and their surroundings. Sounds of sobbing made Allie whirl around. "Veronica, what's wrong?"

"The birds! This will kill them! Think how many of them will die."

"They won't all die."

"Yes, but…"

"The rain will help. Usually rain follows a storm like this. Birds that don't catch a tail wind and coast all the way to California will be taking a bath soon. And think how lucky the other animals are. All the tanks will fill with water."

No response from Veronica.

The stygian blackness they encountered when they entered had become an eye-straining gloom. They sat facing the entrance to the cave, watching the storm. In truth, there was nothing to see except the occasional limb from a tree blowing past and uprooted plants whooshing by in transit. They were silent, each in her own thoughtful uncertainty. Finally Veronica said, "I saw a Black Phoebe before. They're migrants. They're usually back up north by now."

No one commented. Silence again, except for the wind. Gradually, the noise dwindled. In fifteen minutes it was down by several decibels. Kim rubbed her upper arms with her hands. "It's actually getting cool."

A rumbling sound in the distance drew her to the cave's entrance. She shouted back to the others, "Here comes the rain." They joined her at the entrance. Soon, a downpour of rain as dense as the wall of sand had been started to drench the earth. The first drops were strangely tinted rather than clear. "It's raining mud!" Veronica exclaimed.

"The rain is settling the sand and dust," Kim said.

Thunder sounded from miles away, again and again. In the distance, flashes of lightening shot from sky to earth in jagged bolts of blue and yellow. Drops of rain from the eye openings in the cave wall came faster, heavier, and the dirt underfoot became soggy. When the thunder sounded very close they retreated to the back wall.

Allie and Sara tried to make themselves comfortable on the

ground. Veronica stood leaning against the rock. "Is it going to come in here? Is it going to flood the cave?"

Kim answered quickly. "We're on a downward slope here and the wash is just to the east. Over there." She pointed. "The water will follow the wash."

"Then how can we get home? We came up the wash."

"We'll have to hike along the bank. It will be rougher going but we won't get lost. I know the way back, but I brought my GPS just in case. In a gully-washer like this, the terrain can get changed."

"You make it sound easy."

"It won't be. We will have to be careful. The footing will be tricky because the ground and rocks are wet and slippery. We'll buddy up and help each other. We'll be home by noon, if this stops as soon as I think it will."

"I hope it stops real soon. Being inside a skull – this place is creepy."

Sara and Allie had been listening. Sara said, "I know what you mean, honey. I have enough trouble being inside my own head."

Kim smiled at her, knowing her intent to lighten the others' mood. It helped to mentally shake off her annoyance at Veronica's constant questions and concerns. She stood and went to the entrance again. Allie followed.

"I'm sorry I got you into this, Kim."

"Are you kidding? This is more fun than I've had in months. It would be perfect if the others weren't here. Uh, I didn't mean that the way it sounded. It would be perfect if there weren't others here who are frightened and feel unsafe."

Allie simply nodded. They stood watching the rain. The storm lessened in intensity; the sounds of thunder moved further away and slowly faded to nothing but the rain continued.

Suddenly, Kim cocked her head. She turned to face Allie an instant before Allie turned toward her. "You heard that too, didn't you?" Allie asked. "What was that? An animal crying?"

"Sounds more like a human." They both paused again to listen to the noise, thin and reedy, distant and intermittent. After a minute or so, Kim said, "I heard the word 'help'."

"But…" Allie turned to look back at Sara and Veronica as if to reassure herself they were still there.

Kim said, "Don't. Don't say anything to the others. I'm going to see what's up. Just tell them I'm checking things out to see how soon we can head back." Without another word, she stepped outside. The raindrops that hit her were large, cold and hard-driven. She quickly moved out of sight of the others in the cave then turned her head slowly from side to side to locate the direction of the cry for help. Up-hill, and several hundred yards to the north-west.

She began to walk, slowly at first, assessing the footing and adjusting her gait, wiping the rain from her face with both hands and pausing briefly to listen. The sounds grew louder as she hiked; this had to be the right direction. After pushing herself to a faster pace, in six minutes she began to hear not only the shouts, but also made out sounds of panting, breathless curses and an occasional groan. Still, she saw nothing through the curtain of rain.

Watching her footing, she came to an abrupt halt at a dark patch on the ground. Then the illusion resolved its-self. It wasn't ground; it was standing water, a pool about twenty feet by twelve feet across and probably twelve feet deep, a natural tank, a water catchment device created by Nature that made survival for animals possible in this normally parched land. The tank's bottom and sides were of bedrock, slick as glass when wet. During severe droughts such tanks could go completely dry, but these days they were often replenished with water trucked-in by the Fish and Game Department. She had seen this particular tank on a map and knew its name: Charlie Died Tank.

She searched through the curtain of rain. There was a dark shape at the opposite side of the tank, the source of the anguished shouts.

She yelled, "Hey, who is that? Come over here."

No answer, nothing but splashing sounds. Then a dark head came into view, a face red with effort and distorted by fear. A man. A man she recognized. Amos Wagner. Stunned, she said nothing but stood looking at him.

"Don't just stand there! Get me out of here!"

A shudder that wasn't produced by the cold and wet shook Kim's body. *What is he doing here? This can't be a coincidence. Was he stalking her?* She blurted her thought, "What are you doing here?"

"Get...me...out...of...here!"

She stood, paralyzed by a flood of memories: his diatribe about her Apache ancestry, his threat to get her EMT license revoked, and the real possibility that he had tried to kill her.

• • •

Chapter Thirty-Two

Silent now, Wagner desperately clutched at the edge of the tank which had filled to overflowing. The lip of solid rock curved down toward him but in a few areas, soil had encroached on its banks. He frantically grasped at the illusion of solid earth. The shallow layer of soil melted under his hands and spilled into the water. He lunged forward, trying to gain a hold with his fore-arms. Again he failed. Around the tank, Kim saw evidence of many other tries at extricating himself. From the way the water near him roiled, she could tell his feet were trying unsuccessfully to gain leverage on the tank's vertical sides.

She knew from old photographs of the tank that skeletons of big horn sheep and mule deer lay at the bottom. They were victims of drowning during times of excess rain or had starved when trapped at the bottom when the tank was totally dry.

Suddenly, she pictured a human skeleton at the bottom and with it the thought, *I could leave him here to drown and nobody would know. I could tell Allie I saw no one here. What a relief if would be, and if he's the one who tried to kill me, what justice!* She looked at his now-silent struggles and the anguish on his face. Then the thought, *I could actually be enjoying this!*

But she wasn't. This gave her no pleasure at all. As soon as it registered, she shouted to him, "Stop struggling, you horse's ass. Just tread water and I'll get something to help you out."

The rain had dwindled to a drizzle, and finally she could see the desert around her. She spotted a *palo verde* tree with downed limbs at its base. She ran to it as quickly as the wet, rocky terrain allowed. She spotted a five-foot long branch that was almost as big around as her wrist. It looked fairly solid, the green bark indicating it had fallen recently. It felt firm rather than rotting and porous. She carried it back to the tank, dropped it to the ground, and pushed it out over the water. Before she could stabilize it, he grabbed at it with both hands and pulled frantically, hand over hand. It slipped toward him, entered the tank and submerged briefly, surfaced, then floated away behind him. He turned and swam after it, clutched it again. It was too thin to provide flotation but he paddled back toward the bank with it and tried using it in different ways to support a climb out. She watched. At last he gave up the struggle and pushed it away, still treading water. His panting soared to a hoarse scream.

She turned without a word. He screamed again, "Come back! Come back you freaking Indian! Don't leave me in here! Don't leave me!"

She walked to the tree again and saw a branch growing close to the ground that looked shorter but thicker than the other. She tried to wrench it off with her hands, then kicked and stomped on it with her feet until it broke. She dragged it back to the tank, dropped it four feet from the bank and through clenched teeth said, "This time, wait until I stabilize it before you grab it!"

With effort, she rolled a large, heavy rock toward the branch. Then she pushed the limb out toward Wagner. "Wait!" she screamed at him. She quickly rolled the boulder onto her end of the branch and added her own weight by standing on it.

Wagner had only thirteen inches of wood to work with, but it was solid. He grasped it like any drowning man would. Kim saw his arm muscles quiver as he levered himself up onto the branch, then inched forward, slithering along it like an alligator emerging from a swamp.

When he cleared the water up to his waist, she stepped back. He retched violently and vomited the contents of his stomach that were mostly water. He was oblivious to all else but regaining solid earth. He continued to crawl forward until his feet were clear of the tank and collapsed prone onto the wet soil. He lay and panted; she stood and watched. His fingers had the shriveled look of someone in the water for a long time. His cotton shirt and shorts clung to him like a second skin. His sneakers had somehow stayed on through the ordeal. His white socks were now brown with dirt.

His bedraggled condition reminded Kim of her own rain-soaked clothing. She pulled her shirt out in front to relieve the clammy feeling, and tugged down the crotch of her shorts. She felt in her zipper pocket for her car keys. Reassured, she brought her pony tail over her shoulder and squeezed water out of her hair. Then she backed further away from the half-drowned man and mentally prepared to defend herself from attack, although he looked too weak to be much of a threat.

Finally Wagner got to his hands and knees. Head still hanging down, he muttered, "Thank you."

"Think nothing of it, Shit-for-Brains. Now get up and let's go."

Wagner staggered to his feet, the task made more difficult by exhaustion and the heavy covering of wet earth on the front of his body and one side of his face. "Where? I don't think I can walk."

"Try."

He took two steps then stood with hands palm up and face raised to the sky, letting the drizzle wash him. He looked more closely at his palms. They were bleeding from several puncture wounds. He turned. "You! That was a *palo verde* branch. Those damned thorns tore me up!"

With that, Kim reached the limit of her patience and her tolerance. She stepped closer to him. "What do you think they did to me?" She displayed several bloody spots on her own hands. She grabbed his bicep and took a few steps toward the tank, dragging him along. "If you'd prefer, you can go back in for another swim and I'll pull you out with something more to your liking."

His face twisted in horror. He jerked back, stumbled and went down hard on his butt. Looking up at her he gasped, "No, no, I didn't mean it."

Kim sighed, and sat down on the rock. "Do you want to stay here?"

"No!"

"Okay. We're both going to rest a while. Then we're going back to Skull Rock and on the way you are going to clear up a few things that are troubling me." When she rose five minutes later and began to hike back he followed like an obedient child.

Soon the rain stopped completely. The sky showed forth in eternal blue again, permitting only a few scattered clouds for decoration as if proclaiming just another ordinary day, in which nothing at all unusual had happened. It brought a feeling of the surreal to Kim. She couldn't shake it off, and with it the thought that somehow this day held more significant than she could imagine.

Reaching Skull Rock took twice as long as it had taken Kim to reach the tank. It was a downhill walk but Wagner's exhaustion demanded a slower pace. They hiked in silence. In spite of her intention, she was not ready yet or perhaps just reluctant to learn the truth by questioning him.

They finally came in sight of the Rock to see the others standing outside the mouth of the cave. When they were closer Kim noticed Sara's face was both puzzled and frightened, while Allie smiled and nodded at her knowingly. No one spoke until Veronica took her eyes off Wagner and said, "Some woman have a knack for finding a man just about anywhere."

Kim led them safely down the mountain to her car, where Allie was given the job of driving the others home, while Kim turned back and hiked with Wagner to his car. In spite of his protests, she won the job of driving him home. She no longer felt any sense of threat from the man and on the way she pressed for more information about his reason for being in the Kofa. She gained enough information to satisfy her need to understand but the answers were not to her liking. Somehow she managed to contain her anger. Even Wagner didn't deserve to feel its impact. She would save it for its rightful target. It was her turn to knock on Lon's door in the middle of the night.

• • •

Chapter Thirty-Three

A call to Allie told her all the *haboob* survivors were back in their respective homes. Without questions, Allie picked her up where she waited outside Wagner's house and then drove her home in mutual silence.

Kim tended to Zayd while she thought about what she had just learned from Wagner. More than angry, she was furious. Furious at Lon. But he was at work now. She respected him and herself too much to interrupt his day with a confrontation so she used her anger-fueled energy to get through the usual day-off chores in half the usual time.

She skipped dinner and went for a run with her dog. By the time she returned different emotions had risen to moderate her fury and more questions troubled her mind. Sara's words and her own thoughts from early in the day repeated and repeated. Her mood moderated from anger to pensiveness and the plan to barge into Lon's home to confront him seemed less desirable.

As her usual bed time approached she wondered how she could avoid calling him tonight for their routine check-in. She hated the thought of speaking to him. But she had promised. She dialed the number. When he answered she said, "I'm okay but I'm in a bad mood and I don't want to talk right now. Later." She hung up.

After the ten o'clock news she decided to go to bed and try to sleep it off, deal with it tomorrow. At two a.m. she knew it hadn't worked. She got out of bed, showered, dressed and drove to Lon's house near Yuma's Smucker Park.

No light illumined his porch and she couldn't see a door bell. She knocked. No answer. A quick look into the peep hole in the door revealed a shadow approaching. The door swung open. Lon, wearing navy blue boxer shorts and nothing else, pulled her inside with his left hand and kicked the door closed. Only then she saw the gun in his right hand. He dead-bolted the door, put his gun on safety and placed it on an end-table before he spoke.

"Kim, what happened?"

She shook her head, unable to sort and express a flood of differing emotions. Finally she said, "Damn, I don't know where to start. Too much happened."

Lon waited.

"Why did you have Wagner following me?"

"Wagner! Wagner followed you? What did he do? You look okay. Are you okay?"

"I'm asking the questions now. Wagner said he was following Sara, not me. Why didn't you tell me?"

Lon shook his head. "Let's sit down. This could be a long conversation." He pulled her over to the sofa in the living room. "First, I want you to know that having Wagner come anywhere near you was not something I imagined when I initiated the tail on Sara. He didn't hurt you?"

"I'm hurt, but he didn't hurt me."

"I will break every bone. . ."

"I handled it!"

"Okay, I'm good with that. You need to know that we finally got a confirmation on Wagner's whereabouts the night some cowardly scum tried to kill you. He made cell phone calls that night. All pinged from a tower near his house, and a neighbor said she saw him take out the garbage around the time of the attack."

"I wish I had known that yesterday."

"Then let me go back. Kim, last week at Lute's you asked me how I could find someone who might not exist, this Michael friend of Sara's. I decided the best way to find any real person she was associating with would be to follow her. I put it through as a routine duty assignment, the kind that Wagner never does. I'm guessing that someone on the roster couldn't make it today – yesterday – and roped

Wagner into it. So were you with her, with Sara?"

"Yes."

"I didn't know. . ."

"I had never met her until Allie asked me to take her to the place we found her daughter's body. So she could say goodbye."

"You hiked into the Kofa with Sara? Good God! You weren't caught in the sand storm?" She didn't have to answer; he knew. He bolted to his feet, walked around the coffee table, and began to pace back and forth in front of her, seemingly undisturbed by his lack of clothing. She had never seen him like this, this mature, composed and pragmatic man. It alarmed her but she refused to let him see it.

"Oh, for heaven's sake, Lon, don't be so melodramatic. I survived. We all survived nicely, as a matter of fact."

"Why didn't you tell me? Why didn't you tell me you were going?"

"I . . .didn't want you to worry about me."

He stopped pacing. His face softened until she thought he would cry. "Yes, I do worry because I care about you, Kim. And no matter what happens between us, I will always, always care about you."

Tears sprang to her eyes, copious tears she couldn't restrain. They rolled down her cheeks unchecked while all the anger inside her drained away too. The dark, malignant mass of emotional debris that had tried to smother her soul receded, replaced by a feeling of expansion and openness she had never known. She rose and went to him. She embraced him. She whispered, "I'm sorry. I should have told you. I trust you."

"I'm sorry, too. I should have told you." He pulled her in tighter for a long hug and then kissed her. The feeling of connection and sharing of lips and tongues and breath and skin overwhelmed her. She felt her knees go weak. Throbs of desire shot through her pelvis and up through her body, hardening her nipples and raising goose bumps on her skin.

Together, they stumbled back to the sofa and he sat down hard, still holding onto her hands. His hardened penis slipped out of the opening in his briefs. He reached to adjust himself, but her hand stopped him. She looked at his nakedness and felt no trace of fear or revulsion. She unzipped her shorts and removed them while he watched. She took off her panties. Placing her knees on the sofa, she

181 / *Fatal Refuge*

straddled him. His head fell back, his eyes closed, breath coming faster, the pulse in his neck throbbing. She put her hands between her legs and felt the moisture, slick and copious. She rubbed her erect clitoris with wet fingers then held his penis and guided him into her. A brief feeling of resistance, an instant of mingled pain and pleasure. Then she lowered herself onto him completely, without restraint, and engulfed him to the hilt.

• • •

Chapter Thirty-Four

Winston Verbale got into his car, carefully arranged the two Styrofoam cups of hot coffee in the holders and prepared to start the engine. Unexpectedly, he felt the sensations returning, unbidden by the usual memories and pictures in his head. The feelings started in his hands. They flexed sensually, as if imbued with the memory of the soft throat they had pressed into and crushed. Tingling sensations rushed up his arms, moved through his shoulders and shot down the front of his torso in a current of heat. Teasing, they curved around his scrotum like a warm hand, penetrated his rectum with a jolt. His penis jerked erect. He felt his power then, his daring.

His eyes closed and he mentally reproached himself. *This is a work day.* He banished the memories, squeezed his thighs together and allowed the erection to deflate. Yes, he was powerful and daring and also clever. Never mind that the ploy of the "heads" poem had failed. How could he have known the red-haired bitch's mother had been tossed in the loony-bin? He started the car and continued his drive to the office.

Sara Cameron. She had occupied his thoughts every day since he had read the newspapers about the Smith murder and learned Sara Cameron was not in the detention center or in the psych hospital. Evidently they had turned her loose again, a fool who wasted her time writing poems. Why set the whole legal process in motion to deal with someone like her?

But now back to business. He turned off the motor of the

Mercedes, collected the two cups of Starbucks coffee from the holders and entered the office building through the side door.

He entered Allie's office without knocking, placed one of the cups on her desk and sat down in the faux-leather chair.

"Win, I wish you wouldn't, really." She put the phone down and leaned forward in her chair.

"No you don't. You love to start the day with a caramel macchiato and a chat with me." Recently he had been cultivating his relationship with her. He had decided Allie presented no threat to him and could actually be useful. He knew she had counseled Cindy's mother but she had no idea that he knew. And, she had friended the Apache woman who was more than best friends with the detective. The price of a coffee every morning, if it put her at ease enough to talk, was well worth the intel he gathered.

Allie sipped her coffee. "About five hundred calories here, you know." She wiped a bit of foam from her upper lip. "I do enjoy talking to you, Win, but it occurred to me that maybe this doesn't look right to the others. You know how office gossip makes the rounds, even if it's nonsense. One day I'll just buy my own caramel macchiato and lock you out of my office."

He laughed. "That will be the day. You forget I have a master key."

He had started the relationship repair with her by clearing up the issue of the lie he had told about Cindy going back East to care for her mother. He was sure Allie bought his story that Cindy lied. He told her Cindy had actually planned to go back East for breast implant surgery, which he had strongly opposed. Cindy had convinced him to cover for her. That action exposed him to the risk of being fired from his job so Allie must never tell anyone. He had also convinced Allie that he had no idea why Cindy had been at Kofa the day she was killed.

Later, he tried to keep their talks office-related or ask for Allie's opinion about current events, even though such chit-chat made his stomach roil with impatience and boredom. He hated the persistent cheeriness of the social worker/psychotherapist and the willful optimism sweetening her opinions.

Today, at last he found the right time and the right opening to ask the questions he wanted to ask. "So, what have you heard about the investigation of Cindy's murder? You know, I don't think I'll ever be at peace until they get the guy."

"I haven't heard anything – well, not anything more than you have, but. . ."

"But what? Don't play with my feelings like that, Allie."

"Win, I have no intention of playing with your feelings. I'm sure it's nothing, which is why I didn't want to talk about it, but I know some people close to the investigation and lately they both look so happy and upbeat. I asked them if they have new leads on the case, but they won't say. We can only hope it's because the case is warming up. I guess Cindy's mother has been talking with the detective."

"She can't be much help to them, can she?"

"Actually, from what they say, they're very involved with her. I hope she helps them close the case. It's long overdue. It's been more than three months. Now I really have to get to work. Thanks again for the coffee."

Verbale walked back to his office alternately congratulating himself for getting valuable information and questioning what he would do next. *Find out what the mother knows that she might have told the detective? How? And what will I do if it's something or if it's nothing?* Alternate courses of action marched through his mind, eager to be vetted and decided on. When he turned the corner of the corridor, he saw a woman employee standing outside his locked door, a sour expression marring her face. Inwardly furious at the interruption of his thoughts, he greeted her with a smile. He opened the office door for her. With slow and grudging effort he redirected himself to deal with the tedium of day-to-day activities.

• • •

Verbale sat back in his chair at his home office, relishing the plan he had decided on and the steps he had taken to launch it. Earlier that day he waited until Allie went to the restroom, walked into her office, picked up the smart phone on her desk and pulled up the contact file. Finding Sara's name and number was easy. One minute. In and out with the info. It was tough having to wait until he got home in the early evening to call her, but he needed the privacy of his home office for this little act of deception.

"Mrs. Cameron, it's so nice to be able to talk with you and tell you how sorry I am about your daughter."

"Why, did you know her?"

"Yes, of course. My name is Larry Hebo. I'm the head chef at The Diner, you know the four-star restaurant downtown, and I met Cindy more than a year ago. We became. . . close. Very close."

"I guess that means you were her lover. How nice for you, Sinner. Now I'll hang up because I have things to do."

"Wait! Mrs. Cameron, I'm only calling you because Cindy talked about you so much. She wrote you a letter that she said would make things better between you, but she didn't know where to send it. After she died I got it from her desk."

"A letter. Did you read it?"

"No, it was in an envelope, sealed. I'd like to give it to you, and talk to you about her. Ever since she. . .she died, I've been praying that they catch the person who did it, and praying for her soul, too. She hadn't accepted Christ as her savior but she was such a good person."

"A good person. Yes. Are you a good person?"

"I pray to the good Lord every day with gratitude for what I am and the wisdom to become better, Mrs. Cameron. You know, I think it would be so good for both of us to meet and talk about her. Would you come to my house to get the letter, Mrs. Cameron?"

"I think we should meet somewhere."

"Oh. I understand. Well, there's a little chapel on a dirt road just off of Highway 95. We could meet there. Tomorrow morning at five-thirty."

"Been there. It's no bigger than a medium sized room. Why there? And why so early?"

"It's on my way to work, and I have to be to work at six. I do a double shift tomorrow, so I won't be available any later. Besides, it's a holy place. What better place to talk about Cindy and say a prayer for her soul?"

"Does seem fitting. But so early."

"Do you like to sleep in, Mrs. Cameron?"

"No, of course not. I'm an early riser. I'll be there."

"Good. I want us to have a few minutes to talk. As I said, in addition to the letter, there are things Cindy told me about – about her relationship with you – that I think would be comforting for you to hear."

"Okay then. Thank you. Tomorrow." She hung up without saying goodbye.

Verbale smiled to himself. When he keyed in her number he had already decided he would give her the name of the chef at an upscale restaurant called The Diner. When he adlibbed by saying he had a letter written by her daughter it was a last minute flash of genius that would make this particular winning gamble one for the books.

• • •

Chapter Thirty-Five

At 5:00 a.m. on a weekday in July there was little traffic on the highway. Verbale felt sure that people in the few cars he passed would have no reason to notice and remember him. By the time he reached the turnoff to the chapel the sky revealed the reluctant grey-blue glow that precedes the dawn of another sun-scorched day, air stifling as a wool blanket.

He pulled off onto the dirt road and brought the Mercedes to a crawl to prevent a plume of dust. He wanted nothing that would draw attention. He eased the Mercedes into a spot he had selected on an earlier trip. Parked between an apparently unused barn and an empty packing shed the car was virtually invisible from the highway as well as from the field to the north, where agricultural workers might be getting an early start.

He had dressed in overalls with a tan shirt and work boots to make anyone who might notice him think he was just another field hand. He left the car and walked toward the tiny white chapel.

On the other side of the highway green produce with roots in irrigated and fertilized soil basked in the early morning sun for a mile or more in three directions. Behind the tiny church lay a dirt road built for tractors, and an empty field. Far across the field, a farmer's hacienda with a red tile roof. Ahead, nothing but the land in its natural state: flat, dry, hard-packed and strewn with rocks. To the left a winding trail of small trees revealed the presence of underground water, a river bed spanned by the McPhaul Bridge, an eight hundred foot suspension bridge that had fallen into disrepair. Part had collapsed, leaving only a narrow path of metal reaching from bank to bank over the dry sand twenty feet below.

In front of the chapel a sign read "Pause Rest Worship." The neat border of flowers around the building's base, the steeple topped by a cross and three stained glass windows under the eaves gave the Lilliputian structure a look of authenticity.

He pictured the chapel's interior, six pews and a tiny altar holding a guest book. All the privacy and all the room he needed. It would be warm but not oven-hot and airless this early in the day. As he neared it, he felt a surge of power that seemed to rise from the dry soil underfoot but was reminiscent of another day and another encounter with a woman who had interfered with his goals. He had no plan to harm this old woman but perhaps some intimidation and hints of retribution for cooperating with the investigation were in order. He felt his heart beat quicken and the dew of excitement emerge on his forehead and upper lip.

The narrow chapel door was little more than six feet high. The nob turned easily and the door opened without a sound. He stepped inside. The room bore the scent of dust, drying wood and holiness, an ambiance that revolted him. He waited.

"God isn't in there, and neither am I."

The muffled voice seemed to come from nowhere. One step took him to the door. He jerked it open, stepped outside and saw her. The woman, this Sara Cameron, was small, plain, aging and poorly dressed. He looked more closely and decided she was a nondescript nobody with a blank face that said nothing but eyes that appeared to know everything.

"Oh, you're Sara. I – uh hello. I expected you'd come inside." His attempt to collect himself sounded lame in his own ears. He looked around for her car, but saw nothing. "Here, let's go in where it's private," he said, holding the door open for her.

"I'd rather not if you don't mind. Too close for me. I expect we can talk out here. On the north side of the building we'll be in shade." She glanced up at the sun mounting the horizon and walked around the building. He followed her.

"What was it you wanted to tell me about Ruth? And where is

the letter? Cindy wasn't her real name, you know. Tell me about my Ruth."

Bile began to rise in his throat. How dare this woman make demands on him? All his planning, the irony of the setting, the privacy it provided – he had planned it perfectly. Then this slug of a woman threw things off kilter and demanded he talk to her right out here in the open.

"First, tell me what you've been saying to the detectives about her."

"I. . .how do you know that?"

"I know a lot, you old biddy. What have you told them about her and her boyfriend?"

"Do not speak to me that way!" Sara turned to go.

He glanced around quickly and saw no one on the highway or in the fields. It reminded him of the Kofa: they were out in the open but not another person in sight. Without conscious volition his hands reached for her throat. They curled around it easily, fingers and thumbs overlapping around the small column of ropy sinews. He watched her face, eager to see her surprise and then the look of total despair when she knew she had lost, she was dead, and he had won the prize of killing her.

He saw her eyes jerk wide. She tried to pull away, leaning back. Then her clenched fists and both arms came up fast inside the circle of his arms. Her fists grazed his chin then her arms reached full extension upward and outward, breaking the grip of his hands. He was stunned by the swift decisiveness of it. She was free.

She turned to run. He lunged for her, caught her hand and pulled her to the ground. He bent to reach for her, a rush of blood in his ears, his face aflame. He touched but couldn't hold her. She was thrashing, kicking furiously and writhing this way and that like a wild animal. A kick landed on the back of his knee and off balance, he went down. She rolled away from him, scrambled to her feet and ran.

He stood, sprinted after her while a question flashed in his mind, *why did she go in that direction? Why not toward the road, or toward her car?* Another yard and he almost had her – then he stumbled over his own feet encased in the heavy work boots and fell again.

He got up with dirt on his nose and grit between his teeth. Rage increased his speed, after her again. He was close enough to hear her gasps of breath and low moans of effort. In a few second he would grab the nervy bitch. Now he wanted her to look back. He wanted to see the terror on her face.

Instead, he saw her approach the bridge, dodge around the warning sign and chains strung across it. Almost within his grasp, she leaped onto it. She swayed, stumbled. He stopped, transfixed with hope she would plummet down to the empty river-bed. Then she regained her balance and with arms out to steady herself, tight-rope walked the damaged footing toward the opposite side.

Verbale slowed, trotted up to the span panting and now shaking with rage. She was almost a third of the way over. He couldn't follow. He was seventy-five pounds heavier, and not as sure-footed. The bridge wouldn't hold him. He tentatively stepped onto a beam, hoping he could shake her loose. There was no feeling of movement under his foot. The suspension was still firm, in spite of the decrepit condition of the surface. He stared after her, willing her to fall to her death.

Suddenly aware he might be watched, he looked around. Still no one in sight. But it was hopeless. Her car must be parked on the remains of the old road on the other side. By the time he got to his car and drove to where that road joined the highway she would be long gone.

• • •

"I want to speak to Allie."

"I'm sorry, she's not here today. Who is this, please?"

"Sara. Sara Cameron. Tell Allie I have to talk to her now."

"She's not in today, but I'll transfer you to your case manager."

"No, I... "

After two rings a cheerful young voice said, "Hello. This is Judy Squires."

"Who are you? I wanted to talk to Allie Davis."

"Yes, the receptionist told me. But Allie isn't here today. I'm Judy Squires, your case manager."

Sara was about to hang up the phone but as frightened as she was, her natural aversion to rudeness checked her.

"Sara, I'm sorry I haven't had time to call you and introduce myself. Maybe we can meet and get acquainted later this week."

"Why?"

"I'm your case manager. I can help you with things that concern you. I can drive you places you need to go or I can get food for you from the food bank if you're running short – things like that."

In spite of her desire to be polite, the pitch and volume of Sara's voice rose. "I don't need food. I need someone to protect me from the guy who's trying to kill me. Can you do that?"

"Trying to kill you?"

"Yes. Earlier today. He tried to choke me but I ran. His name is Larry Hebo."

"Who?"

"Larry Hebo. He said he's the cook at a restaurant called The Diner."

"Sara, I need to meet with you about this, now. Are you at home?"

"Yes, with the door locked."

"I'll be right there – ten minutes at most. Don't go anywhere."

"I'm not about to leave this room. Didn't you hear me? The guy tried to kill me! You sound like you're young enough to be wet behind the ears, and you're telling me what to do?"

"I'm sorry, Sara. I don't mean to be bossy, but I'm your case manager. Uh – I'll be right there."

Sara hung up the phone. She stood paralyzed by fear and uncertainty. So she was a "case," someone who needed advice from a girl probably young enough to be her granddaughter, a person who wanted to give her a hand-out of food, an act of charity she didn't need. Just because her brain didn't work like everyone else's, did they think she was stupid? Did they think she was helpless?

She began to pace the room. In only five paces she reached the wall and had to turn. Five paces back, turn again. Then again. Then again, *not fast enough, not long enough. This isn't helping. This is frustrating!* She clenched her fists, let out a low-pitched, guttural cry of anguish, pushed over one of the chairs at the table, reached for the throw pillows on the bed and tossed them against the far wall. She reached for the back of the other chair, grasping the wood until her fingers grew numb. Her mind, too, went from frantic to numb and empty.

Then a name inserted itself into the emptiness. She heard the name "Michael," repeated and repeated in her mind, in that voice, in Michael's own voice, as if he was reminding her of himself, calling for her to reach out for him.

• • •

Chapter Thirty-Six

The voice of Michael saying his own name was not welcomed by Sara. Shocked and angry, she pushed the voice away, refused it. Maybe she even said it aloud, she wasn't sure. "Go away!" Gradually the name faded. Her mind returned to seeing and feeling and sensing the room and all that was around her. Her breathing slowed.

A knock at the door. She pushed the curtain aside to see a tall, slender woman in her twenties with a purse hanging from her shoulder and a briefcase in her hand. The woman looked back at her through the window. "Sara, it's me, Judy."

Sara opened the door and the woman came in. Judy Squire's face was heart-shaped, unlined and pink. Her fine, light brown hair was cut short with bangs above alert blue eyes. She wore a loose denim jumper over a short-sleeved white shirt. Disc-shaped ear rings in blue and blue cloth shoes completed her look.

Sara saw the young woman glance around at the disarray in the room. Her face and manner changed, even more serious now. She righted the overturned chair and indicated for Sara to sit down. She put her briefcase down on the worn linoleum floor, hung her purse on the back of the other chair and sat down. "I can see you're upset, Sara. What can I do to help?"

"I don't know. You wanted to come see me. You tell me what you can do."

"Well, did you call the police after the man…the man tried to kill you?"

"I was afraid to. They told me not to make trouble. They said they didn't want to have to arrest me, they never wanted to see me again."

"Why do you think the man tried to hurt you, Sara? Have other people tried to hurt you like that?"

"No. I don't know why he did it and no one was with him."

"No, I mean other times before…have people tried to hurt you or follow you or sort of…sort of persecute you at other times?"

"Sort of? Sort of? What are you saying – that I imagined it? It was something I imagined?"

"No, no, I didn't say that. So, tell me what this man looked like, Sara. Maybe we can figure it out."

"Nothing to figure…oh, all right." She described Win Verbale in detail, and repeated the name he had claimed was his. "His name is Larry Hebo."

Judy didn't try to hide her disbelief. "But, Sara, I know him. I know Larry Hebo, the daytime cook at The Diner. He doesn't look anything like that. He's short and heavy set, and has dark… But there are a few other guys who work in the kitchen there. Maybe it was one of them, just using Larry's name."

"How could I know that?"

"Sara, have you been taking your medications?" Judy turned to look on the counter by the sink, then at the bedside table.

"Medication? I'm not talking about my medication. What do drugs have to do with this?"

No response from Judy.

"I know what you're thinking, and I did not imagine that someone tried to kill me! He did!" She put her hands to her neck and rubbed the sore places where Verbale's thumbs had pressed hard.

Judy's eyes followed the gesture. She said, "Yes, your neck looks a little red there."

Neither spoke for a long moment. Finally Judy asked, "Sara, Allie isn't available, but you know Dr. Sirota, don't you? Why don't we go talk to him about this?"

"Yes, I know him. A psychiatrist. A nice man. But I'm not going anywhere right now. I don't feel safe out there anymore."

"Okay, but I'm going to talk to him and maybe he can figure out something to make you feel better."

"What can he do? I'll feel better if I never see Larry Hebo again. Will you just listen to me for a minute without asking me anything?"

Judy said, "Yes, of course." When Sara had told her story in detail, Judy said, "Thank you for sharing all that with me. But don't worry. I think you're very safe here." She retrieved her brief case and purse and walked to the door. She turned to give her new client a smile. "Take care of yourself, now," she said.

Her fake smile evaporated a second later. She walked to her car with her mind in turmoil. Larry Hebo was her older sister's husband. She often entered the kitchen when she was at The Diner for lunch, and she knew most of the staff, even the evening workers. None matched Sara's description of her attacker. The woman must be decompensating. Her paranoia no longer in remission, Sara must be delusional again.

Judy asked herself silently why she hadn't contacted this relatively high-risk client before. The answer was the same as most of her similar inquiries: *because my case load is impossibly high and I don't have time.*

When she reached her car she turned on the motor, cranked up the air conditioning and lifted her i-pad from the brief case. In a few key strokes, she had access to all Sara's current psychiatric records. They showed what she suspected, that Sara hadn't seen the psychiatrist in almost a month and Allie even longer.

An hour later she entered Dr. Sirota's office. When she finished relating what had happened in her first contact with Sara, he leaned far back in his chair, looked up at the ceiling. "I'd almost rather believe someone did try to kill her. Damn! What caused her to regress that much?"

"I don't know. It's the first time I've seen her."

"Because there's no question about not taking her medications. The injection I gave her lasts a month and she's not due for another until five days from now. It's the newest and best anti-psychotic drug on the market. She did so well on it for almost three months."

"I know. But her room was a mess. She had trashed it. And besides the fact that my brother-in-law *did not* assault her, she didn't make any sense, talking about a church and a bridge and a car like a black hearse. Then she said that God told her the man who attacked her was the same man who killed her daughter."

The muscles around Dr. Sirota's eyes tightened, deepening his crows' feet and the wrinkles in his forehead. "I guess it's not surprising. With her tenuous grasp on reality, learning about her daughter's death was more than she could take. But we gave her a brief reprieve, didn't we?"

Judy felt touched by the psychiatrist's need for reassurance. She nodded, blinked back tears and cleared her throat. Looking into Doctor Sirota's face she mused that his lower lids drooped in a way that reminded her of a sad clown.

He spoke again, his voice softer and slower. "Well, it may be only a brief reprieve but let's get her in here. There's always something else we can try in these atypical cases."

• • •

Chapter Thirty-Seven

It was Monday, August eleventh, the last day of the "dog days of summer." Most of Yuma's heat-enduring public had no idea how the phrase "dog days" originated. Most would say it referred to rabid dogs, once terribly common on the streets in late summer, but it was coined in the lexicon of astronomy and describes a cosmic event. Every year between July third and August eleventh, the "dog star" Sirius rises in conjunction with the sun, as if to challenge the sun's celestial prerogative.

On the morning of this August eleventh, Allie woke very early with an unsettled feeling. She lay in bed trying to identify specifics and assign cause to her emotional discomfort. The annoying buzz of the alarm clock sounded. She rolled over, turned it off and got out of bed. When she finished in the bathroom, she came back to sit on the edge of the unmade bed.

Winston Verbale would bring her coffee again this morning. What was wrong with that? The answer came like a rebuke from a well-meaning friend. "Because he's been pumping you!" Yes, exactly. He usually turned the topic to the Cindy Cameron murder, trying to gain more information about the investigation. Why? What had been niggling at the back of her mind was that his curiosity had a different flavor than a natural interest in the death of someone who had been close to him.

So, again, why? Could he be involved somehow? Could he have killed her? She had discussed the possibility with Kim but she couldn't imagine it. A second later she told herself sternly that many things that couldn't be imagined were real. In many cases of murder, rape or sexual abuse, the perpetrator's friends and relatives were shocked and unbelieving. They couldn't imagine the person they knew so well doing such a thing. More likely, it was that they *wouldn't* imagine it. They didn't see it when it was right under their noses or didn't believe it even when incontrovertible facts spelled out the truth.

But Win – just last week she had accidentally walked in on him in the bathroom. The look of surprise on his face was still vivid in her memory. It had seemed – off somehow, contrived. A month before, a staff member confided in Allie about the same kind of event, saying she couldn't talk to HR about it because the person she walked in on was the HR director. And of course, Debby Smith, traumatized by her bathroom encounter with Win and then, poor woman, a murder victim. Wait! What did Debby and Cindy have in common? Winston Verbale. And Debbie had been murdered just a week or so after Verbale had learned she would take the city council seat he lusted for.

The sequence of memories and their association kicked Allie from diffuse uneasiness into the realm of shocked reality. The man she thought she knew was a paraphilic, a sexual deviant, a pervert. And also, very possibly, a murderer, the murderer of two women she knew and liked. Cindy had been a gentle, empathetic woman who took pleasure in small things and loved to provide pleasure and healing to others. That was how she had viewed her career as masseuse. And Debbie – she was a vulnerable woman but bright and capable with a lawyer's grasp of political nuances. She would have made a good council member.

Literally laid low by the realization of Verbale's true character, she fell back onto the bed then rolled over into a fetal position while she tried to process it. When she allowed the thoughts in, their logic became apparent. Although his motive escaped her, Verbale had had the means and the opportunity to kill Cindy. If he had committed the murder it would explain his strange reaction when she told him Cindy was dead, and it would explain his prurient interest in every detail of the investigation. And Debbie Smith? His motive, if it was Verbale, was perfectly clear and totally debased. He wanted the council seat enough to kill for it.

Finally, logic brought emotional surrender. She lay flat on her back and stared at the ceiling. How could she have been so wrong about him? Why hadn't she seen it all before now? After many minutes of dealing with self-condemnation she rallied her self-respect. Confusion gave way to determination. She wouldn't think about Debbie Smith and what had happened to her. It was too much. Her first concern and her debt of friendship was to Cindy.

• • •

Verbale didn't want to go to work today, not with this feeling that he had lost, that he was losing. The humiliation of his encounter with Sara Cameron had shaken him. He forced an internal dialogue that it hadn't changed anything; he had given her a false name and in any case law enforcement would never credit the word of a crazy person. The antithetical thoughts that followed were that if she ever saw him again she would raise an embarrassing alarm that could eventually lead to a very bad outcome for him.

He coached himself with familiar warnings about quitting on a losing streak, appearing normal, being able to hide his feelings like the best poker players in the world. At eight a.m. he entered Allie's office with a cheery, "Morning, Sunshine." He put the cup of flavored coffee on her desk. All she could do was smile back at him while the thought of his arrogance, his monstrous duplicity, released a flood of acid in her stomach. His falsity and the thought of what he had done to her friend sickened her while she struggled not to let it show. When he left her office she took the paper cup to the bathroom and poured the brew down the sink.

Her mental turmoil escalated throughout the day. She had to do something. Confront him? Tell someone? Who? Kim, the police, a sheriff's deputy? Tell them what, that she suspected him because he brought her coffee every morning?

She was able to put aside her concerns to focus on each of her clients in their turn, but in idle moments her own inaction tormented her. Finally, she questioned why she had mentally condemned him when the legal system would claim he was innocent until proven guilty. There had to be a way she could confirm her suspicions before she shared them with anyone else. In the last minutes before five p.m., she had it. She left her office and started down the corridor, instructing herself not to hurry because he never left at quitting time. She spotted him through the glass windows, still at his desk. *Yes!*

"Allie, hi." He put down the papers in his hand then did a slow double-take when he saw her face. "You look excited. What's up?"

"Yeah, I guess I am excited. I knew you'd want to hear this. I just had a call from my friend, the one who's close to the Cameron investigation, and she said they're about to wrap it up! They have solid proof of who did it. Of course she wouldn't tell me who, but she said detectives are talking to the judge right now to get a warrant for his arrest."

Win blinked, blinked again. "Well that's great. And it's about time. It's been – how long now?" He didn't wait for an answer. "They should have solved it long ago, but I guess that's the state of law enforcement, they take their time without any consideration for the victim's loved ones." He leaned back in his black leather executive chair and crossed one leg over the other. "It's about time they got it together," he added, then sat staring at her.

Allie's thoughts were that Win never crossed his legs like that. More telling, his words sought to place blame rather than praise for the investigators in her imagined scenario. She said, "I guess we'll have to wait until they arrest him. . .whoever. . . to really celebrate. Well, got to get home now."

"Yes! Keep me posted, please."

Allie was confident in her ability to read body language, nuances of voice and expression and listen to what people *didn't say* as well as what they did say. She walked out to her car feeling stunned to have what she knew was the truth confirmed. In her mind, Win had confirmed his guilt as clearly as if he had confessed it.

• • •

When she was out of sight, Win stood on legs that felt inadequate to support him. Unable to react further, he automatically returned the wave of several office workers as they passed his office. He turned and looked around but was unable to register what he saw, unable to compose a coherent thought. Then it came. As of this moment he no longer controlled the game. Someone else had taken over and now he and the game inhabited a different world, a different universe, where the game would be fatal to the loser.

Think, think! What should I do? What followed was that he was on the defensive now. He had to defend himself. He had thrown away the 45 he used to kill Cindy, tossed it into the river; the shoes and clothing he dropped in the Goodwill bin. Then the week he returned from his alibi trip to Costa Rica, he bought a little 22-caliber pistol.

He jerked open the top drawer of his desk, grabbed the key to the lower drawer, unlocked it and retrieved the little 22 and immediately held it behind his back. He silently cursed the glass walls and door of his office while he tugged out the tail of his short-sleeved dress shirt and tucked the gun into the belt at the small of his back. He relished its hardness against his skin. The sensation dominated him while he locked his office door.

Another employee leaving for the day caught his eye. *That person walking down the hall,* he told himself, *I could kill him now. I could kill six people with no effort at all.* The thought was both reassuring and tantalizing.

In the car he leaned back in the seat; the gun pressed uncomfortably against his spine. Should he put it in the glove compartment? No, he needed the feel of it, pain or no pain. He reached for the button to start the engine, but then he asked himself, "*Where will I go? Home? They might be there, waiting for me. Who could help me, hide me? No one. No one I trust enough. It's time to cash in and go.*

He started the engine, checked the gauges; the gas tank was almost empty. He fought the urge to gun the engine anyway in a headlong race for Mexico. The San Luis port of entry was less than twenty miles away. Instead he drove to the nearest gas station, the shabby one with second-rate fuel he never used, and filled the tank. Back in the car, he told himself he had time, time to go home to get his laptop and other things, things that might incriminate him: a lock of the fat woman's hair, stiff with her blood. *Think, think, don't panic. Get it together.* Doubt and fear crowded his mind. He struggled with the decision. It was like the recurring nightmares of being an unrecognized nobody in a crowd of celebrities and it produced the same effusion of cold sweat.

Finally he leaned forward and patted the dashboard of the car. The car would take him to Mexico, then maybe, after a few years, back to California with a new identity and then . . .

• • •

Chapter Thirty-Eight

Dusk had overtaken the last dog day of summer, the time when the sun released its last, weak rays before twilight, the time highway patrol officers call "dusk, dinner, and death time," when most fatal road accidents occur.

Near the intersection of Highway 95 and West County 15th Street, just yards north of the place the Highway cuts through the north-west edge of the Cocopah Indian reservation, Verbale pushed the speed limit heading south, fleeing toward the border and freedom. Anger, fear and hope vied for dominance in his mind but for now, at least, he felt in control. The glare of the setting sun to his right would extinguish itself in just a few minutes, bringing the dark of night to make him safer. The intersection of Highway 95 and County 15th Street near Avenue B was nothing that would slow him; the smaller roads held stop signs.

Something in the corner of his eye – he turned his head, a pickup truck came at him from the left, the driver's face startled. He jerked the steering wheel right. The truck veered left. At the same instant both drivers knew it was too late. A loud "crunch" and a jolt when the sides of the vehicles touched, then the truck careened across County Avenue B and onto the shoulder. Win's black Mercedes bounced onto the shoulder of the dirt access road and onto Reservation land. A jarring stop, an instant of brain-numbing shock.

Breathless, Verbale assessed his body's condition and decided he was not injured. But his car! Anger jolted him. His car was damaged, his beautiful Mer-kaaa-deez now with an obscene dint in its beautiful black skin, no longer pristine! His head jerked toward the offending vehicle and its driver. He leaned forward to touch the gun at the small of his back.

Then he remembered the game, the deadly game, and this was not part of it. It didn't occur to him that the man had probably been blinded by the setting sun, didn't see the stop sign and if it had occurred it would not have mitigated his rage. His plan of escape came into focus again to dispel the fog of rage. Killing was a luxury he couldn't afford even for the pleasure of destroying the other driver, the stupid clod.

Then it hit him. Was his car still okay to drive? He gunned the motor, let the Mercedes roll forward a few yards to check its soundness then began to turn back toward the highway.

Movement from the truck caught his eye. The young driver climbed down from the cab, apparently unfazed, and looked at his rear fender. Verbale could see a new dent-and-scrape on the truck with a few flakes of black paint decorating its faded blue. The man headed across the road toward him. Win had no intention of talking to this ignorant farmer who probably intended the mundane exchange of insurance information. Furious but on track again in spite of this hellishly bad luck, he pulled the steering wheel hard left into a U-turn that would take him back to Highway 95 south.

The sound of a siren, an East Cocopah Tribal Police car barreled toward him, braked hard, sending up a spray of dust, turned across the road and blocked his way. It was too much. He was so close, so close to freedom and now this! He cut the engine and slapped both palms to his face. Pent up terror and rage erupted from his mouth. He screamed and screamed and screamed.

• • •

205 / Fatal Refuge

Chapter Thirty-Nine

At the fire house, Kim and her EMT squad number three partner, Jim, sat in the day room drinking iced coffee. After five o'clock on this noon to midnight shift there hadn't been one call-out when usually there were three or four.

The day room décor had been designed to simulate the cozy ambiance of a private home, featuring easy chairs, sofas and a few potted plants but concrete floors covered by throw rugs, high ceilings and speakers on the walls betrayed its real function.

Kim sat at a desk in the corner while Jim had slumped into the room's only recliner. He levered the chair back, creating a picture of innocent indolence. His recent attempt to grow a goatee had not matured and masculinized his face as he had hoped; the blond fuzz on his chin softened his appearance even more.

"Hey, Latte," Kim said, "maybe the reckless drivers and wife beaters are worn out by the heat."

"Let's hope. I'm not as unquenchably thirsty for mayhem as some of your former partners." Still in recline, he reached for the glass of coffee sweating droplets of moisture, and bent his head down sideways to take another sip.

Kim nodded. "I noticed. When you became the new half of Squad Three we wondered if we'd have to put the Newbie on tranquilizers. Those first few weeks, I think I heard you praying for no call-outs. You've finally learned how to relax."

"You did okay by me, Straight-Up, trained me good. I feel like

I can handle whatever they throw at us." He put his glass down and turned his head toward her. "And speaking of confidence," he said, "you look totally rad today. What's up?"

Kim laughed. "So I'm feeling good. Nothing's up."

"Only money or sex could make someone as happy as you look and I'll wager you're still as poor as me." He turned away and reached for his glass again.

Kim rose from her chair, the wooden legs screeching on the floor. She went to smile into her partner's face, one hand on the back of the recliner. "I'd say that's a little too personal and none of your business, Latte. One hard push and you'll be on the floor wearing your coffee."

He sat up fast. The recliner squealed then thumped while his coffee sloshed. He wiped his hand on his uniform then put the glass down on the end table and stood. "Sorry, Kim." He held both palms up and toward her.

"Don't ever go there again kid," she said. She turned and went to the bookcase, wondering if there was something to read that was good enough to relieve the enforced idleness of this shift. She saw Jim still stood looking at her.

"So, Kim, whatever happened between you and Amos Wagner? I haven't heard anything lately about him out to do you dirt."

She sat down in an easy chair. "Good to know. He and I came to an understanding."

"He didn't get your license pulled, like he was bragging he would."

"If he had, I wouldn't be here. He made a complaint to the Board, but then he retracted it. He hadn't given them anything to document it in the first place, so they dismissed it."

"Justice triumphs again." He picked up his glass to salute her. She nodded and opened her book. He put the glass down and went back to the recliner.

Unable to focus on the novel, Kim turned to watch him. His eyes closed while she mused about his embarrassingly accurate comment. Her relationship with Lon was now much more than a friendship or even the modern version of friends with benefits. They were seeing each other almost every day and spent most nights together at her home or his. Their sex was an exploration of passion and joy she had never suspected lay within her and they seemed to understand each other without explanations.

She looked at Jim's face and idly wondered if he would ever be so fortunate in his relationships. His face smoothed to contentment in ultra-slow motion, his jaw easing lower, lips parting. Soon his deep and slow rhythm of breath told her he had fallen asleep.

She rose from the chair, dropped her paper-back novel on the end table and began to pace, unable to release feelings of tension so inappropriate for a quiet day.

For a reason she didn't understand her thoughts turned to Apache ancestors, among them Cochise, Geronimo and the woman warrior, Lozen. What intense, exciting days and what desperate, tragic times those had been. She tried to imagine herself there and then, but couldn't complete the mental picture of who and how she would have been. Still, it was interesting to speculate that she had been born too late and was meant for those days instead of these.

An alarm sounded. It startled her out of her reverie and shocked Jim awake. The duty sergeant's voice blared from the intercom, "MVA, two vehicles, with injury. Intersection of Highway 95 and County 15th. Law enforcement on site. Squad Three respond."

• • •

The sounds of Verbale's screams stopped the uniformed Cocopah officer in his tracks. Fresh from two years of junior college and on the job three months, he had dealt with only a few accidents, fender-benders with no injuries. This one was different. He spoke into the radio fastened to his shoulder then continued toward the black car, wondering what terrible injury could make a man howl like that. He noticed body damage on the passenger side of the car and looked through the glass at the driver, bending and craning his neck to see the man's injuries. He couldn't see the blood and gore he expected. Then it must be the poor guy's legs and feet, he decided. He waded through knee high weeds and clods of dirt to the driver's side and reached for the door handle.

Fear replaced Verbale's anguish. His hand came up in a split second. He locked the door. Then it hit him. This was a tribal policeman who didn't know anything about him. It was the Sheriff's deputies who wanted him for murder. Chances were slim they even had a warrant yet, much less put out a BOLO. Here was good luck embedded in the bad. He unlocked the door, unfastened his seat belt and got out, smiling at the officer. "I'm all right," he said. "But I have an important meeting in Sonora, in Mexico, and I'm running late."

"Aren't you injured?"

"No, not at all."

"Why were you screaming?"

"I told you! I have important business to take care of in Mexico."

"So you were late for a meeting. Were you speeding?"

"No, no. That guy ran the stop sign!" He gestured to the opposite side of his Mercedes where the driver of the truck now inspected the damages.

The officer motioned for the other driver. Standing between both, he interrogated the young man briefly. When he was satisfied the second driver also denied injury he began to take notes, meticulously recording names, license numbers and other details.

Win looked from the young farm worker to the dark skin and round face of the officer. He barely suppressed the urge to punch them both, to jump into the patrol car and speed away, do something, anything. His mind raced while he trembled with frustration and impatience. He glared at the young driver who dipped his head and fixed his eyes on the ground. The distant wail of an ambulance siren grew louder, closer. Within seconds, all three men turned to see it roll onto the dirt access road.

When Kim was satisfied she was well away from traffic on the highway and the county road she stopped. Jim immediately unfastened his seat belt, climbed down from the shotgun seat beside Kim and went around to open the back doors and prepare to give aid. Kim sat looking through the windshield at the three men who stood talking. She picked up her radio. "Squad Three reporting. Hey, Dispatch, I thought you said injury. These guys are all vertical and breathing. What's up?"

"Roger, Squad Three." The Dispatcher's voice sounded more bored than resentful. "The call came in from the Tribal police. Check it out then terminate if appropriate."

She walked toward the three men. The officer turned and stepped toward her, obviously relieved to see another responder on scene. They greeted each other with a quick handshake and exchange of names, then she asked, "So who's injured?" She glanced over at the pickup truck on the far shoulder of the road. "Someone trapped or lying down in there?"

The officer responded. "No, just these two guys. I thought Mister Verbale here was injured but he says he's fine. I'll call the Sheriff's Department now. The truck is on their territory."

For Kim, the name Verbale sparked instant recognition. "*Lon's murder suspect!*"

Verbale let out a piercing scream. Officer and truck driver jumped. Win clutched his belly and bent forward. "Ohhhhh. I think I am hurt. Ohhhhh!" He took a few steps toward Kim. She reached to grab him before he collapsed. He leaned on her, groaning. He lifted his chin toward the ambulance to indicate his intent, and began to walk toward it with Kim supporting him.

Kim didn't like it; something was wrong here. The guy hadn't looked injured or shock-y to her. He might be a fraud, hoping for an insurance payout like some she had transported. But, no, this was different. This man might be a murderer.

They reached the cab of the ambulance and continued back to the open rear doors. Out of sight of the Cocopah officer and the other driver, Verbale reached to the sweat-drenched small of his back and pulled his gun. He pressed the barrel into Kim's right side and leaned into her, rotating his wrist. The gun barrel twisted into her side as if it would bore through her skin into her rib cage. He whispered in her ear, "Don't say a word."

Kim gritted her teeth, full of self-reproach. In spite of her suspicion he had taken her off guard. His closeness made her shudder and her lip curled at his odor, stale coffee breath and fermenting sweat. She said nothing, determined to stay calm.

When they reached the back of the vehicle. Kim knew her partner probably saw only a man who appeared about to collapse and her with a strangely blank face. She knew Jim was prepared to unclamp the gurney from the floor, lift it out and jump down to help his partner stabilize and load the victim.

Verbale growled, "Stay where you are, you little fairy, or I'll kill your mom here." Jim froze, staring at the gun pointed at his crotch. He clutched at the hand-grip just inside the doorway and didn't move.

• • •

Chapter Forty

Win squeezed Kim's upper arm hard, released it and gave her a shove back toward the cab. "Get in and drive, and if you say or do anything I don't like, I'll kill your pretty partner and put the next one in your ear."

"Drive, drive where?" she asked, her mind a whirlwind of other questions.

Verbale hesitated. In the ambulance, the border was no longer an option. Border Patrol officers would ask to see doctor's orders and other documents allowing them to enter. California was the only alternative. The Colorado River formed the state border and the bridge was only seven miles away on Interstate 8. Highway 95 didn't intersect directly with 8, but connecting roads could take him there.

"North on Ninety-five," he said, then glared at Jim. "Get back!" He gestured with the gun.

Kim started toward the cab, hoping for a split second opportunity to get them out of this horror. When she looked back she saw the gun trained on her until she opened the cab door.

She climbed in and quickly turned back to look through the window-sized opening between the cab and the patient compartment. Verbale somehow kept his right arm extended with the gun pointed at Jim while he grabbed one of two metal grips near the doorway to lever himself up. Then he was inside, closing the rear doors.

Poor Jim. Kim thought he looked hypnotized by the dark hole of the gun barrel. He backed up again until his legs hit the EMT's leather seat. He collapsed onto it. The seat faced the rear doors and was almost in back of the driver's seat so Kim couldn't see his face any longer but knew he was staring up at Verbale. She put the vehicle in gear, breathing hard with the full realization of the danger she and Jim had been sucked into. They were being hijacked, kidnapped.

She turned on the headlights and flashers, punched on the siren and pulled onto the highway headed north. She felt her mind scurrying for a solution. Then she remembered something from EMT training, something she thought she would never have to do. She saw in the rear view mirror that Verbale wasn't watching her. Holding her breath she slowly reached for the radio on the console to her left. She picked up the hand set, pressed the button and said, "Squad Three reporting. Nine, nine, nine. Repeat, Squad Three reporting nine, nine, nine."

The words meant nothing to Verbale but the urgency in her voice and Jim's change of facial expression did. Reacting instinctively, he smashed the gun butt into the EMT's face. His trigger finger contracted and the gun fired.

Kim flinched then braked to a hard stop. She looked back through the window to the patient compartment, expecting to see her partner had been shot. The bullet hadn't struck Jim, it had entered the ceiling of the compartment, but she saw Jim's body slowly sink down in the chair. Blood oozed from his smashed cheek. He was unconscious.

Verbale stepped forward and stuck his arm through the window to the cab. He shoved the gun against Kim's ear. A sharp inhale; the barrel was hot. "What did you just say, Bitch? What was that?"

"Nothing! I was just checking in." She looked back and saw Jim's white face. She demanded, "Why did you hit him? He didn't do anything."

Verbale turned and fired a bullet into the unconscious EMT's leg. Kim saw the leg recoil on impact but Jim made no sound. Verbale leaned through the opening again, screaming, "That was your little twit's leg, Bitch! Tell me the truth or the next will go in his head! And get this crate back on the road. Now!"

Kim turned and pulled the ambulance onto the road again. "Just don't hurt him anymore!" she screamed. A shudder coursed through her body followed by a stronger surge of anger. "He's done nothing to you! It was me. It was the signal that's going to bring every police car and Highway Patrol within fifty miles! We have to stop. If you surrender they won't hurt you."

"Give me that!" Not waiting for a response, he leaned forward, reached across her arms to grab the hand-set and yanked it out of the connection, striking Kim's grip from the wheel. The vehicle swerved onto the shoulder, rocked, threatened to overturn. They careened passed two vehicles pulled over on the opposite shoulder, the drivers' faces masks of fear seen in a split second. Kim's hands groped back to the wheel. Careful not to over-correct, she regained control of the ambulance. She exhaled. They were not going to die – not right now anyway.

Verbale had been thrown against the wall by the near-overturn. He regained his balance and darted to the window. He stuck the gun through it. "You are not going to stop! Move this cracker box!" When he didn't feel enough acceleration he yelled, "Floor it, you stupid Indian!"

Kim pressed the accelerator harder. "It won't go any faster. It has a mechanical governor."

"What?"

"A governor that limits the speed. It won't go any faster than sixty-five miles an hour. They're built that way."

Finally, Verbale was silent. Kim pictured Jim, shot and pistol-whipped, lying untended on the stretcher behind her. She needed to get to him, needed to help him. Anguish crept into her mind, slowly filling it while she envisioned the worst. The fear grew corrosive, her courage and resilience faded, leaving a sense of unreality, an omniscient view of Jim, Cindy's murderer Verbale, and she, barreling down the highway at sixty-five miles an hour, three people in a metal box on wheels.

Oh, her mind was going someplace else, the way it had when she was a child being abused!

She shook her head and sat up straighter in the seat. She couldn't do that now! She needed to be in control of herself as well as the rig. Fully aware again, she saw an intersection ahead but the shoulders of the road were almost invisible. Full darkness had engulfed them. She yelled back to Verbale, "I'm going as fast as I can, but there's going to be traffic ahead. I can't keep up this speed."

There was no answer but she heard him moving around in the compartment. She glanced in the rear view mirror. She saw Verbale tuck the gun into his belt, grab the still-limp body of the young EMT and heave it onto the gurney wrong-ended, head toward the rear doors. He fastened the three straps around the bleeding EMT. A memory from Kim's training came to her, "Secure three, over nipples, navel and knees." She yelled at him, "What are you doing? Why are you putting him on the cot?"

Glancing back through the window as often as she dared, she saw him reach over the gurney to the side wall and yank open a storage cabinet door, then another. He grabbed boxes of gauze, opened them and wrapped the EMT's unconscious form with lengths of the stuff, knot after knot, hands pulling hard. He lurched back to the window and pressed the gun against Kim's neck again. "See what you did, Bitch? You almost got your little tit-sucker killed. Do not swerve again like that. One more time and I'll blow your brains out. Turn off the siren and the flashers."

When she did, the sound of other sirens replaced theirs. Verbale let out a sound like the bellow of a wounded bull and then a string of expletives. Up ahead in the darkness were the unmistakable blue beacons of many Yuma City patrol cars. They told Kim her radio message had been received and understood. Help was up ahead.

"Turn!" Verbale screamed. "Turn right!" East 16th Street was only yards ahead, but Kim braked hard and made the turn. There ahead another blue light flashed – one patrol car turned sideways blocking the narrow road, two officers standing to the side, guns drawn.

"Keep going! Stop and you're dead!"

Kim took a deep breath while time turned into slow motion. She steered the ambulance as far left as possible onto the shoulder. It tilted precariously. As they sped past she saw the patrol men's faces, painted blue by the light. Every feature and expression imprinted in her mind as clearly as if she had stared at them for an hour. Their faces said they saw her too, they understood, and they didn't have much hope for a successful ending to this one.

The ambulance approached Avenue A, pushed again to its maximum speed, creaking and swaying in protest. There was much more traffic now, Yuma city traffic, shoppers or workers about their daily routines. Kim switched on the siren again. Verbale did not object. She slowed for the red traffic light, then safely through the intersection, they approached South Fourth Avenue. The Interstate was next, the highway to California. Kim knew it was Verbale's goal, but if they made it across the bridge, maybe the California Highway Patrol would be waiting for them. She had to hope.

Verbale seemed glued to his spot at the window opening, gun pointed at her. "Take Interstate Eight west," he commanded. She moved into the left lane. The intersection ahead was an underpass, Interstate 8 overhead, well lit by twenty foot tall sodium-vapor street lamps. Clearly visible, she saw an unmarked car and a tall, slim man standing beside it. Lon! He held the 20-gauge pistol-grip shotgun he kept in the trunk. Her eyes riveted on him, she barely noticed two white Arizona Highway Patrol cars flanked the entrance ramp, blue and red dome lights glaring. A long cylindrical object filled the arms of one tan-uniformed officer. Suddenly he tossed the thing across the on-ramp – a spike strip to flatten their tires.

"No!" Verbale screamed. "Straight, go straight!" He reached through the opening as if to grab the steering wheel. Elbowing his hand away, Kim swerved into the right lane. Then they were through the underpass, continuing on Highway 95 headed east, north-east with not another California border crossing ahead for eighty miles.

This was Verbale's second chance at escape denied. He was silent. What did that mean? Kim was more uneasy than if he had continued to scream and wave his gun at her.

City traffic and busy intersections flashed past, making them slow but not stop. In ten minutes the traffic was behind them but sounds of sirens, their own and others, continued a nerve-assaulting wail. She looked in the rear-view mirror and saw two Arizona Highway Patrol cars – maybe the ones with the stop-sticks – and maybe there were others further behind. Was Lon now in pursuit, too? Yes, she was sure he had chosen to enter this hellish chase. Her concern for both Jim and herself was eclipsed by her fears for him. She took a deep breath. Her white-knuckle grip on the wheel tightened even more. She glanced over her shoulder but Verbale was not at the window opening. "What about Jim, what about my partner?" she yelled. Her voice rose with anger. "I want to stop and check him."

Verbale's back was turned. Maybe he had been trying to count the number of cars following them with blue lights flashing. "Blue light special," he muttered.

"What?"

"I'll give them a blue light special." He turned toward Kim. "You can slow down now," he said. "I'll check your friend."

Kim slowed. She leaned to the right and back far enough to see Verbale through the window. He bent over the still-unconscious EMT. Verbale didn't know how to check vital signs. What was he doing? He bend over and pulled the red handle on a rod that secured the gurney to the floor. He waddled, wide-stanced for balance, toward the back doors. Then she knew. He had unlatched the floor clamp that held the gurney in place. She braked hard. The cot rolled forward, struck the wall behind her. She let up on the brakes. The ambulance was still traveling fast. The gurney rolled back carrying its unconscious victim and shot out of the open rear doors. Crash! It bounced hard on the pavement, bounced again, then continued down the road speeding away from them as if under its own power, streamers of gauze trailing behind.

• • •

Chapter Forty-One

Warring objectives exploded in Kim's mind. Kill Verbale. Get to Jim. Make sure Lon was safe. She brought the ambulance to a full stop, screech of brakes, stench of burnt rubber and metal on metal. She jumped out of the cab and ran around to the back. Verbale was prone on the floor, scrabbling for the gun that had flown from his hand. She grabbed an ankle with both hands and yanked hard, but a split second too late. His hand closed on the gun. Pulled toward the door, he twisted upright to elude her grasp. His free hand caught the door frame. The hand with the gun swung forward and smashed into her forehead. Kim's knees buckled. The red glow of the tail lights dimmed, gave way to flashes of light then a dark fog.

The next thing she knew, Verbale's left arm was across her throat, pulling her upright and in front of his body, tight against him, the gun to her temple. This was it; she would die. Then – what was he waiting for? The blackness dissipated from her vision and she saw. Some of the pursuing vehicles had stopped a hundred yards back. She could make out people in uniforms hovering over the gurney that held Jim's inert body. Relief flooded her.

Then she saw two County Sheriff's vehicles that joined the chase when the ambulance left the city limits stopped ten yards away, and Lon's unmarked Crown Vic. Four deputies, three men and a woman had scrambled from their patrol cars and stood facing her and Verbale. In front of them was Lon, now holding his handgun. Five guns clutched in ten hands were trained on her because she was

Verbale's shield.

"Put the gun down, Verbale!" Lon screamed. "Let her go. Give it up now."

Verbale pulled Kim tighter and backed away toward the cab of the ambulance. Her eyes fixed on Lon. His expression sent palpable waves of love and anguish to her, then turned to Verbale with contempt for the man and a steely determination that said he would defeat the man at any cost to win back her life.

It sparked in her a stronger need to fight Verbale, grab the gun, kill the murdering scum, but she was gasping and struggling just to breathe against the pressure of his arm. Her head swam in pain and her knees were rubber. Step by step, he dragged her backward, then pushed her into the open door of the ambulance and across the seat to the other side while he climbed in. He shifted the gun to his left hand, put the vehicle in gear, and pealed out, cab door still open. Kim looked into the side view mirror. Lon Raney and four deputies scrambled for their vehicles.

Her next conscious realization was that she was still in the shotgun seat of the ambulance, slumped painfully against window and door. She put her hand to her bleeding head and struggled into a seated position. A slow self-assessment finally reassure her she had a concussion but not a fractured skull. She would be okay but she needed to stay awake.

She looked at Verbale, sitting forward as he drove, intent. His left hand held the steering wheel, his right hand on his thigh held the gun, the barrel pointed at her. Out of the windows all she could see was a dark landscape with no signs of habitation. They must have passed Araby road and South Fortuna Road. They were headed north, toward Yuma Proving Ground, then Kofa, then Quartzite and the California border. A glance in the rear view mirror showed three sets of headlights close behind. *Bless him,* she thought, then *bless the deputies, too, the Old West posse that never gives up.*

She closed her eyes and wondered how long ago it had been since she and Jim sat in the ready room at the fire station drinking iced coffee, feeling bored. It felt like this nightmare had gone on for hours but it couldn't have been more than thirty minutes or so. Whatever, Lon would figure out a way to end it. Her head ached. At least Jim was safe now – if he was still alive. She looked at Verbale's dark profile. Nausea overwhelmed her. She leaned forward and vomited on the floor.

Verbale turned. "You disgusting bitch. If you weren't my lucky escape card, I'd kill you now."

She sputtered and spat on the floor, pulled a handkerchief from the back pocket of her uniform and wiped her mouth. "Luck is the last thing I am for you, Verbale, you murdering excuse for a human being. I have a concussion and I'll vomit if I need to."

He looked at her as if he had never seen her before.

"Where do you think you're going?" she continued. "You'll never get through Quartzite and onto Interstate Ten. Even if you did, they'd be waiting for you. They're quirky over there in California but they don't like women-killers any more than Arizona does."

Verbale glanced over at her again. Was that a flash of doubt in his face? "Shut up, Bitch, or I will kill you now," he growled.

"You would. You murdered Cindy Cameron, didn't you? But why? We can't figure out why."

He was silent.

"She was a wonderful person, so much better than you could even understand. She was too good for you."

Without warning, his right fist that held the gun slammed back toward her face. She dodged. The blow missed, striking the window. She reached up for the gun and wrenched it from his hand. He let go of the wheel and clawed for the weapon with both hands. With no one steering, the ambulance careened to the right and bumped off the road into the desert. Verbale's foot was jammed against the accelerator while they fought. The ambulance careened across the rocky terrain, tossing and bouncing them while both their hands clutched at the weapon. Then it was gone, fallen to the floor. Where?

A violent collision. Something crashed into the windshield sending a shower of safety glass over them. The rig had plowed into an eighteen-foot tall saguaro cactus, cutting it in half. The top section slid across the flat roof, carving a foot-wide dent, emitting a screeching sound like a thousand pieces of chalk across a thousand blackboards. The impact had slowed their headlong rush. Then came a banging, rending sound from the vehicle's undercarriage, metal against rock.

The battered ambulance lumbered forward. The engine coughed and died. The vehicle continued its movement by momentum only. The headlights and dashboard lights blinked out. The rig was totally disabled but hadn't yet come to rest while Kim and Verbale were tossed against each other and the dashboard. Kim tried to sit upright and gather her senses. Verbale now slumped against the steering wheel looking dazed. The gun was not in either of his hands. She couldn't see in the dark but frantically felt around the floor. Nothing.

The ambulance rolled forward a few more feet and listed slowly toward the passenger side. If it landed that way, Kim would be trapped. She jerked open the door and tumbled out onto the ground. She stumbled, eyes straining in the darkness to make out her surroundings. No matter, this was her chance to escape. She turned in the direction they had come. Less than a mile away, one set of high beams appeared to be moving toward her across the desert. Lon in his own car, or one of the Yuma County Sheriff's patrol cars? She started toward it.

Without warning, Verbale's dark silhouette appeared in front of her but his back was toward her. He, too, was looking at the vehicle trying to reach them. Did he have the gun? If not, she would take him on, finally, and beat him senseless. The thought inflamed her mind with pleasure. She wanted it, wanted to punish him, beat the last spark of life from his miserable body for what he had done to Jim, and her, and before that to Cindy. She couldn't see his hands. Had he recovered the gun? Should she take the chance?

Before she could decide, he turned to the left and crept away up hill. The desert was faintly lit by a quarter-moon, and silent except for metallic popping and groaning sounds from the disabled ambulance and faint hum of the approaching vehicle's engine.

Then Verbale's voice. "Hey, Indian bitch! Where are you? Come on over here, I won't hurt you. You're my ace in the hole."

She sank into a crouch and willed herself to silence.

"Didn't you like it when I grabbed you? I felt your tits."

She held her breath.

"Don't you want me, Squaw? We'll do it good here in the dark. I promise I won't tell your boyfriend."

The taunts rolled off her back, meaningless as static on a radio. Either he had the gun or he was foolish enough to think he could beat her down in a one-on-one fight. She looked down at her feet to place them carefully and quickly, getting closer so his voice, still taunting, grew louder.

She stopped and looked back to the approaching vehicle thinking, *It's Lon, coming to help me.* But the lights were stationary now. She stared, willing them closer. They didn't move. The rescuer's vehicle had also been conquered by the desert.

She stood, trying to catch her breath and rest until the pain set in, a dozen bumps, bruises, and scrapes nagging their hurts at her, pulsing into her woozy, pounding head. *My vision should be better*, she thought, even with nothing but the quarter moon to light the way. There seemed to be a fog in front of her eyes, dotted with pinpoints of light flashing like distant stars. *The damned concussion. And I am thirsty, so thirsty.*

A whirring sound overhead startled her. She looked up but couldn't see anything except night sky and stars. A large night bird? A distant helicopter? Then, whoosh! Instinctively, she squatted down. What was going on? Another whoosh and then a flash of light. Was she hallucinating? No, the light revealed desert landscape and other objects looming there. A saguaro or the silhouette of a man? She couldn't tell.

She waited for another sound and another flash, long minutes of dark and silence. Nothing. What should she do? She knew this area was the Yuma Proving Ground, where military weapons had been tested since the 1930s. She might be standing in a real danger zone. But Verbale was what mattered because if he had the gun he was the clear and more immediate danger. Where was he? If she stayed here another flash of light might reveal him but if she moved now she might walk right into him.

Without conscious thought she stood, spreading her arms wide, and began to turn slowly in a circle, remembering Lozen and her prayers to the creator. A tingling in her fingers stopped her. There! She couldn't see him, yet she was certain he was there coming toward her. Her arms dropped to her sides. Enough. Mentally she entered an alternate reality of invincibility, a trance state before an adrenalin rush. She would fight him, gun or no gun.

Whoosh! Whoosh! Two flashes of pale blue light, sparks, then two pillars of fire. She gasped and stared as columns of yellow and then blue flames danced against the dark sky. While she watched they revealed their fuel. One fiery pillar consumed a six-foot tall saguaro with a mechanical object embedded in its spiny flesh. The other pillar of fire engulfed a six-foot tall man, his arms straight up in the air, waving, jittering, then collapsing onto himself, down to the ground, a pile of smoldering flesh and bone. The stench of burning plant, human flesh, plastic and metal filled her head and sent her, too, spinning to the harsh desert floor.

• • •

"She's over here!" Kim opened her eyes, closed them again quickly against the flashlight beam. She looked up again through slitted lids. Lon!

She blinked and whispered, "Thank you for coming."

"You saved the last dance for me, Baby, that's all that matters," he said, and cradled her body closer. Safe at last, she felt her muscles relax into his and looked around, trying to orient herself. It was still dark, stars still winking in the sky, but so many man-made lights, so many sounds. A deputy approached. Seeing Kim he repeated Lon's call, "Over here," and waved his flashlight. Slowly, wary of becoming dizzy, Kim sat up more and turned her head to look around. The scene was incomprehensible.

• • •

Chapter Forty-Two

She turned on her side to face him in the bed and caressed Lon's naked legs with the arch of her foot. It was Saturday, a day off for him and one of her last recuperation days from work. She said, "I don't remember much after that until after we left the hospital and got home. I remember Zayd fussing over me. He wouldn't leave me alone, trying to lick every cut and scrape on my body. Finally you got me into that hot bath. It hurt like hell, but it helped."

"I'm surprised you remember that much. I think your brain was still addled. When we got you to the E.R., you wanted to check out A.M.A." He stroked the hair back from her forehead, avoiding the bandage that covered three sutures.

"Yes, I knew I had a. . ."

"Yeah, a 'little' concussion. How is that different from a 'big' concussion?"

"Actually, a *mild* concussion which is different from. . . Oh, never mind. Just don't scold me, Lon. I know it wasn't smart to try to leave the E.R. against the doctor's advice. They did the CT scan and I'm fine."

"Yes, you are fine." He leaned over and kissed her lips. As if reluctant to leave them, he gently pulled her lower lip with his front teeth before releasing her. Eyes still closed, she responded with a hum of appreciation, "uummm."

Abruptly he propped himself up on one arm to look down at her with the intense blue/green eyes that tolerated no falsehood. "But are you ready to go back to work on Monday?"

"Yes, of course. Nothing's changed about work – or my feelings about it. But I need to know what happened out there at the Proving Ground. What went on during the time I was unconscious? You can help me with that, can't you?"

He leaned against the headboard and started to speak, but now she was staring at his upper body, the golden brown hair on his chest, the curve of his shoulders and biceps; then she put her hand out to stroke his forearm. His eyes acknowledged her desire and honored it. He made love to her again, slowly, tenderly.

Afterward she started to ease out of bed, but Lon's arms around her naked waist pulled her back. "Hey, I thought you were asleep," she said.

"The ungrateful, unimaginative man falls asleep after lovemaking. Those of us fortunate enough to bed a goddess are neither."

"And why do you fortunate ones remain awake?" She eased back under the sheets.

"To anticipate more heavenly bliss."

His face so close to hers gave her the gift of knowing intimately its every texture and angle, his eyes and mouth soft and moist. "Ah, heavenly bliss, such as an encore?" She kissed his cheek. "I'm not sure I could endure more bliss right now. I still have those unanswered questions, remember?"

He groaned but rolled out of bed, went to the dresser to pull on underwear then came back to sit on the edge of the bed beside her. "Okay, back to the Proving Ground. I'm not supposed to know this, so of course neither are you. What the Army and Air Force are doing out there is supposed to be top secret. But the Deputies and I saw more than the project officers ever expected to be seen.

"There were other civilians, too, weren't there?"

"They called in some military security men who were still in their civvies. It wasn't hard to figure out what they're doing. They're testing drone-mounted laser weapons to shoot down mechanical drones. And I don't mean over in Syria or Iraq. There's illegal drone activity right here in the States threatening civilian air craft and who knows what other targets. They see it as a real threat."

"Drones to shoot down drones. I guess that makes sense. Was it the drone or the laser that killed Verbale?"

"I can't say for sure. It was probably the laser, from the way you described it to me. By the time I got there, he was nothing but a pile of stinking ashes. Of course it was an accident. I mean, the laser was targeting the drone."

Kim nodded, able to make more sense of what she remembered.

"You and Verbale sure raised hell out there that night. If he hadn't been. . .dead. . .and if you hadn't been injured, you might still be sequestered on base getting grilled by the FBI, the NSA, CIA – the whole damn alphabet."

"So I'm supposed to be grateful for trashing my rig, getting tossed around like a cork in a washing machine, battered and concussed?" He smiled, kissed her and the subject was closed. It was enough for her to take in for the moment.

They showered together and prepared to go out to dinner. Kim pulled on a yellow cotton dress, smoothed a little gloss on her lips and started to brush her hair but she was still preoccupied and pensive.

Lon must have sensed her distraction. He hugged her from behind and said, "You know you did everything right, Kim. That's why you survived, concussion and all. He would have killed you the minute he decided he didn't need you."

"I know. I just wish I could have stopped him before he hurt Jim."

"Jim will be okay soon enough."

"They're releasing him from the hospital to a rehab facility tomorrow. He needs some physical therapy to get the strength back in his leg." She put her hairbrush down and turned to hug him. "I knew you would come."

"What else could I do? You are the most important thing in the world to me."

They dined that evening at Romero's Riverside, the best Mexican restaurant in town. They lingered over coffee and a shared dessert, flan garnished with caramel sauce and fresh fruit. After the last bite Lon sat back in his chair smiling.

"That's a self-satisfied look," Kim said. "What *other* marvelous things have you been doing lately?" She raised an eyebrow, up and up again, and he knew she was referring to their time in bed. He laughed.

"Well, in addition to your recovery, I'm celebrating the end of the Debbie Smith case."

"That was quick!"

"Detective Reed and I found evidence in Verbale's house: his little trophies from her body. Along with his DNA they collected in her home, that clinches it."

"Wonderful. But what about Cindy Cameron? We know he killed her. Allie said when she lied to him about a warrant being issued for the murderer, he gave the clearest set of guilty tells she's ever seen."

Lon dropped the spoon he was using to stir his coffee. "And that's what almost got you killed!"

"Lon, she feels terrible about it. She couldn't have known what he would do or that it would involve me. She said she's the queen of unintended consequences, and that was the worst consequence of them all."

He didn't respond except to shake his head. He signaled for the waiter and paid the check. They walked out into a mild, breezy night hand in hand. He pulled her close and they continued to the car, arms around each other's waist. He opened the door for her then hesitated. "About Allie," he said. "If she's your friend then I guess she's my friend by association."

"A friend once-removed." She gave him a quick hug.

He continued. "We were talking about Cindy before. Her case and Smith's are officially open, but we've stopped working them. DNA on the sneaker came back. Verbale's was on the inside. There is such a thing as conviction in absentia but I don't think they can convict a dead man. Let them do their legal contortions over it. Let's just be glad he is dead."

"I'm more glad they found that rifle in his closet. Knowing he's the monster who tried to kill Zayd – and me – means I don't have to watch my back and you have no more excuses for worrying about me."

The conversation stuck in Kim's mind, provoking old lines of thought. When they reached Lon's home she settled Zayd for the night and changed the sheets on the bed. They watched the late show but when they lay down to sleep she couldn't stop her mind from churning. After hours of listening to Lon's soft breathing, hours of feeling warm and grateful but still fighting her thoughts, she turned and glanced at the clock on the bed stand. Four a.m. No use. She sat up in bed and said, "I didn't enjoy seeing Verbale die that way."

Lon stirred. She said it again, louder. He turned over to look at her, brushing his face with his hand. "What? What did you say?" She repeated the words. He sat bolt upright. "Why would you say that? Who said you enjoyed it?"

Kim's lips pressed together into a straight line. "Maybe that I should . . or would. . .or. . ."

"Whoa. Let's talk about this." Lon rubbed the sleep from his eyes and took her hand. Together they got out of bed and padded into the living room, she wearing only bikini panties, he in pajama bottoms. He pulled her down onto the worn leather sofa where a few months before they had made love for the first time. He didn't question her. He looked into her face and waited.

"Sure, I like the excitement of being an EMT," she said. "But I don't have the love of blood and gore that some of the techs do. The adrenalin rush comes one time in ten. The other nine times it's just a challenge. I like it because I'm helping someone, not enjoying someone's pain. I like it because I'm using important skills and I'm active instead of sitting at a desk all day."

Lon had no idea where that had come from or where she was going. He just nodded.

"I did lose it when he. . .when Verbale pushed Jim out of the ambulance. I wanted to kill him but I don't think I would have." She stopped. For the first time since sitting down she looked at him. His face was open, his eyes alert and accepting.

And so it came out. She talked about being victimized by a pedophile, about how, why and who had shot her in the thigh, about her fears and shame and about "…collective karmic guilt – that's what Allie calls it."

An hour later she stopped talking in mid-sentence. She shrugged her shoulders, sighed, and leaned into him. Lon embraced her, kissing her face many times.

"Thank you. You listened."

"Of course I did, to every word. Thank you for trusting me because now I understand so much more about who you are. I get how you've come to this place in your life and I'm grateful as hell that I'm here with you. You've carried a heavy load since you were a kid. First your struggle with your Apache ancestry then the molest. It's more than anyone should have to deal with."

"I know others who've dealt with worse, Lon. We all have our demons."

"I've known for a long time that there were things in your past you needed to let go of."

She raised her chin to look into his eyes. "Yes, and I have. But I want to go home soon and talk to my parents, my mom, see my friend Crystal. Will you come with me?"

"The 'meet the parents and best friend test'. I'd be delighted, thank you." He grabbed her hand and pressed it.

"And there's something else I need to do now. I need to go back to where I found Cindy's body."

"Go back to Kofa?" Finally Lon was surprised. "Why? You went there with Allie and Sara Cameron. How can going again help you?"

"I'm not sure. But Cindy's mom went there for what Allied called closure. I think it helped her. I want closure, too." She eased out of his grasp and stood.

Now she could see Lon resisting. "What? It's – it's not even dawn yet. Let's take some time to get ourselves together and go this evening."

"It doesn't matter when. I'm going."

"Then I'm going with you. And Zayd." He stood, as if the matter was closed.

"I could be out there for hours, Lon. I can't say when but I'll know when it's over."

"Then that's when we'll come back with you," he said.

Chapter Forty-Three

Sara has found a new place to park for the night, fearing they know about Betty's Kitchen and will look for her there but she no longer feels safe and at peace anywhere. Memories of the attacker who tried to strangle her haunts her in dreams that come during sleep and in waking hours. Even memories of the would-be do-gooders at the Clinic are no longer reassuring.

It is early morning and she is drifting in the space between wake and sleep. *The river*, she thinks or dreams, she isn't sure, *the Colorado, the force of nature, the giver of life, the tamed and used and fought-over and damned and diverted and polluted and exhausted, depleted, indomitable river. The river and I flow. On the river I float. I and the river. I am the river.*

The first rays of sun find their way through the windows onto her face. She abandons the dream, stirs from the bed of the truck, crawls through to the front, unlocks and opens the door. The river's murmur is almost inaudible but bird calls are clear and jubilant. By mid-morning their chorus will reach a symphonic finale.

She looks around to see who might be watching. She sees no one but knows they are there. She walks barefoot a few yards away and finds a spot to hide among the jojoba bushes. She digs a small hole with a stick, and urinates into it. Back at the truck she hauls out her water jar, washes her hands and face, then brushes her teeth, careful to let all the waste water fall onto a flowering weed where it will do some good.

It has been ten days since she decided not to go to the clinic for her monthly shot of mind-control. She feels quicker and clearer already and that endless craving to eat and eat is gone. Invisible anchors on her body and mind are lifting and yet the residue of fear from being attacked torments her. Every day she re-lives the day a stranger tried to kill her. She will not drive by the place it happened or go near the restaurant where he works. And the reason Judy Squires, the girl who claimed to be her case manager, denied his name and where he worked is unanswered. The girl even denied he tried to kill her! She must be part of the conspiracy, one of the war-lovers.

When she left the tiny apartment the Clinic had provided she took almost nothing except the clothes on her back and the cell phone the Clinic people had given her, "for emergencies," they said. The phone has been buzzing many times a day, every day until the last two. Allie and the others at the Clinic are the only ones who know the number. They are calling to tempt her back, back into the fold where she doesn't belong. She could turn the phone off or take out the battery or even throw it away but she hasn't done that. The sound is annoying but it holds some trace of reassurance. Some of them meant well. Soon the battery will die and she will be left with her thoughts only.

She settles into the driver's seat and munches an apple for breakfast. She is free again, herself again, free to choose where to go and what to do. The Yumans have proven to her that they are not deserving of salvation; she has searched and searched but the nine hundred righteous do not exist here. In this place her daughter was murdered and she herself was nearly murdered. Let them deal with their mortal danger by themselves. Let them try to prevent the coming apocalypse in this very evil and dangerous world.

Thus ruminating, she waits to learn what she will do and where she will go next. Soon words come to her, words of a poem written long ago about her home in Oklahoma. They sing in her mind:

I may return again someday
to these rolling hills where miles reveal me. . .

"No!" The voice is both familiar and commanding. The rest of the poem escapes her. "Michael?" She looks around and sees no one. "Michael?" Chills creep up her spine and she shakes them off. She waits but hears only sounds of the natural world. Suddenly she feels strangely lonely as well as a little frightened, emotions she detests. Quickly, she begins to tidy herself by combing her hair and then tidies the truck. Yesterday she bought a full tank of gas; today she will have the oil changed.

The phone in her pocket rings. For some reason, instead of ignoring it again, she looks at the caller I.D. Kim Altaha. Yes, the Indian girl. Impulsively she answers.

"Sara! Thank you for picking up! We've all been so worried about you."

"Nothing to worry about, Kim. I been taking care of myself since I was twelve. Anyway, what are you doing up at this hour? Going to work?"

"Yes, later. But I woke up this morning thinking about something besides work. Sara, you know that Allie and Dr. Sirota and Judy Squires all want you to come back?"

The voice comes again. It is Michael's familiar, deep baritone, "No."

"No," Sara says and it's not as if she is repeating, it's as if the first "no" is her own.

She hears Kim's sigh. "I didn't think you'd come back. Alright, but I need to tell you something. Sara, I've been wondering how much farther your truck can go and what you would do if it gives out in the middle of the desert. I don't want to scare you about that, but I've been thinking that I need to buy a new Jeep. I want you to have the one I'm driving now. It's got only fifty-five thousand miles on it and it's in good repair. I'd feel better knowing you were driving something safe."

To Sara the idea is so unexpected it sounds unreal; she can't quite process such a generous offer. Her mind goes blank.

Michael's voice, "No! It's a trick, you stupid woman."

"Well, I. . .let me think. . ."

His voice is loud, with a knife-like edge. "They don't want to help you. They want to pen you up again and control you. Say no!"

"No, I can't," Sara says into the phone. She struggles to get the next words out. "Thank you anyway, Kim." With trembling fingers she keys off the phone and drops it at her feet. She takes a deep breath, and waits for her companion.

When he comes into sight, he is walking fast, talking harshly, not as she remembers him at all. "Old woman! Why did you get involved with them? What did it get you? A bed to sleep in and a telephone. Then they sent someone to murder you! Throw the phone away or I will." Without waiting he picks it up and throws it far down toward the river.

"Michael, please don't be angry with me." She is trembling, but somehow it's alright, somehow there is security and familiarity along with the fear. With Archangel Michael to help her she will be safe. He is her protector, her gift from God.

He speaks again. "Now get in the truck and shake the dust of this place from your feet, foolish woman."

West, the thought comes to her and she knows why. Court-ordered by the State of Arizona to receive mental health treatment in Arizona, the Clinic can actually send the police or sheriff's deputies to bring her back to the inpatient unit, back to mind-control medication, back to that tiny trap they called an apartment. But in California, or even north in Utah, they have no power over her at all. Michael likes that. She does as she is told. She walks to the truck and gets in.

• • •

Chapter Forty-Four

Kim spent the rest of the day making sure her uniforms were clean and pressed, getting ready to go back to work. After dinner Lon stowed two backpacks filled with water and supplies in Kim's Jeep, and put Zayd in the back seat. They drove with the windows down, enjoying the recent blessing of cool nights, saying little. When they parked at the trail head Kim said, "You and Zayd stay here, please."

Lon's face hardened and she knew he was about to protest. She said, "You can stay here and wait for me or you can go home and come back. I have my smart phone and there's reception from down here. I'll call when I'm ready."

"We'll wait."

She set out carrying a powerful flashlight and a bottle of water. She didn't need to turn on the flashlight and forgot she carried water. She reached the site without knowing what she would find or what she would do there. The first thing she saw was the little white cross Cindy's mother had set up. It lay fractured on the ground, nothing left of the mass of purple flowers Sara had placed there. The woman's anguished and remorseful words echoed in Kim's mind. She stood quietly. A shudder shook her body. The site felt as grisly and damaged as it had the day she found Cindy's body lying there, face down in the dirt. The wrongness of it came to her again, echoing the emptiness inside her. The spirit of the place was wrong.

And her spirit? Guilty and angry. She had felt remorse at seeing Cindy's body, a dead woman in the wilderness, shades of her tribe's recent history of warfare, part of that racial guilt she had claimed for herself and mingled with personal guilt from her own past errors. And she had felt anger, anger at the White man whose invasion of this land had set it all in motion.

She unlaced and removed her sneakers and socks, pulled the scarf from her pony-tail and climbed atop the boulder. She stood and turned slowly, looking up into the pale blue sky, at stars winking on as the sun began to set. The play of colors on the western horizon held her for long moments as they swelled from pink and yellow to crimson and gold, then faded to grey as the sun slipped away.

Twilight, the time when the earth pauses. She looked down at the high desert landscape and saw no movements. The heat and intense activity of day was over but the dark, predatory energies of night had not yet emerged. The evening breeze stirred away the last of late summer's warmth. The rock beneath her bare feet had been hot. Now it felt cool. She looked up again, at bats and nighthawks soaring, at the stars in the great vault of the darkening sky, and felt small. Then she looked down at the earth, at rocks and pebbles, cacti and ground insects, and felt large.

An early September full moon rose in majesty from behind the mountains. She let its light bathe her face. She thought of Sara's ceremony of farewell to her daughter and felt some comfort, as Sara had. She remembered her resolve to help find Cindy's killer and she and Verbale had found each other, the fated joining of intended victim with killer. But fate had turned killer into the recipient of justice; the trail of evils Verbale perpetrated became the hell-fire that swept back and consumed him.

She looked at the desert floor, softened by the glow of the eternal moon. Yes, the earth's soil could be dirtied by blood and the moon's dust could be sullied by man's footsteps; but the spirits of earth and moon could not be desecrated by man, no matter man's heedlessness and cruelty.

She closed her eyes. After many minutes a vision sprang up. In her vision she has found her soul tree! She makes a small fire nearby and begins to dance around her soul's twin in the form of a tree. She dances in celebration but suddenly the fire sends sparks to ignite her soul tree. In her vision it becomes a torch, a funeral pyre, her twin soul extinguished. She feels the fire inside herself. It burns away anger and guilt inside her, both inherited and self-inflicted. As it consumes it purifies, leaving freedom and possibilities.

Then the vision was gone. She opened her eyes. She remembered what Lon had said to her, here in the Kofa. He told her that first responders were either lovers of life or lovers of death. The knowledge entered her, with perfect clarity and perfect certainty, that she was a lover of life.

As night settled in, peace inhabited the cells of her body. Her eyes accustomed to the dark. She saw nightlife: scorpions crawling on rocks, pack rats, bats and nighthawks. She saw coyotes loping about their business but they didn't see her, a watcher transfixed by the watched.

A cloud passed over the moon. More clouds built, far away to the southwest. Then lightening, at first with no sound, just distant flashes from sky to ground and from cloud to cloud, a sense of moisture and tension growing in the air. She watched as clouds moved closer, concealing the moon, absorbing its light. The crash and roar of thunder came closer, deafening. Bolts of lightning flashed a split second behind the roar. She stood, absorbing sound and light. A few drops of rain fell on her face followed by a pelting torrent; and still she stood.

Soon she was soaked to the skin, hair wet, shirt and shorts dripping. Gradually the flash and noise of the thunderstorm faded away. Rain water, too, drained away, moisture evaporated and absorbed by thirsty desert air and earth.

Something was happening inside her, something leaving her, something filling her, and it was good.

Mingling into the soft murmur of desert nightlife a drum beat sounded in her ears, the drum beat of a Native Sun-Dance she had attended years before. She listened intently. She heard it, felt it, absorbed it and then became one with it. In her body the vibrations were subtle but defined, "boom-boom, boom-boom, boom-boom." She jumped down from the rock. Slowly she began to dance, toe-heel, toe-heel, moving and swaying, turning and circling in a dance of redemption.

THE END

CPSIA information can be obtained
at www.ICGtesting.com
Printed in the USA
LVOW04s1045031215
465175LV00002B/3/P

9 780996 940801